THE CEILING MAN

PATRICIA LILLIE

ISBN-13: 978-1541264137
ISBN-10: 1541264134

Printed by CreateSpace
Ebook edition published by Kindle Press

This novel was inspired by my short story "Abby" published in *Deep Cuts: Mayhem, Menace, & Misery,* edited by Angel Leigh McCoy, E.S. Magill, and Chris Mars. New York: Evil Jester Press, 2013. Parts of that story appear here, in slightly different form.

Cover photography used under license from Shutterstock.com.

www.patricialillie.com

For Liz & John,
Thank you.

1.

[BLEVINS]

THE FOG DID NOT ARRIVE ON LITTLE CAT FEET. IT ROLLED IN fast and heavy and smothered everything in its path.

One moment, Blevins lounged by his small fire. He leaned against the backpack stuffed with his scant belongings and enjoyed the clear night sky, if not the chill. *If it gets any colder, I'm going to have to get myself arrested.*

The next, the stars disappeared. The moonlight vanished. He couldn't see—or feel—his fire a few feet away.

"Well, this bites the big one." No one listened. He just wanted to hear the sound of his own voice.

What was that? A cough?

The shroud of dense air muffled the sound, made it hard to place. Maybe he hadn't heard anything at all. Maybe he wasn't alone.

"Hey! Who's there?"

No answer.

"You'd better keep your hands offa my shit!" *Bastard better not touch my bike.*

Around people, Blevins made a point of watching, of knowing exactly where they were and what they did. And dogs. He always watched the dogs. He never knew what those crazy fuckers might do.

"Whoever you are, stay right where you are. I have a knife." He didn't, but if he couldn't see whoever was out there, it didn't hurt to scare them a little.

There's nobody here. Blevins refused to be spooked.

He concentrated on his list of people who'd pissed him off that day. A nightly ritual, it always comforted him, filled him when he was hungry and alone.

That bitch at the laundromat threw him out and didn't even give him a cup of coffee.

"Come on. One cup of coffee for a homeless guy?"

"Leave now. Or I call the police." Bitch had the phone in her hand as soon as he walked in the door.

He wasn't ready to go to jail. The nights were cold, but it hadn't snowed. Besides, she let that idiot Danny with his stupid shopping cart sit inside and get warm. She probably even gave him coffee. He called her some choice names before he left. Blevins was pretty fucking proud of his vocabulary.

That creep at the desk at the Y.

"You can't be begging money from our members."

Like they couldn't afford to give him a buck or two. The Y might as well be the country club in this crappy town. When he let loose with his mouth, those preschool teachers grabbed their kids and ran. The little brats were there for an education, weren't they?

The damp worked its way through his coat, and he shivered. The stench, where did that come from? Part overflowing Port-a-Potty and part sunbaked road kill—Blevins had a strong stomach, but he gagged.

Another noise. Blevins still couldn't locate it. Was someone laughing at him?

"God. What's that smell? Is it you?"

Still no answer.

He went back to his list-making.

That place on Main Avenue, he couldn't remember what it was called.

He didn't go in, just stood outside the huge windows and watched those fancy-ass bitches fawn over their plastic-draped customers. The one from the desk came out and told him to leave. His ugly face pressed against the glass made the drowned rats in the chairs uncomfortable.

When the fog lifted and he could see where he was going, he'd break some windows. Hurling rocks and watching glass shatter always made him feel better.

The last time he hit the laundromat, he used the big neon OPEN sign for a target. Even turned off, the sign made for a little extra fun. He couldn't remember if they replaced it along with the window, but he hoped so.

As fast as it appeared, the fog lifted.

He was right. He wasn't alone.

Blevins hated mirrors and avoided them, but he was sure he didn't look as bad as this guy. He looked like he was a month dead and didn't know enough to lie down and admit it.

"Christ, you're one ugly bastard."

The other didn't answer.

Blevins watched the still, expressionless stranger. *I bet I can have some fun with this guy.*

"I think we're gonna be friends," he said.

The other finally spoke.

"Blevins, you are my new pet."

2.
[CAROLE]

LIFE WITH A TEENAGER WITH AN AUTISM SPECTRUM DISORDER was, on the best of days, quirky. I knew things could be much tougher. High functioning, low functioning—it was all attempts to slap generic labels on individuals, and Abby fell somewhere in the middle. Other than periodic meltdowns, we had it relatively easy and learned to deal with, if not understand, the way she worked.

There were the non-sequiturs.

In Tim Burton's version of *Charlie and the Chocolate Factory*, Grandpa Joe is talking about working for Willie Wonka, when out of the blue, Grandma Georgina says, "I love grapes."

I loved that scene and so did Abby. She and Grandma Georgina had similar conversational skills. At noisy family gatherings, Abby might bring all discussion to a halt by loudly announcing, "In third grade, I sat behind David Besom. He had red hair."

Her father or I looked at her and quietly said, "I love grapes." It was a signal. Repeating lines from a movie or a book or whatever to mean something else is a common ASD behavior—*scripting* is the jargon. Jim and I often found it expedient to speak Abby's language. Fewer words, more meaning, and she always got it. Abby did know, by other people's standards, she was not quite right. She was okay with that.

There was what we called Abby's Pause Mode. On her way to the kitchen, the bathroom, her bedroom, she stopped, usually in the middle of a doorway. She stood stock still and grinned her lopsided grin until Jim or I said, "Hey! You stuck?"

"Noooo." She laughed and continued on her way. If we were busy and didn't notice she was on pause, she retreated to Abby-land. We found her stopped, still grinning, but no longer still. She swayed, front to back, elbows bent, hands in front of her body. Her fingers danced, her eyelids fluttered, and, if it'd been too long, her eyes rolled back in her head. Once she made it to Abby-land, it was harder to call her back.

"Abby!" Wait a beat. "ABBY!"

"Huh."

"You stuck?"

"We haven't had any snow days this year." Her replies were mundane and often of the grapes variety, and we assumed they had something to do with whatever happened in Abby-land.

We went with it the best we could. "Nope. And as far as I'm concerned we don't need any."

"I want at least one." She grinned and moved off to wherever she was headed before her little holiday.

And the obsession. At times, I obsess. Everyone does. Although I've had friends who carried it to the point where I wanted to suggest medication, they were all slackers compared to a teenager with ASD.

Something small to most of us—a postcard reminding us it was time to have our eyes checked—consumed Abby's attention.

"Did you make our eye appointments?"

"When are you going to make our eye appointments?"

"You really should make our eye appointments."

"We need our eyes checked."

On and on, until I said, "Yes! I made the appointments!" Obsession over eye check-ups led to obsession over the dentist, the ear doctor, and the anything-else-she-could-think-of doctor. Regularly scheduled maintenance was very important to Abby.

When she was excited about something, anything, the obsession became the only subject of conversation for weeks, even months.

"Abby, did you empty the dishwasher?"

"Twyla's birthday party is in three weeks."

"Abby, dinner's ready!"

"I'm going to wrap Twyla's present in red."

"Abby, do you know you're a banana?"

"I think I'll wear my new jeans to Twyla's party."

"It's okay, Abby. I love bananas. A lot."

"Twyla's favorite color is red."

There was more, some of it, like the rocking, typical ASD behaviors. Some of it, Abby specific. Being on the spectrum wasn't her only issue. Mentally and emotionally, in some ways she was twelve. In others, completely seventeen. It kept things interesting.

Our life had a rhythm. An odd rhythm, but it worked. It was my excuse for not noticing sooner something was wrong. Most people with typical kids would have caught on at the first sign of weird. Weird was our way of life, and we took it all in stride.

MY OWN PARTICULAR OCD was paying bills—god knew, it wasn't housework.

In the early days of our marriage, when money was tight, Jim took care of all the financial stuff. I hounded him constantly. *Was the electric bill paid? When was it due? How much was left in the checking account?* And in those days, we had to write a check, put it in an envelope, stamp it, and mail it, all early enough for some nameless drone to process it by hand. In the interest of staying married, and quite possibly saving my life if not my sanity, I took over the family finances.

Bill paying and account balancing became easier with online banking, but remained a high-stress time for me. When I was at the computer paying bills, lightning could strike the house and as long as the electricity stayed on, I'd never notice.

Even so, when I looked up and saw Abby in my office doorway, I knew she hadn't been there long, maybe a minute. Not long enough for her to go from simple pause to deep Abby-land, yet there she was, already into the eye-rolling stage.

"Abby? Abby! ABBY!" Three *Abby*'s deep was bad.

"Huh."

"You stuck?"

"He's moving."

Not one of Abby's stock answers. I wasn't sure I'd heard her correctly. "What?"

6

"He's hungry."

"Who's hungry?"

"Idunno," she said. And shrugged.

In Abby-speak, that word—and it was one word—combined with a shrug didn't mean she didn't know the answer. It meant she either didn't want to or couldn't find the words to talk about it, and it was always her final answer.

She walked away.

"Hey!" I called. "What did you want?"

She stopped and turned back. She looked puzzled.

"Did you need me for something?"

"I forget," she said. She gave me her crazy-wonderful grin.

Like the proverbial elephant, Abby never forgot. Anything. Ever.

"Why don't you take your dog for a walk?"

And there was The Mighty Samsonite.

That dog could hear the words *walk* and *out* from the farthest corners of the house and, I swore, teleport herself to our feet, ears perked and butt wagging—she was an Aussie, no tail—ready to go. She hadn't learned to stop and grab her leash along the way, but I suspected it was only a matter of time.

"Sami, come," Abby said.

Whenever I needed a short break from parenthood, I sent the two of them out for a walk. It was good for all three of us, and as long as Sami was with her, I knew Abby was safe.

"SOMEONE IS TORTURING the kid again," Jim said.

I looked up from my book. "Can you tell what she's singing?"

"I can't even tell what language it is."

Abby loved music. Getting her an iPod seemed like a good idea at the time. We didn't realize with the buds in her ears, she would sing along even louder and, if possible, more off-key than we were used to. She was upstairs in bed, and the noise filled the house.

Sami whimpered and laid her head on Jim's knee.

"Ahhh, is the girl hurting da puppy's ears?" He scratched the top of her head.

"Don't talk baby talk to the dog. She's well past puppy-hood," I said.

Jim grew up in a pet-free household and was leery when I insisted we get our first dog. He promptly fell in love and turned out to be the world's biggest marshmallow with our pets. Five years ago, when we got Sami, I sent them both to obedience training and hoped Jim would learn some discipline. It didn't work.

"She'll always be my little puppy," he said.

"You are damaging her dignity," I said.

He laughed. "You're worse than I am."

"Nobody is worse than you are." Sami's whining grew insistent. "I think it's more than Abby's singing. I think she needs to go out."

Sami bounced.

Aside from their big brown eyes and lack of tails, Aussies are known for their ability to out-bounce Tigger.

"I'll take the widdle doggy-kins outs," Jim said.

"Now you're just trying to annoy me."

"Is it working?"

"For a big, bad cop you really are a pansy." I turned my attention back to my book.

I made it through a couple of pages before the back door opened. Sami shot through the living room and flew up the stairs. I heard her land in Abby's room. Jim followed at a slower pace.

"What was that all about?" I asked.

"I'm not sure. She got weird while we were out there."

"That wasn't very long."

"Well..."

"What?"

"I don't know. She was fine until we got to the middle of the backyard, then she glued herself to my leg and growled."

"Was there something out there?"

"I'm not sure," Jim said. "I thought maybe I saw something by the garage, but—I don't know. First I thought it was a shadow, then I thought it was a dog, then I thought it was a person, and then it was gone. And Sami took off for the house."

"The full moon was last week, so it wasn't a werewolf."

"Thank you for that."

"Coyote?"

People had coyote troubles on the other side of town, but not on our side. Our wildlife problems were usually groundhogs or skunks, and not many of those thanks to our neighbor's extermination program. Pete trapped them, gassed them, and disposed of the bodies in dumpsters all over town—Jim pretended not to know anything about that last part. On the other hand, we were close to the river, so who knew what might wander up.

"Maybe," Jim said. "Or maybe it was just a shadow."

"At least you had the Mighty Samsonite for protection."

"And whewa is my widdle luggage dog?"

"Keep it up, and you're sleeping on the couch tonight."

A FEW DAYS later, I got a call from Abby's teacher. Daytime calls from Ms. Colley were always bad and usually meant Abby had a meltdown.

"What's up?" I closed my eyes and hoped for only a minor meltdown. Things were crazy at work, and I didn't have time to go get her.

"Um, I have a sort of odd question," she said.

"I'm Abby's mother. Define odd."

She laughed. "Good point. Has Abby been watching movies that she's not ready to cope with or process?"

I panicked. My first thought was sex. Attempts to discuss the subject and explain appropriate and inappropriate behavior to Abby were frustrating. I could never tell how much she understood or how much she already knew. She was seventeen, and she was obsessed with the idea of having a boyfriend even though she didn't fully grasp the reality.

The previous year, thanks to a pregnant cousin, she figured out that one doesn't have to be married to have a baby. She told everyone she knew—and a few people she didn't know—she wanted one. Dealing with the backlash was loads of fun.

"What kind of movies?"

"Oh, the scary, gory, bloody, spattery kind."

I was relieved. Bad movies I could deal with. I was fairly sure Abby would never take an ax to a cabin full of teenagers.

"Not that I know of. What happened?"

"Abby disrupted the math lesson with...lurid talk," Ms. Colley said.

"The two things she kept repeating were, 'He rips their throats out,' and 'When he eats them, their insides get splattered all over.' No matter how many times I told her to change the channel, or just to stop, she kept going."

Change the channel was Ms. Colley's version of *I love grapes*.

"She didn't stop until Twyla cried. Then Abby cried, and they both had meltdowns."

I was speechless. And appalled. We both knew Abby didn't—couldn't—just make things up. She could only lie in reply to yes or no questions, and she was bad at that. She could repeat verbatim things she heard or describe in great detail things she saw or did. Even when she went off on a tangent and imagination came into play, the what-ifs were always easily attributed to something we knew she'd heard, seen, or done.

"Are you still there?" Ms. Colley brought my attention back to our conversation.

"Yeah. I'm clueless. We don't watch many blood-and-gore movies and never when Abby's around. Besides, she's pretty self-censoring. If we watch anything that gets scary or makes her uncomfortable, she goes to her room and puts in an *Anne of Green Gables* DVD. Maybe she watched something on Netflix when she was home alone. I'll check into it. Do you need me to come get her?"

"No. They're both sitting in the Quiet Corner now. I think Abby feels bad for upsetting Twyla. They seem to be comforting each other. I just wanted you to know what happened."

We hung up, and I thought about it. I dwelled on it—Abby-level dwelling. We didn't have cable, so television was limited to Netflix, only hooked up in the living room, and DVDs. I wasn't getting any work done, so I opened my Netflix account and checked the list of recently viewed items. Nothing there I didn't recognize, nothing that explained Abby's storytelling.

When I got home, she was at the kitchen table doing a word search puzzle.

"Abby, what happened at school today?"

"Nothing."

"Don't tell me *nothing*. Ms. Colley called me."

"Twyla does not like moving pictures. They freak her out."

I understood that. Twyla couldn't cope with television or movies. Her parents kept the television in a locked cabinet and only watched it when she was asleep or gone.

"What does that have to do with what happened at school?" I asked.

"I should not have showed her moving pictures. It was mean."

"What are you talking about? What moving pictures?"

"Idunno." Shrug.

Great. "Abby, we really need to talk about this."

"Mom. I really need to finish this." She went back to her puzzle, and that was that.

I checked her room. Maybe somebody at school lent her a movie. I looked in her player and at her DVD collection—*Anne of Green Gables, Emily of New Moon, A Little Princess*, all I found were the sweet, slightly sappy movies Abby liked. I checked her known hiding places. All I found was a half-eaten bag of chocolate chips. One minor mystery solved. I knew I bought those. The room was a mess. Unless I dismantled and reassembled it, I wouldn't find the DVD, if it existed.

After Abby was in bed and we were alone, I told my husband about Ms. Colley's call. Jim couldn't come up with an explanation either. We decided to take the wait-and-see route and not worry until we were sure there was something to worry about.

It had worked for us before.

3.

[CAROLE]

Most days, I loved my job. The other days involved dealing with budgets, grant proposals, or my mother-in-law, and it was Evelyn's day at the Senior Center. My mother-in-law didn't come to the Center for the services or the activities or the company. She came for the chance to annoy me.

Evelyn was a strong woman. When Jim was an infant, his father abandoned them. Neither of them ever saw or heard from him again. His mother raised him on her own. It wasn't easy, and I had a lot of respect for what she went through. However, I didn't like her, and I didn't feel at all guilty about it. She didn't like me either.

It was a given that I wasn't good enough for her golden boy. Nobody was or ever could be. She adored Abby but remained convinced all of my daughter's problems were my fault because I waited until I was "too old to be having babies" to have one. Her darling boy was, of course, in no way responsible for that decision. If only I was a better housekeeper, a more devoted wife, a more attentive mother—the list went on—Evelyn could relax and enjoy her dotage. I tried not to take it personally, usually without success. Even if a miracle occurred and I became a cross between Mother Theresa and Martha Stewart, I would never measure up.

When Jim was around, Evelyn's behavior toward me was passive-aggressive, snide little comments with double meanings. She was Jim's mother, so I smiled, reminded myself to breathe, and took it. When she was at the Senior Center—my turf, no Jim—she turned on the flat-out aggressive. I still smiled, reminded myself to breathe, and took it. I liked my job.

When she hit the lobby, I was in my office with the door closed, buried in a grant proposal. I still heard her.

"Can't anyone run the vacuum around here?"

I hit save on the proposal. If I didn't go out and greet her, there might not be anything left of the Center to fund. The paid staff knew it was me she was after, but I'd already lost too many volunteers over her.

"Evelyn? How are you? You look nice today." I added an extra dollop of syrup to my voice.

She stood at the bulletin board and read the list of the next month's activities. "This is the same old stuff. Didn't you even look at the list of suggestions I gave you?"

I'd tossed it on my desk and forgotten about it. It might have slipped off into the wastebasket.

"I did. It's wonderful, but you know I need to run it by the Board before I can do anything." Sometimes I hated myself.

"Oh. Well. Did I tell you I'm talking to Catherine Marlowe about being appointed to your Board of Directors?"

There was a good reason Jim said I was never allowed to own a gun. Syrup. I tried to remember the syrup. "Really? How wonder—"

That idiot Blevins walked in the door.

Port Massasauga was officially considered a city. In reality, we were a large town, just large enough to have a few city-type problems. One of which was a small homeless population. Some of them were mentally ill, some were drunks or druggies, some just down on their luck, and some were all three. Then there was Blevins, who was a sociopath. Or a psychopath. I always got the two mixed up. Whatever he was, he was a nasty piece of work.

Shelly, at the diner, used to feed him for free every night. They had a deal. He came in at the end of the day, and she fed him while they cleaned and got ready to close. He might take the trash out as token payment, but usually he just ate. The arrangement came to an end last November. He showed up in the middle of the evening rush and demanded food. When Shelly told him to come back later, he went ballistic. He yelled. He swore. He tipped over tables and generally scared the paying customers. She called the police, and Blevins went to jail.

When spring came, he showed up at the appointed time and expected dinner. When Shelly told him the deal was off and he needed to leave or she would call the police, he was outraged.

"But it was winter! Time for me to go to jail!" Blevins hated being contained in good weather but got himself arrested as soon as the snow started to fly. After the Salvation Army, the only homeless shelter in town, banned him, it was pretty much his only option.

Shelly had a restraining order. Just walking through the door was enough to get him arrested. He left, but not quietly. Blevins's mode of communication was, to say the least, colorful.

That night, the diner's plate glass window was shattered. She replaced it. The next night, a rock went through the new window. On the third window, Shelly spent the big bucks on unbreakable glass. It was cheaper than continual window replacement.

I asked Jim why the cops couldn't do something. Everybody knew Blevins broke the windows. He reminded me *everybody knows* isn't enough. They had to catch him in the act. The one time they caught him, he didn't go away for long. Blevins broke, but he didn't enter. No matter how expensive it was, vandalism wasn't as serious a charge as breaking and entering. He was mean. He was nasty. He preyed on those he saw as weak, but he wasn't entirely stupid.

"I need money." He headed straight for Mrs. Gardner, the meekest of the three women in the lobby. She shrank away and clutched her purse.

"You need to leave. You know you're not allowed in here." Blevins didn't scare me. He was all about intimidation and sneakiness, not outright assault.

"Can you at least give me a cup of coffee? I need coffee." He was at the urn before I could answer.

"Take your coffee and leave. Otherwise, I will call the police," I said.

"I can't believe you are giving him coffee! He has no right to be here! And he stinks!" Evelyn's screech and fingernails on a blackboard had a lot in common.

I wasn't giving it to him, more like letting him take it, but she acted like I invited him to tea. Her feathers weren't just ruffled. She puffed up with rage.

Please don't explode. I don't want to clean up the mess. I watched Evelyn turn purple with fury and didn't notice Blevins next to me until I smelled him. She was right. He stank.

"You're a real bitch." He took a mouthful of coffee and before Evelyn could reply, shot it all over her. If he were a comedian, it would have qualified as the best spit-take ever. For about three seconds, he was my hero.

"Coffee sucks anyways." He dumped it on the floor and splattered all three of us.

"You need to leave. Now, or I'm calling the police." My wet shoes washed away any hero-worship.

Blevins let loose with one of the rich streams of invective for which he was famous. It was almost poetry. His last line as he went out the door was "Nice fucking windows."

BY THE TIME I got everybody and everything cleaned up and settled down—and got rid of Evelyn—I was a good hour behind my self-imposed schedule. On my drive home, two hours later than usual, I thought about dinner. I had no desire to cook, but I'd already played my one pizza card for the week.

Abby loved to cook. Except for a few simple things, she needed supervision, which took as much or more energy as doing the cooking myself. As for Jim, he was a disaster in the kitchen. I'd told him many times my next husband would be both rich and a gourmet cook. I didn't know which was a higher priority.

Dinner needed to be something quick and easy. I tried to remember what we had to throw into a pasta salad—and saw Blevins on his bike. Whenever I passed him on the road, I fought the urge to run him down. Most of my fellow Port Massasauguans admitted to the same urge. Blevins still lived only because no one would believe running him down was an accident, and prison jumpsuits weren't flattering to any figure type. The memory of him spewing coffee all over Evelyn bought him some goodwill. When I passed, I gave him more than his bicyclist's three feet. I almost waved at him.

Abby and Jim met me at the door. Jim's grin was as loopy as Abby's. They were up to something. He took my coat and briefcase, and Abby led me to the dining room. The table was set with my vintage Fiesta Ware. Something was on the plates covered by napkins—the good linen napkins.

Oh, god. More laundry.

"Sit down. Don't touch anything until Daddy gets here." Abby pointed me at my chair. As soon as Jim joined us, she whipped the napkin off my plate.

A peanut butter and dill pickle sandwich. Jim and Abby loved them, but I didn't see the appeal.

"The pickles count as vegetables," Jim said. "By the way, my mom called." He winked, and Abby giggled.

Abby was a sponge for other people's moods. After a weekend with Evil-lyn, she came home sullen and critical of everything. Go figure. After time with my parents, who took the grand-parents-are-more-fun-than-parents philosophy as gospel, she came home glowing, in love with everybody and everything.

She was happy and mirrored Jim's silliness. It was one of her clear days. I needed to sit back and enjoy her and the ridiculous sandwich before she caught my crankiness, but all I could think about was jammies, a good book, and as soon as she and Jim weren't looking, the bag of Oreos stashed in the back of the cupboard.

"Well. That was delicious." Not as delicious as the Oreos would be, but they didn't need to know about my hidden treasure.

"Stay put," Abby said. When she got bossy, she really got bossy.

"Is this going to take long?" My comfy pajamas were calling my name.

"Just sit." She and Jim went to the kitchen.

I relaxed a little while I listened to them in the other room. Something hit the floor, followed by an *oops* and more giggles. I tried not to think about the mess they were making. With any luck, Sami would clean up the floor.

"Brownie Sundaes!" Abby was back. Jim was right behind her with a loaded tray.

She stuck a bowl in front of me. A ginormous slab of brownie topped with ice cream, hot fudge, whipped cream and, oh yes, a cherry.

I loved my family. Peanut butter, dill pickles, and all.

ABBY AND JIM both called it an early night and left me downstairs alone. I curled up on the couch with my book and enjoyed the quiet. The night was freakishly warm for the time of year. The door to the sun porch stood open, and Sami lay on the porch enjoying the night air.

Sami growled.

At first, I thought it was the big orange cat from across the street. He loved to sit just close enough to the house to get Sami riled up. Once Sami worked up a good frenzy, the cat washed his butt. When one of us humans finally bellowed *Enough* at the dog, the cat got up, stretched, and sauntered away, his work done.

I waited for the barking, but it never came. Just the deep growl. I put my book down and got up to see what was going on.

Sami went crazy. She ran through the house and hurled herself at the back door—then she barked.

Insane barking. *Timmy's down the well barking. There's a clown car in the driveway barking.*

She ran back through the living room, halfway up the stairs to the landing and barked at the window. Back down, back to the porch. She barked, ran to the back door, and repeated the process.

I was almost to the porch when she barreled at me, head-butted me, and grabbed my pajama leg in her teeth. Unless I wanted ripped pants, I wasn't going anywhere.

"What the hell is going on?" Jim stood at the bottom of the stairs.

"I have no idea. Something out front set her off. I don't know what. She won't let me move."

Jim headed for the porch.

Sami let go of me. She growled, lunged, and snapped.

One time when Sami and I were getting out of the car, the mailman came around the corner of the house and startled me. No blood was shed, but Sami sent him home for a change of underwear. Until then, although I knew she took her people-protection duties seriously, I'd never seen her spring into action.

Dogs have forty-two teeth—ten more than humans have, but still only forty-two, not the hundred and forty-two they look like when they're all bared and snapping.

Sami flashed them all. More frightening than the teeth, she bared them at Jim. Jim, the puppy-loving marshmallow, source of treats and Frisbee fun and all things good in doggy-world.

"Sami. Sit!" It didn't work. She barked and snarled and displayed an alarming number of teeth. Neither of us wanted to try to get past her.

Then it was over. She slumped and hung her head, like someone hit her off switch. I swore I heard her sigh.

"What was that all about?"

"I have no idea," Jim said.

We went to the porch and looked out the windows, but saw nothing to explain Sami's freak-out.

Jim got a flashlight. "Stay here," he said.

"Yeah. Like that's going to happen." I followed him out the door.

We searched the front yard and walked all around the house. We found nothing out of the ordinary, not even a big orange cat.

4.
[BLEVINS]

"THIS IS BORING." BLEVINS AND THE OTHER HID IN THE shadows of the tree line.

"Wait."

"They have beer, and I don't." The other promised him a good time, but so far they just stood around and watched a bunch of rednecks party. The yahoos were having fun. He wasn't.

"They also have a gun."

"So? I'd rather have beer. And I don't see no fucking gun," Blevins said.

"Watch."

"I can't see nothin."

"Shut up and pay attention."

Blevins groaned. If he humored the ugly son of a bitch, maybe he'd get bored and they could go find some real fun. Break windows or something. He shut up and watched.

The once white doublewide had turned to dirty gray with pieces of its faded red trim missing. Rotted plywood covered two windows. Blevins squatted in abandoned buildings in better shape. On one corner hung an American flag and on the opposite, a Confederate flag, both survivors of a few too many winters. The trailer's front yard held two barbecue grills and a rusted burn can, but the men gathered around a bonfire. One sat in a rickety lawn chair. Two more stood nearby. Empty beer cans littered the ground.

Blevins didn't recognize any of the three, but he knew one of the two pick-up trucks parked in the yard. While he was on his bike that afternoon, the jacked-up Ford F-150, tailgate covered in Pennzoil decals and stupid bumper stickers, passed him. The driver laid on the horn and cut close enough to run him off the road. He hoped it was parked there every night.

He'd be back. Before he smashed the windows, he'd flatten the tires.

Bits of talk and wood smoke drifted his way.

"Hey. Mopey. You need to cheer up. She's not worth it." The man in the *Show Me Your Tits* shirt kicked Mopey's chair. The chair teetered—Blevins waited for it to collapse, but Mopey regained his balance and righted himself. Mopey reached down, grabbed Tits's ankle, and with a quick jerk, dumped him on the ground. Blevins laughed.

"Asshole! You made me spill my beer!" Tits had a point.

"She always said she hated my friends," Mopey said. "I think she meant you."

"I like Mopey," Blevins said. Maybe there'd be a fight. At least they were finally doing something besides standing around.

"Shut up," the other said.

"Everybody chill." The guy in the biker jacket took a beer from a blue cooler and tossed it to Tits.

Blevins liked the jacket, but didn't mention it. He was sick of being told to shut up.

"I'll cut him some slack tonight, being that he's broken-hearted and all," Tits said, "but if it wasn't for that...I have an idea." He stumbled up the three steps into the trailer.

"Maybe he'll fall on his face on the way out," Blevins said. "I know. Shut up."

"Then do it," the other said.

"Look! Stress relief." Tits was back. The beer was gone. Instead, he held a gun.

"I don't like guns. We're gonna get shot," Blevins said.

"Don't worry about it." The other was one cool motherfucker.

"Where'd you get that?" Biker Boy was impressed.

"My old man left it to me." Tits waved the gun over his head.

"Your old man is still alive."

"Yeah. He doesn't know he left it to me."

"He's gonna kick your ass."

"Not if I'm holding this." Tits fired once into the sky, then again into the fire.

"Ooooo. Fireworks. Can we go now?" Blevins said.

"Wait." For the first time, the other's voice held a hint of emotion. Blevins wasn't sure what it was. Not quite excitement. Anticipation?

"Hey, Mopey." Tits looked as if he might kick the chair again but thought better of it. "Try this. It'll make you feel better."

Mopey waved him off and took another pull of his beer.

"Lemmee try it." Biker Boy held out his hand, and Tits gave him the gun. He turned it over and examined it. "M1911. Niiiiiiiiiice." He let off two shots into the fire, took aim at the Confederate flag at the far corner of the trailer, and put a hole in it.

"Hey! Asshole! That's my Bocephus flag! Give it back!"

Biker Boy laughed and handed Tits the gun.

"Shit. It's already got one hole in it." Tits pointed the gun at the flag, fired, and missed.

Biker Boy was practically doubled over laughing. "You oughta sell it to me."

"Hell no. It was my grampa's. Had it in the army or something."

"Army? What army was he in? The booze-hound brigade? Hey! Don't point that thing at me!"

"Watch your mouth. Besides, it's empty," Tits said.

"Didn't your old man teach you anything? Never point a gun at a man unless you're willing to kill him. Loaded or unloaded. And it's not empty."

"What makes you think I'm not willing to kill you? And it is too empty." Tits lifted his hand and ticked off his fingers with the barrel of the gun.

"He's counting on his fucking fingers," Blevins said. "It's his gun. He oughta know what's left in it."

"He does. Or did. Watch," the other said.

"Six shots," Tits said. "It's empty."

"And one in the chamber. You shouldn't sell it to me. You should give it to me. You're too fucking stupid to keep it." Biker Boy opened another beer.

"Tits oughta shoot him," Blevins said. "Fucking know-it-all."

"Shut up and watch."

Mopey looked up from his beer. "I'm pretty sure it's empty."

"Ha. Another country heard from. I'm telling you, it's empty. Look." Tits put the gun to his temple and pulled the trigger.

Blevins heard the pop and watched. He watched the blood spurt from the wound and pour from the man's mouth. He watched the gun fall from Tits's hand and the body sink to the ground.

"Shit," Biker Boy said.

Mopey puked.

Blevins smiled. "Cool. How'd you know that would happen?"

"I made it happen." The other shrugged.

"Stop shittin' me."

No answer from the other.

"Fucking idiot just can't count. Couldn't count." As much as Blevins wanted to believe, he couldn't quite wrap his mind around what the other was—or wasn't—saying.

One corner of the other's mouth twitched in something that almost passed for a grin before it disappeared.

"Seriously? You can do that?"

Still no answer.

"I wanna do that." *Way better than breaking windows.*

"Later. I'm hungry."

"I might have enough for a burger. Maybe fries." Blevins pulled a handful of change from his pocket.

"I need more. Let's go."

Blevins and his new best buddy walked toward the two survivors.

5.

[CAROLE]

I DIDN'T KNOW THE MEN INVOLVED, BUT I KNEW WHERE IT happened.

What a lot of people thought of as Port Massasauga was part of the township, not the city. Just outside of town, Workman Road was township. It was heavily wooded, and the homes were widely spaced. A few were nice—and expensive—houses built by Port Massasauga newcomers, but most were trailers, and not the tidy well-maintained variety. They were peeled-siding, plastic-and-duct-tape-on-the-windows, Christmas-lights-up-all-year-around trailers. Some sat just as they were when hauled in decades ago. Some had ramshackle additions. Front yards were overgrown and filled with trashcans and rusty cars on blocks. Most had satellite dishes on their roofs, and at night the curtain-less windows lit up with the glow of giant-screen televisions.

The newcomers campaigned to have Workman Road annexed by the city. They wanted city zoning regulations enforced and the eyesores on their bucolic road cleaned up.

Most reports of gunshots on Workman Road—the reports always came from the newcomers—turned out to be out-of-season hunters or rednecks letting off steam. This time, the county sheriffs found three men dead. The newspaper called it a suspected murder-suicide.

THE MISTERS DONATHAN, Hensley, Bartone, and Pekonen, four

of my favorite Senior Center regulars, were back from their second suspension for gambling on the premises. All in their eighties, they enjoyed bragging about being on probation at the Senior Center. Old man bad-assery at its finest. They played poker for toothpicks. If anyone asked, they claimed it was pinochle. They sat in the corner, and the cards were out. I had a hunch the toothpicks represented more than toothpicks and headed over to remind them a third strike meant they'd need to find another place to hang out.

Just short of their table, I stopped. Eavesdropping on fogey chatter was always entertaining and sometimes enlightening, one of the small perks of my job.

Entertaining didn't fit their subject. I didn't understand why women had the reputation for gossip. Old guys were the worst.

"I heard some animal got to 'em. Musta been huge. They were devoured. Ripped apart." Mr. Donathan dealt the cards.

"Don't be an idiot. If anything got them, it was a fox," Mr. Hensley said.

"It was one of them black bears." Mr. Bartone had a thing about black bears. Every summer, one wandered into town, and he worried until the snow fell. Sometimes later.

"What I don't get is why the guy with the hole in his head was all in one piece. And you keep dealing this crap, you could end up with a hole in your head," Mr. Pekonen said.

"I got enough of 'em already," Mr. Donathan said. "Maybe he watched the other two get eaten and shot hisself just to get the picture out of his head."

"Especially if it was a black bear," Mr. Bartone said.

"That doesn't even make sense. Don't you read the paper? Fold." Mr. Pekonen tossed his cards on the table.

"What? You believe everything they put in the paper? You're a moron. Call." Mr. Hensley said.

"He shoulda shot the bear first. I'm out." When Mr. Bartone got started on bears, he had a lot in common with Abby.

"Where do you guys get this stuff?" I asked.

"Oh, we listen," Mr. Donathan said. "You should too. You wouldn't believe half of what goes on around here."

"She's married to a cop. She knows what's what," Mr. Pekonen said.

"That's right. You got any juicy stuff for us?" Mr. Bartone perked up.

"No, and you know I wouldn't tell you if I did. Interesting variation of pinochle. I always thought it used more cards. If any money changes hands, make sure it's after you leave here." I left them to their game.

I discounted half their talk—okay, ninety percent of it—but I knew the Workman Road events were uglier than the official newspaper version. They always were.

The township was county sheriff's jurisdiction, and I was glad Jim was a city cop. In almost twenty years with the police, Jim saw terrible things. He seldom shared them with me, but when he needed to talk, I listened. Even then, I suspected he spared me the worst of the details. The rare Port Massasauga murder was usually drug related—ugly, but clean. The domestics bothered him, especially when children were involved, and the air got tense around the house. The Workman Road mess involved rednecks, not children, but still sounded nasty enough to make for tension at home.

In the afternoon, Ms. Colley called again.

"Well, at least this time we know what inspired her," she said.

Abby didn't start it. Devon did. He lived in one of the new houses on Workman Road and probably just repeated things he'd heard at home. Although Abby might have seen the front page of the paper, I knew her additions to the conversation were nothing she heard at home.

"Some of it was the same things she said last time, about ripping their throats out and splattering them all over," Ms. Colley said, "but this time she added, 'those two were just a snack,' 'he only wants the live ones,' and 'wait 'til he gets really hungry.' The weird part—she sounds so matter-of-fact about it all."

For a kid who hated scary stuff, blood and guts storytelling was out of character.

The ability to hold two completely different ideas in her head at once or make two plans and the inability to see the conflict between the two was typical for Abby. I found myself saying, "Abby, you cannot go to the A-Tech next year and stay in Ms. Colley's class at Creekside at the same time," or "Abby, if you are spending the weekend with your grandmother, how are you going to spend the night at Twyla's house?" or something similar on a daily basis.

Most of Abby's dual track thoughts made sense in an Abby-way. If she could picture two sets of events, both were real and connected for her. Sometimes I had to strain for the connection, but to her it was obvious. I long ago accepted that I would never completely understand the workings of Abby's mind, but I couldn't find the connection between what I thought of as Abby-normal and the new Abby-gruesome.

When I told Jim about Abby's latest round of storytelling, he didn't say anything.

"Okay. What are you not telling me?" I asked.

"She probably just picked up on some of the gossip. I bet the school was full of it."

"The Center certainly was. Is the stuff about an animal true?"

"I really can't tell you anything more than what you read in the paper."

"You know, that is exactly why so many cops end up divorced," I said.

It wasn't a city investigation, but cops talked—to each other. I was pissed but knew better than to press him for more information. Something about Ms. Colley's call disturbed him. From the look on his face, trying to get him to tell me what would be as futile as trying to get Abby to talk after an *Idunno* and would only piss me off more.

"Why don't you take the dog out," I said.

THE NIGHT THE lights went out, Jim and I were out to dinner with friends. Abby was home alone—sort of. At seventeen, she rebelled at the idea of a sitter.

"I am not a baby," she said.

My line between over-protective and irresponsible parenting was blurry, especially after Abby hit adolescence and it started moving. We left her alone after school. As far as I was concerned, that earned me a shiny gold star in the *Encourage Independence* category. Leaving her alone after the sun went down was a different matter. She didn't agree.

"I am seventeen. Seventeen-year-olds do not need babysitters.

Seventeen-year-olds are babysitters."

We compromised—my euphemism for getting sneaky. When Jim and I went out for an evening, Pete's wife Livvy dropped in for a visit and acted surprised to find us gone. She and Abby loved each other, and Livvy usually brought cookies. Even if Abby tired of socializing and went up to her room, Livvy stayed until we came home. Someday, Abby would figure out what was going on, but since Livvy was a neighbor and a friend, she hadn't yet. At least, she hadn't told us so. Maybe she just liked the cookies.

At the restaurant, we waited about fifteen minutes in the dark. When the electricity didn't come back on, we made our apologies and left. Not only did we want to check on Abby—even though I was sure Livvy was there—a prolonged power outage meant alarm drops and people getting the stupids. There was a good chance Jim would be called in to work.

Between Friday night traffic and no streetlights, our ten-minute drive home took over a half hour. When I asked what good it was to be married to a cop if you couldn't use lights and sirens when you needed them, Jim snorted. I made the same joke often.

The house was pitch dark. Abby didn't answer when we called, but Livvy met us at the back door, flashlight in hand.

"I didn't get here until the lights went out," she said. "I had to let myself in. She didn't answer the door." Livvy had a spare key to our house. "She's in her room. She did acknowledge me, but didn't want to come downstairs, so I gave her a flashlight and left her there. The dark didn't seem to bother her. In fact, she seemed pretty happy with the situation." Livvy'd known Abby since she was a toddler and knew better than to push for typical reactions.

"Oh yeah. There's cookies on the kitchen counter. Chocolate chip with pecans."

Livvy and Pete were the best neighbors in the world. We thanked her, and she left.

Jim grabbed a flashlight, and we headed upstairs. Abby sat cross-legged on her bed. Her fingers danced. Her eyelids fluttered, and her eyes showed only white. To anyone who didn't know her, it would look like a seizure. We knew she was deep in Abby-land.

Both Jim and I had always assumed Abby-land was a happy place. When there, Abby always smiled. She looked downright blissful. Sometimes, I wished I could join her there. We never wanted to call her home and were sorry when we were forced to.

That night, however, she looked anything but blissful. Her lips were pinched, a tight straight line. On one side of her jaw, a muscle throbbed. Her forehead was furrowed, her eyebrows knit into a uni-brow. She appeared lost in intense—and worried—concentration.

"Abby! ABBY!" We both tried to call her back, but she continued to rock, unaware of our presence. Rocking was supposed to soothe her. Often, watching her rock soothed me, but there was no comfort in that night's rocking. She ramped up the speed, the motion jerky rather than rhythmic. It hurt to watch her, and whether she needed it or not, I needed to bring her back to us.

I reached out to shake her, something we tried to avoid. Before I touched her, she stilled, and the lights flashed on. Her face was slack, her expression blank.

"He is finished," she said, her words as empty as her face.

"What? Who's finished?" Jim asked.

"The ceiling is red. Twyla would like it."

"Abby. Look at me. What ceiling?" I struggled to keep my voice calm, steady.

She looked at us then, and her face lit up with her big, loopy, Abby grin. "How was your dinner? Was it good?"

"Abby—" I lost the struggle, and Jim interrupted me.

"We didn't get to eat. The lights went off before we even ordered our food."

"Me too," Abby said. "Sandwiches?"

Tuna on toast wasn't in our plans for the evening, but it was one of Abby's specialties and she enjoyed making it for us. Jim took his first bite and pronounced it delicious. Abby glowed.

It was a normal family night. A happy family night. I relaxed and went with the flow. Whatever was going on with my daughter, I couldn't solve it then. Better to concentrate on Abby's sandwiches and Livvy's cookies.

The next day, Jim went to work, and Abby and I spent the day doing

Saturday things. We half-cleaned the house and shopped for Twyla's birthday present, a weird fleece pillow supposed to look like a pizza. I thought it was hideous, but Abby assured me Twyla would love it. Abby decided she should bake a batch of her Killer Brownies.

"They will be a surprise for Daddy," she said.

I never argued with brownies.

Whenever I tried to bring up the previous night, all I got was "Twyla would like the ceiling" or "There will be five of us at Twyla's party. That is just enough." Pushing her resulted in an *Idunno*. We were having such a good day I decided not to force it.

I was one of the last to hear what happened during the blackout.

Evelyn called. She asked for Jim, but when I told her he was working, she deigned to speak to me.

"I hope you are planning a good dinner," she said. "With the day he is no doubt having, he'll need it."

I was a crap housekeeper, but nobody ever accused my family of being underfed. *She's Jim's mother. Be nice.*

"Abby made brownies. Why?"

"You haven't heard? Oh, that's right. You're too good for television. The Connors family. Dead. All of them. They found them late this morning."

I knew the Connors. Not well, but Marnie was in my Lamaze class when I was carrying Abby. Although our girls were the same age, we seldom saw each other after they were born. Kyra and Abby didn't move in the same circles. Kyra was a cheerleader and on the Creekside Homecoming court. The two younger boys, red-headed twins, were hell-raisers. The month before, they took a 1969 Mustang for a joyride, totaled it, and were arrested for under-age drinking and grand theft.

"Nobody was hurt," Jim told me, "but the car. God, that was painful."

Evelyn was still talking. Once she got started, she barely stopped for breath. I only half listened. She was prone to exaggeration.

"I need to go. The timer's going off. Time to take the brownies out of the oven." They were cooling on the counter, but I wanted off the phone. My mother-in-law was not the most reliable source of information. I wanted to check the local newspaper online. Maybe their report would be less melodramatic.

The *Telegraph's* website had a short paragraph, no names, no details, just "Port Massasauga police are investigating..." and "More details in tomorrow's edition." Local television stations had the story. Channel 19, true to form, sounded like Evelyn wrote their headlines. *Family of 5 Slaughtered! Small Town Atrocity!* I didn't want to play the videos with Abby around, and the articles were more innuendo than news.

Evelyn needn't have worried about me feeding her son. I had meatloaf and mashed potatoes—comfort food—ready, but by the time he got home, after midnight, he had no appetite. He did need to talk.

He sat still—rigid—his head down and his voice toneless. "They were...ripped apart. All of them. The kids. Like something ate them. And the blood. So much blood. On the floor. On the walls."

He was silent for a moment, then raised his head and looked into my eyes. "There was blood all over the fucking ceiling."

Sometimes, when the brain is hit with something it can't handle, it shuts down.

A black wall slammed down inside my head. My senses—the sound of Jim's voice, the glare of the room lights, the lingering smell of brownies and meatloaf—became physical, solid, heavy, pressed against me, smothered me.

I wonder if this is how Abby feels when she has a meltdown...

When I could breathe again, I realized Jim was next to me. He held my hand, and we sat in silence for I don't know how long. It felt like forever.

6.
[BLEVINS]

TURNED OUT LEATHER WASN'T ALL THAT WARM. BLOCKED THE wind, but not much more. Didn't matter. Blevins liked his new jacket. Made him feel tough. Strong. But when he thought about the night he got it, things went fuzzy. His head hurt.

He remembered Tits and the gun. Fucking awesome. He even remembered what the gun was—M1911—and he didn't know shit about guns. He remembered walking toward the men and standing in front of them.

"Your buddy was pretty fucking stupid, huh?" he said.

Biker Boy and Mopey were upright, but otherwise not much difference between them and Tits.

"Hey? Anybody home?"

The men stared straight ahead. Blevins couldn't figure out what they were looking at. All he saw were trees. Boring.

He snapped his fingers under Biker Boy's nose. Not a flinch. Good thing. If the big dude woke up, he could snap Blevins in two without breaking a sweat.

"Hey, Mopey. She still hates your fucking guts." He waved both hands in front of Mopey's face. "Maybe I'll pay her a visit. See if she's lonely and in need of a real man." No reaction. "What's wrong with them?"

"You want the jacket?" the other said.

"Uh, sure."

"Give it to him."

Biker Boy took off his leather jacket and handed it to Blevins. Too big, but he didn't care. "I want Mopey's do-rag too."

Mopey pulled the red bandana off his head and held it out.

"Holy shit. Did I do that?"

"No, not yet," the other said.

Blevins took the bandana and stuffed it into the pocket of his new jacket. Do-rag or snot-rag, he'd decide later. "How long they gonna be like that?"

"Long enough."

"I gotta take care of something."

He let the air out of the Ford's tires. He smashed the windows. He did the same to the second truck. Might as well. Who was going to stop him? When he finished, he felt *good*. Energized. High. He went back to the fire.

Blevins remembered going back to the fire, but then things got cloudy. Foggy, like the night he met the other, but inside his head.

Mopey and Biker Boy. Where were they? He couldn't find them. The smoke. He remembered the smell of smoke and beer, mixed with something sweet. And wet dog. He swore he smelled wet dog. And copper. Something smelled like pennies tasted.

The harder he tried to see Mopey and Biker Boy, the more his head hurt and the thicker the fog got.

"Let's go." The other stood in the doorway of the trailer. He wore clean clothes. His hair was wet.

"A shower? I want one," Blevins said.

"No time. Let's go."

"One second." Blevins took two beers from the cooler. "Want one?"

"No. Come on."

He stuffed one beer into his jacket pocket and popped the second. "Now we can go."

They walked back to town. Blevins hated walking.

"What happened to those guys?"

Silence.

"You need a bike. I can get you one." Town was full of unlocked garages.

The other looked healthier, sort of. A little less dead, at least. Even with the shower and clean clothes, he still smelled putrid.

"What's your name?"

"Doesn't matter," the other said.

"What do I call you?"

"Doesn't matter."

"How about if I call you Rat Bastard?" Blevins drained his beer and tossed the can away.

"Doesn't matter."

"How about if I call you Ugly?"

"Doesn't matter."

He opened the second beer and decided to call the guy Ugly, but only to himself. Ugly might decide it did matter, and Blevins didn't want to piss him off.

UNBELIEVABLE HOW MANY morons left their cars unlocked. Some stupid bitch even left her purse on the seat. As far as he was concerned, it was a gift. Not a lot of money, but enough for beer and Ho Hos. Ugly'd been missing for a couple of days, so he didn't have to share. Ugly never wanted any of his food, but there was always a first time.

Maybe Ugly moved on. Or got himself arrested.

With his belly full of beer and cake, Blevins didn't care. He stretched out and went to sleep.

"Wake up."

He recognized the stink. Ugly was back. "Go the fuck away," he mumbled.

"Get up. We're going for a walk," Ugly said.

"Fuck you. I'm sleeping."

"I said get up. Now."

Blevins rolled over and ignored him. The kick to the middle of his back jarred him awake. He sat up. "Stupid motherfu—whoa."

To the west, flames lit the night sky. Maybe the whole town was on fire.

"Where?" Blevins asked.

"Pallet yard."

Until the morning he overslept and got caught, Blevins spent rainy nights in an outbuilding at Forest Savers. Not only did the asshole who found him throw him out, the next night all the sheds wore heavy chains and padlocks.

Forest Savers didn't have big glass windows, but they did have a football field sized yard full of old wood pallets waiting to be recycled. Tinder. Blevins tried to set it alight but only managed to get one stack going before some shithead saw it and called the fire department. Forest Savers hired a night watchman.

He wanted to get the whole yard going at once and make one badass fire. It was on his bucket list.

Ugly'd done it.

"You can wake me up anytime."

"Count on it," Ugly said. "Come on."

He got up and went.

Cops blocked off the streets around the fire, but the bike trail was packed with morons snapping pictures with their cell phones. Blevins loathed crowds. "This is close enough."

"They're not going to notice you," Ugly said, but he stopped at the edge of the mob.

"They always notice me." He counted trucks from eight fire departments. This was one crazy fire—bigger and better than he'd dreamed.

The crowd grew. He was surrounded. "We need to go. I'm gonna get blamed for this."

"You're safe when I'm with you," Ugly said.

Blevins wanted to believe him, but people stared at him. The weight of their gazes crushed his chest. Strangled him. He gasped for air.

A guy with a camera interviewed a fat kid.

"My cousin said he saw two guys starting it," the kid said.

"Did your cousin talk to the police?" Camera Guy asked.

"Nah. He hates cops."

"What about the night watchman?"

The kid laughed. "I heard he was a crispy critter. A sizzle burger. A human torch."

Camera Guy shook his head and turned to Blevins.

"We need to go." Blevins choked, the words razors in his throat.

"Not yet," Ugly said.

Camera Guy moved closer. He stopped to talk to a blond woman, but Blevins knew the guy was after him. Staring at him. He trembled. His knees threatened to give way. He tried to move, but his feet stuck to the ground. His ears rang. The back of his head pounded.

Camera Guy moved again.

The glare of the fire burned his eyes. Beer and Ho Hos threatened to come back up. Camera Guy was almost on top of him. He needed air.

"Let's go," Ugly said.

Blevins moved. He still shook. His heart thumped and his head ached, but his feet worked. Ugly pushed through the crowd, and he followed.

"Wakey-wakey."

Ugly never let him sleep more than an hour at a time. Sometimes less. After the first two nights, Blevins wanted to throttle him. Slug him. Teach him a fucking lesson. He tried, but somehow he never got ahold of Ugly. The bastard looked like a sick old man. Worse than when they met. How did he move so fast?

Blevins worked out a plan to kill Ugly while he slept. He imagined bashing the dickwad's head in with a rock. He even had the rock picked out.

He was psyched, until he realized Ugly never slept. At least not when Blevins was around.

Blevins tried to shake him. He changed campsites. Ugly found him. He tried sleeping in the park. Ugly found him—if the cops didn't roust him first.

Day or night, whenever and wherever he slept, Ugly found him.

"Come on, boy, sit up," Ugly said.

No use fighting. When he did, Ugly kicked him. He didn't need any more bruises. He opened his eyes.

Daylight. The bastard let him sleep all night. Didn't feel like it.

"Here. I brought you a present." Ugly held out a McDonalds cup.

He sat up and took it. Coffee. He wondered if Ugly'd done something to it. Spit in it. Pissed in it. He didn't care. It was coffee.

Coffee with lots of sugar, exactly the way he liked it.

"There's more." Ugly tossed him a wrapped sandwich.

His mouth watered at the smell of grease. He tore off the paper and stuffed half the egg sandwich into his mouth.

He was savoring the last crumbs of biscuit when it hit him. Ugly never had any money.

"How'd you get this?"

"Bought it."

"Where'd you get the cash?"

"Business transaction."

Blevins took a swallow of coffee and looked around. "Where's my bike?"

"You don't need it."

"Fuck you, asshole." He dropped the coffee and stood. "Where is it?"

"I don't like bikes."

"I'm gonna kill you!" He leapt at the other.

Next thing he knew, he was flat on his back. Ugly sat on his chest, his hands around Blevins's neck. No pressure, but Blevins felt them, like a collar.

He fought. He bucked and kicked. He grabbed Ugly's arms and pulled.

Ugly stayed calm and rode him like a kiddie ride at the county fair. The bastard was heavier than he looked.

Blevins stopped fighting. "Go ahead. Squeeze."

"I could take you now." Not a threat. An indifferent statement.

"Then why don't you?"

"You're not ready."

"Fuck you." He spat in Ugly's face.

Ugly contracted his hands—not much, just enough to hurt.

Blevins grasped at the fingers on his throat. He couldn't get a grip. He pounded Ugly's chest.

"This is good," Ugly said, "you were getting boring." He tightened his hold on Blevins's neck.

He clawed Ugly's face. His eyes—he'd take out the fucker's eyes.

Ugly squeezed.

Blevins's head roared. He longed to give up, cry uncle, let Ugly know he'd won, but his body wouldn't let him. Against his will, he twisted and kicked. He clutched Ugly's wrists. They didn't budge.

Where did the sick SOB get his strength?

Black spots invaded his vision. His tongue swelled, filled his mouth. He met the other's eyes and looked away. *I give up.*

Ugly released him.

Icy-hot air burnt his throat, and his lungs filled with pins and needles.

"You'll be ready soon." Ugly got up. "You need a fire. You'll freeze to death."

Blevins stayed where he was. "Did you get much for it?" His throat was raw. He sounded like a frog.

"Enough for your breakfast."

Fuck.

THE NIGHT AIR nipped at his face and raised goose bumps under his jacket. Snow was on its way—he smelled it. He should build a fire, but even thinking about it wore him out.

It was time to go away for the winter. He knew what he needed to do. Break a window. Piss in a planter on Main Avenue. Get caught and get locked up. A nice warm bed and three meals a day. Without Ugly.

He'd do it tomorrow.

He said that every night.

Ugly told him not to worry about it. "This will be your best winter ever. I promise."

But, he was freezing and Ugly was nowhere to be seen.

His list. Time to make his list.

He strained to remember where he was and what he did during the day. All he saw was Ugly.

Ugly. Life was good before he showed up. Where was he? Blevins hated him for not being there. He hated himself more for caring.

"Oh, Blevins. You missed me."

"Where you been?" Blevins tried to sound nonchalant.

"Preparing."

"For what?" He looked up. Ugly loomed over him. "God. You're a mess." He slouched and pulled his jacket up around his ears. The smell of wet dog turned his stomach.

"Look at me."

"No," Blevins said, but he couldn't help himself. He looked into the other's eyes.

"Time for you to go."

Blevins tasted pennies and heard faraway screams.

He didn't realize they were his own.

HE STOOD AND stretched. Rolled his shoulders. A little tight, a little stiff, but new shoes always were.

Anger. Blevins was a very angry man. It tasted like honey. And hatred. More than he expected. He basked in its glow.

Best of all, deep inside, he still heard—felt—Blevins's screams.

Blevins. Yes. He could be Blevins for a while. With any luck, a long while.

But first, sleep. Feed.

And then, the girl.

7.
[CAROLE]

IT'S HUMAN NATURE TO SEARCH FOR MEANING IN COINCIDENCE.

I told myself Abby's newfound interest in gore had no meaning. Somebody—a classmate, a kid on the bus—told her a story. Halloween was past, but winter was still the time of year for spooky stories. She heard something and latched onto it, and we had to wait it out. Even when her obsessions seemed to go on forever, they eventually faded. The latest would too.

The Connors family's murder was a coincidence. Poor timing.

A murdered family equaled coincidence. I was a horrible person, but I knew it, so it was okay.

Still, when I found Abby paused in a doorway, on her way to Abbyland, I tensed.

"Abby!" I didn't intend to snap, but I did.

"Huh."

"You stuck?"

"Noooo."

No hungry man. No red ceilings. We were back to our usual ritual. Coincidence, I convinced myself. Meaningless coincidence.

The Mighty Samsonite, on the other hand, developed issues. The hard-on-the-carpet kind of issues. She stopped asking to go out. She spent most of her time in Abby's room—except when she came downstairs and left a surprise in the corner of my office.

The dog who lived for walks sat down at the end of the driveway and wouldn't budge. Abby couldn't get the leash on her. Jim and I got her leashed, but we had to drag her to the backyard. Outside, she planted her feet and refused to go near her designated poopatorium or do what we took her out to do.

I stood with her and hauled her around the yard for an hour. Nothing. Ten minutes after we came in, I found her peeing in the corner of my office.

Jim thought it was hilarious.

"You're the one who insists we have a dog," he said, like he had nothing to do with it.

"Wait 'til I train her to aim for your shoes."

My daughter was her usual self. My dog was screwed up. My husband was a snot-ball. Life was...normal.

Normal was good.

I stopped grinding my teeth and considered buying stock in the Dog-Gone Odor Remover company.

Just call me Cleopatra, dwelling on de Nile.

ON MY BEST days, I'm not a morning person.

Abby didn't need my help getting ready for school. I got up because she liked to have me there. Our morning routine involved my physical presence but little active participation on my part. Jim's morning skills were sharper than mine—he got up and got to the caffeine first—and he took care of parental trivialities like lunch money.

He also kept my coffee cup filled. I loved that man.

If Abby was in a chatty mood, Jim handled the conversational heavy lifting. I might chime in with small talk, but mostly I cuddled my coffee cup and supplied agreeable noises and rote responses on an as-needed basis.

Abby made peanut butter toast for all of us.

It wasn't one of my better mornings. I hit the snooze button twice. The heavenly scents of toast and coffee finally lured me out of bed.

"It's about time," Jim said, his mouth full. "I had to eat your toast."

"You're a good man." I headed for the coffee pot. Since I was so late, I was willing to pour my first cup myself and let him chew.

Abby spread peanut butter on two more slices of toast.

"He was really hungry," she said.

"Then it's a good thing he got my toast."

"Not Daddy. The other guy."

I stopped. "Who?"

"Aunt Nancy and Uncle Kyle will be sad."

"Abby, who was hungry?" Jim asked.

"Twyla would like the ceiling, but I do not think Aunt Nancy will."

"Abby. Look at me." Jim upped his serious-dad voice to near cop-mode. "What are you talking about?"

"Idunno."

She shut down. Jim tried but couldn't get another word out of her. When the school bus arrived, she left without saying good-bye.

I'D KNOWN NANCY and Kyle pretty much all my life. They weren't really Abby's aunt and uncle, but we'd all met in kindergarten and remained good friends. They were family.

"Four kids? What were we thinking," Nancy said. "We need a vacation. A kid-free week."

She and Kyle arranged a second honeymoon.

"This time, I won't come back pregnant," she promised.

Her mother stayed with the children.

When none of the kids showed up for school and no one answered the phone, the school contacted the police. The dispatcher sent a patrol car to check on them.

Port Massasauga was like that.

It happened sometime during the night and nobody, not a single neighbor, heard a thing.

"As soon as the call came in, I knew," Jim said. "It was just like the last time. Worse. Those kids. Their grandmother. So much blood... the ceiling. How did she know?"

Abby never slept through the night. She woke up, got out of bed, and spent an hour or so at her computer. Sometimes, she sat in her bed and sang.

Or rocked herself to Abby-land.

I TOOK SICK leave from work. I slept while Abby was at school.

Ms. Colley would keep Abby focused in class. She wouldn't let her rock herself to Abby-land. The bus ride both to and from school was short, too short for anything to happen. I hoped.

At home, I watched.

"He's hungry."

Every time I caught her rocking or swaying or slipping away to her secret world, I stopped her.

"He's hungry," she said.

"Who?" I asked over and over but never got more than *Idunno* in return.

Nights I spent in the big chair in the corner of her room. Whenever she woke up, I made her lie down. We talked about silly, safe things, or I read to her.

We've read aloud to Abby since the day we brought her home, long before we knew anything was different about her. When she hit toddlerhood and still didn't sleep through the night, our midnight story sessions were the only thing that calmed her and kept me sane. When we began having her tested for developmental issues, somebody in the parade of doctors—they all ran together after a while—suggested we use the time for only non-fiction. View it as an educational opportunity. Expand her vocabulary. At the very least, only read stories based on real world needs. *This is the Way We Brush Our Teeth* or something equally boring. The doctor was concerned she wouldn't learn the difference between fantasy and reality.

Abby would have none of it. She liked *stories*. Folk tales were her favorites, followed by anything with talking animals. A story with both—*The Three Bears, The Three Little Pigs, Red Riding Hood*—was a bonanza. When she got older, she liked the classics and didn't want anything set in the modern world. We read *Little Women,* the *Alices, The Secret Garden*, and *Heidi* so many times I could recite them from memory.

We started *Little Women* again. I hoped it would keep us both calm and sane and keep me awake.

As far as I knew, there was no rocking or visits to Abby-land for a week, nor were there any more red ceilings in Port Massasauga.

Jim and I didn't discuss it.

ABBY GOT HER snow day. I'd sat awake in her room all night. Since she was home, I couldn't go to bed in the morning. I was tired and cranky, and to make matters worse, it was the day of our eye exams.

"Maybe they are there," Abby said for the fiftieth time.

"Everything is closed." My last shred of patience was slipping away.

"Maybe just school is closed. You should call. Maybe they are there."

"They called us. They're closed. I need to reschedule our appointments."

"You should call now. Please?"

"Abby. No one is there to answer the phone."

"Maybe they are."

"ABBY. They. Are. Closed. I'll call tomorrow. DROP IT."

She never dealt well with being yelled at. She stiffened and went into pause mode. She swayed.

"ABBY!"

"He is very angry," she whispered.

"WHO? ABBY, WHO IS ANGRY?" I couldn't stop yelling.

"Idunno." She shrugged and ran to her room.

I wanted to curl up in a ball and cry—or run away from home—but I followed her upstairs.

She sat on her bed and rocked.

"ABBY."

"Huh."

Her *huh* was a relief. She was still in this world. I pulled myself together and dredged up some cheerful. "I'm sorry I yelled. We have a snow day. Let's make the most of it. We'll bake cookies. Brownies. Watch movies. Make mac and cheese."

Mac and cheese always got her attention.

We spent the day on all those things and anything else I could come up with to keep us busy. The whole time, I spewed a stream of happy chatter.

No pauses. No rocking. No time to think.

Perky did not come naturally to me. The day left me drained.

Jim and I shared the night shift. Two hours asleep, two hours on watch. Although I couldn't fall sleep on my breaks, I struggled to stay awake on my watches. I was almost sure I managed it. Almost sure there was no rocking.

There was no real talk in our house the next morning, only grunts and monosyllables, the conversation of the sleep deprived.

Until Abby left for school. As the bus pulled up, right before she went out the door, she turned to me and grinned her loopy grin.

"Twyla's birthday party is today," she said. "She loves red. But no moving pictures. And five is just enough."

The door slammed and she was gone before I could ask, "Enough for what?"

LIKE ALICE, ABBY always said what she meant and meant what she said, and often left me feeling like the March Hare while I tried to sort it out.

The first time she made a pun, I practically threw a party.

She and I were visiting my mother-in-law. Sometimes, I couldn't avoid it. Abby sat on the couch. Evelyn's cat, Stella, curled up on the couch back next to Abby's head. Her purr was turned up to eleven.

Evelyn and I made small talk. Since any conversation with her was a minefield, I concentrated on avoiding the explosives. Abby was in her own world.

"Stella has fine motor skills," Abby announced and collapsed in giggles.

She knew exactly what she said. She started physical therapy when she was five.

I laughed and played it cool in front of her. In my head, I did the happy dance to end all happy dances, then ran to the other room and called her father. Jim was as thrilled as I was. I didn't think Evelyn got either the joke or the significance.

Five.

Twyla's party was at school, scheduled for the end of the day. Twyla, Devon, Abby, Ms. Colley, and Mrs. Lamb, the classroom aide. Five people at the party.

Just enough.

The school had a guard, a city cop nearing retirement, on the grounds. The doors were locked. Nobody could get in unless the guard hit his magic-buzzer button and let them in.

Nothing could happen. I needed to go to bed, get some sleep, and stop worrying.

Five is just enough.

Compared to me, the March Hare was the picture of mental health. Sleep wasn't going to happen.

I sent Ms. Colley a text and poured another cup of coffee.

There would be six at Twyla's party.

I TOOK THE shortcut on Betchel Road. None of Port Massasauga's Most Influential Citizens lived there, so it wasn't a high priority for the snow crews. It was barely plowed and hadn't seen a salt truck. The midday sunshine turned the snowstorm leftovers into a mess of wet, slush-covered ice. Another route would have been wiser, but in the Land of Lake Effect Snow, we took risks—and had four-wheel drive.

Between my lack of sleep and the overload of caffeine, I was in worse condition than the road. I locked the Jeep into 4WD, slowed down, and concentrated on where I was going. I didn't need to get there fast, just to get there.

Blevins stood in the middle of the road.

Even as I jammed on the brakes, I knew it was the wrong thing to do.

I swerved and lost control.

8.
[THE CEILING MAN]

THE GROUNDS BEHIND THE HIGH SCHOOL OVERFLOWED WITH teenagers. They shouted and laughed and threw snow at each other, but if the girl was among them, he didn't find her. He skipped from head to head. Weak minds. Open to him. Not all, but enough. The ones shivering in their shirtsleeves, too cool or too tough for coats, were his favorites. He made a few drop and roll around in the snow. Their classmates shrieked with laughter. His inner-Blevins was amused, but that didn't take much.

They were sheep, easy prey. Young, tender, and quite possibly delicious. He longed to cut through the flock, but he was here for the girl, not fun and games.

"Teenagers are mean little assholes," Blevins said.

«*Pot. Kettle.*»

"Huh?"

The bell rang, and the herd trickled into the building. He searched for his target, but he was too far away. The jumble of too many undisciplined minds hid her. He'd find her when he was inside. She was different. Once he was near, she'd stand out.

She would recognize him.

Access to the building was more complicated than he expected. In the past, he could walk into a school or anyplace else he wanted, but the place was a fortress. None of the side doors, including the one the sheep used, budged. He headed for the front entrance, like an invited guest.

A uniformed guard sat on the other side of the glass doors. Old guy. Fat. Sleepy. Looked like he was counting out the days until retirement. A pushover.

«*Let me in.*»

The guard looked up from his magazine and laughed.

"Blevins. You asshole." The man's thought might as well have been a shout.

"He's an ass," Blevins said, "and not too bright."

If he was dimmer than Blevins, he must be a vegetable.

«*Open the door.*»

He wasn't a vegetable. He resisted.

«*Let me in.*»

The rent-a-cop paled and swayed, but his hand went out and the door buzzed and unlocked before he collapsed and hit the floor.

If the guard hadn't fought back, he might have survived.

Wasted snack food, but the girl was his goal.

"This is so cool," Blevins said.

«*Shut up or I won't let you watch.*»

The Blevins-remnant obeyed.

He wasn't prepared for slamming doors and alarms, but he enjoyed them. The empty hallways were easy to navigate, but fear permeated the air like steam. A drug, it distracted him, made tracking the girl harder.

Harder, but not impossible.

He didn't need to search. She found him, and he homed in on her like a beacon.

9.
[ABBY]

At 9:32, Ms. Colley says, "Abby. Shush. No more talking about the birthday party until party time. You've brought it up fifty times already."

She is wrong. It is only thirty-two times, but I do not argue. If I argue, I know I will say *birthday party*.

At 11:14, Ms. Colley says, "Abby. Your mom is going to join us for Twyla's party. Won't that be fun?"

I do not answer. I am shushed and cannot talk about the party.

It is 12:37. The bell will ring at 12:40. At 12:40, Twyla's party will start. At 12:40, I can talk.

The clock is very slow. Maybe it is broken.

"Abby. You're making me seasick," Ms. Colley says.

She is telling me I am rocking. The rule says, "No rocking in class." I sit straight and still.

It is 12:39. My mom is not here. She should not be late. She has one minute left.

The bell rings. It is 12:40.

"Birthday party time!" I say. That makes thirty-three, but I do not tell Ms. Colley.

"Woot! Woot! Party time!" Devon shakes his butt.

Devon and I hang up the *Happy Birthday Twyla* banner, and Mrs. Lamb gets the presents from the closet.

Twyla picks one. It is not mine, but I try to be patient.

"NO," Devon says. "Cake first."

At Devon's house, birthdays are cake then presents. Twyla and I say presents then cake. There are two of us and one Devon.

"No, Devon. We voted. You lost. Presents first. It's on your list," I say.

Devon looks at his list. When Devon writes it on his list, it is final.

"Do not mess with the list," Devon says.

Twyla is already unwrapping her presents. All of them are wrapped in red paper. Red hearts. Red stripes. Red polka dots. All of them are red.

She likes my pizza pillow best.

We sing *Happy Birthday Dear Twyla*. Devon sings so loud I almost do not hear the intercom say, "Dooooop. Doop-doop. Dooooop. Doop."

I know what that means.

Twyla hugs my pizza pillow. She wears the red hat and scarf Mrs. Lamb made for her.

Devon does not notice the alarm. He sings, "You look like a monkey and you smell like one too."

Ms. Colley locks the door and turns off the lights and pulls down the window shades.

"Everybody to the Quiet Corner," Mrs. Lamb whispers.

We go. She follows us and brings Twyla's birthday cake.

Ms. Colley slips the green paper under the door. We are all safe and accounted for.

Mrs. Lamb cuts the cake. "Shhhh," she whispers. "We are going to play a game. Everyone eat your cake and be as quiet as you can. First one to make a noise has to wash the dishes."

"That game is not on the list," Devon says. "I am in charge of games, and I did not write that one on my list."

"You have to wash the dishes," I say. I am the second one to make a noise, so it is okay.

"No. No games not on the list." Devon is not happy.

"It is okay, Devon," I say. "The plates are paper."

"Everyone shush," Ms. Colley says. "Code Red. Remember what we practiced."

My mom is coming. Where is she? She should not be late.

"CODE RED LOCKDOWN," Devon says. He is not shushed. "HOSTILE INTRUDER ALERT."

"Devon, shhhhhh," Ms. Colley says. "We must be quiet."

Ms. Colley is trembly. I do not think this is a drill.

My mom is not here. Nobody gets in or out during Code Red.

Twyla has her second piece of cake. When she eats, she is messy. Her mouth and chin are covered with red frosting, but she is shushed. Twyla is always shushed except when she screams.

"Step One," Devon says. "All Faculty, Staff, Students, and Visitors must IMMEDIATELY proceed, if possible, out of line of sight of windows and doorways and to the nearest classroom or secure space." He is rocking.

The rule says, 'No rocking in class.' Ms. Colley does not say, "Devon, you are making me seasick." Maybe a party does not count as class.

I hear screaming. It hurts my ears.

It is not Twyla screaming. Mrs. Lamb screams, but her mouth is closed. She stands at the door. Her hand is on the lock. I do not know how she screams with her mouth closed.

"Step Two," Devon says. "Lock classroom doors. If there is no lock, barricade the door with available objects. Close all window shades or blinds if applicable. Stay away from the windows and doors." He is not shushed.

Mrs. Lamb is not shushed, and she is hurting my head.

"Devon, be quiet," Ms. Colley says. She should tell Mrs. Lamb to be quiet.

Twyla's face is all red. My mom is late.

I put my hands over my ears. They hurt too much and I cannot make them stop.

"NONONONONONONONONO." I scream too.

Mrs. Lamb stops screaming. She is on the floor and shushed now, but my head still hurts.

"Abby, shush," Ms. Colley says.

The door is closed. He is on the other side. He tries to open the door, but Mrs. Lamb does not unlock it before she falls down. I think he is angry.

"Step Three," Devon says. "After the classroom or office doors are secured, the Faculty or Staff member present will slide a colored reporting sheet—a green sheet for all safe or a red sheet for medical or other emergency problems or Students or Staff members unaccounted for—under the main exterior door of the classroom or office leading to the hallway."

He wants me to let him in. If I let him in he will make the ceiling red.

My mom is supposed to be here. She says I am a banana, but it is okay. She loves bananas. And grapes.

Twyla loves red.

I think there is enough red already.

"NONONONONONONONONO." I scream again, but this time, I keep my mouth closed too.

10.
[CAROLE]

FOUR-WHEEL DRIVE ISN'T ANY HELP ON ICE.

When I hit the ditch, the Jeep rolled. I thought twice, but wasn't sure. After the first, everything blurred.

My head ached and blood dripped into my eyes. When the airbag went off, I hit myself in the head, and my ring left a gash in my forehead. I'd probably end up with a black eye. The good news—I wasn't upside down. The shattered windshield was still in place. As far as I could tell, I was still in one piece.

Blevins. *Did I hit him?* He wasn't on his bike. *Of course not, you idiot. The road's a mess.*

Abby. I needed to get to the school.

Five is just enough.

Sirens came my way and went right past. If they were looking for me, they had bad directions. I dug around and found my purse—in the back seat—and took out my phone. *No Service.* Of course not.

My door wouldn't budge, and the passenger side was no better.

Breathe. Take your time. Think. Breathe. I crawled over the seats and got a back door open.

"Blevins!" He didn't answer. I was about to leave the scene of an accident and felt obliged to at least make a token effort to find out if I hit him. The Jeep's damage appeared to all be from rolling. No blood in the snow. If I didn't find him dead in the ditch, I was good.

I wore boots, but they were boots for warm cars and salted sidewalks, not for trudging through a field of drifted snow, and certainly not for crossing ditches full of freezing water and slush. By the time I made it to the road, my boots were ruined, my toes frozen, and my head wasn't the only thing hurting. Still no sign of Blevins.

"Blevins! You jerk! Are you here? Alive? Dead? Hey!" Had he answered, I might have killed him.

It took me some time to get my bearings. I was directionally challenged under normal circumstances. When I hit the brakes—*stupid move*—the Jeep spun around and skidded into the other lane before going off the road. I was lucky no one was around to hit me head-on. Blevins could be in the ditch on the other side, and if I was going to hitch a ride to the school, I had to get over there anyway.

Getting across the ice and slush would be an adventure.

I remembered the extra boots in the Jeep. Warm, waterproof boots with heavy duty treads. The boots I kept stashed for emergencies. Like this one.

Shit.

It wasn't like I was going back for them.

I hoped any cars that came my way would be driven by sane and sensible types. Slow drivers. Drivers who would see me in time and not end up in the field with my Jeep. Or run me down. I almost made it to the other side before I slipped and fell. Getting up was impossible. Every time I tried, I ended up back on my knees. Or my rear-end. I gave up and did the butt-slide over the last few feet.

Blevins wasn't laying in the ditch on that side either, at least not where I could see him. I hollered for him one more time and got no reply. *He's probably somewhere warm and dry by now. Next time, I run him over.*

Adrenalin from the accident had propelled me forward, but it was running out fast. I shivered from the cold, from nerves, or more likely, from both. My feet burned from the wet and cold. I cut my hand when I fell, and the ache crept up my arm to my elbow.

I reached for my purse to try my phone and realized I'd left it in the Jeep. With the nice warm boots. I didn't know what time it was. I quit wearing a watch years ago. With all the gadgets bearing the time, it seemed redundant. Silly me.

I wasn't crying. The cold made my eyes water.

The party must have started by now.

I had to get to the school.

Walking hurt. Not just my feet. Everything. Along with the tears, my nose ran.

It's the cold. I'm not crying.

Sooner or later, a car would come, but I couldn't wait. I stopped searching for Blevins. If he was dead in the ditch, I'd either find him or I wouldn't. I didn't much care.

Tromping through the packed snow alongside the road took work, but it gave me traction. I didn't want to end up on my ass again. Two cars came and went. The drivers either didn't notice me waving my arms like a windmill and screaming at the top of my lungs, or they were just dicks.

What time is it? The party.

The third car stopped—Macey, Twyla's mother.

"Good god. What happened to you?" she said.

"I wrecked my Jeep." I didn't tell her about Blevins, afraid she would want to go back and look for him.

"Get in."

I did. The car was an oven, but I couldn't stop shaking.

"Are you going to the party?" *Macey and me make seven.*

"You haven't heard?"

"What?"

"The school's on lockdown."

My tears weren't from the cold.

11.
[ABBY]

"Abby. ABBY," Ms. Colley says.

"Huh," I answer.

"All clear. Repeat. All clear." The intercom speaks in Principal Halstead's voice.

"Are you with us?" Ms. Colley says.

"Step Seven," Devon says. "Do not evacuate the building even if the audible fire alarm is heard. This could be a ruse to get people into the hallways. DO NOT respond to anyone at the door until Administrators announce ALL CLEAR. After the ALL CLEAR signal is given, remain in your room until an Administrator or Police Officer knocks. Do not open the door until the Administrator or Police Officer slides identification under the door."

The clock says 2:47. My bus leaves at 2:40-on-the-dot.

The bus driver says, "If you are not in your seat at 2:40, I'm leaving without you."

I am not in my seat and neither are Devon and Twyla. If my mom is here, she will drive us home.

She is late and she is not here.

"We are left behind," I say.

Ms. Colley kneels next to Mrs. Lamb. She gets up and slips the red paper under the door.

"Classrooms or offices bearing red papers will be opened first," Devon says.

"He is gone," I say.

"Who?" Devon asks.

"The Ceiling Man."

"Abby, who is the ceiling man?" Ms. Colley is still trembly and her words are trembly. I think that is a bad thing and I cannot find my words.

"Idunno," I say.

Devon writes *The Ceiling Man* on his list.

Twyla sticks her finger into the cake and eats red frosting.

I think Twyla needs a new favorite color.

12.
[THE CEILING MAN]

As Blevins would say, *fuck.*

He hid in the woods behind the school and licked his wounds. Whatever the girl did to his head was bad, but his ego had taken a worse hit.

He swore he heard Blevins laugh at him.

"Ha ha, asshole. Taken down by a little girl."

He wasn't down. Slowed a bit, maybe. But not down. Never down. But he was right back where he started, and the girl was still alive.

"That was supposed to be fun," Blevins said. "You said it would be fun. All we got out of it was a fucking headache."

«We? You're only along for the ride.»

His host irritated him, but the girl was problematic. He wasn't sure exactly when he first noticed her watching him. Maybe before he arrived in this podunk town. He'd only run across a few watchers over the years. Most considered him a nightmare. Not the girl. In the beginning, she simply watched, not emotionless but not afraid either. Accepting. If anything, he sensed pity. *He's hungry.*

He should have hopped into Blevins and moved on, but the pity pissed him off. She wasn't quite right, even for a human. He got that. Who was she to look down on him?

She didn't feel sorry for him anymore.

"Taken down by a little girl."

«Shut up.»

Blevins snickered.

The idiot had more gumption left than he should. *Annoying.*

Sirens. Shouts. People were coming. Searching for him. Searching for Blevins. His host had a well-earned reputation. The guard wouldn't be talking, but someone else might have seen him and no doubt recognized him. Identified him. The police were looking for Blevins. For him.

"I am pretty famous around here," Blevins said.

Another reason to move on, leave Port Massasauga, and forget about the girl.

A cloud of fear and panic surrounded the building and billowed toward him. He wanted to breathe it in, enjoy it, but it was time to leave. Worn out from both the jump to Blevins and the battle over the old woman, he needed rest.

"A battle you lost."

«*Shut up.*» It wasn't a battle. It was a skirmish. The girl didn't know what she did. She ran on instinct, like the animal she was, but she intrigued him. He couldn't leave yet. She was a loose end, and loose ends bothered him.

The sensible route was to get rid of her and move on.

"Tried that. Didn't work," Blevins said.

«*Temporary setback.*» Not even a setback. There was more to her than met the eye. Maybe she was more than meat. Maybe she had something else, something he could use.

Blevins's teeth—his teeth—chattered. He needed to find a warm place. Regroup.

New plan. He'd figure her out. He'd break her. And then, after he took what he could, one last meal in Port Massasauga. She'd locked in on *five*, but the number meant nothing to him. Nice full meal, but that was all. She was one of three. She wouldn't see him coming.

Dogs. He smelled dogs.

"I hate fucking dogs," Blevins said.

«*You've stooped that low?*»

"Huh?"

«*Still an imbecile.*»

13.
[CAROLE]

The Creekside Parent Handbook asked that parents not go to the school during lockdowns and promised authorities would provide timely updates on the situation. They shouldn't have wasted the paper.

Every student with a cell phone—which didn't include Abby—called their parents the minute the alarm sounded. Most parents dropped everything and headed to the school. Some of them made it to the parking lot before the roadblock was in place. We weren't among them.

Five is just enough. We're too late.

"Crap," Macey said.

If she hadn't stopped for me, she might have made it inside the barriers. *Five.* Twyla was in there too.

"I know the guy on the barricade." Not well, but I'd met him at police department picnics. I didn't know if Rodgers was the type to cut me some slack because I was Jim's wife or go in the opposite direction.

"You look like you need medical attention," Macey said.

"I'll play it up." Even in the warm car, my shivering made talking hard.

"I really don't think you need to."

I got out of the car. My knees buckled, and I ended up, once again, on my rear in the snow.

"Hey. We need some help over here!" Macey jumped up and down and screamed.

"I'm okay," I said.

"No, you're not."

She caught Rodger's attention. When he reached us, I tried to stand and didn't make it. Macey was right. I didn't need to act.

I heard her say something about Betchel Road and an accident, and the next thing I knew, I was sitting in the back door of an ambulance wrapped in a blanket.

"What's your name?" An EMT pointed a light in my eye.

"Why are there ambulances here?"

"Standard procedure. What day is it?"

"Friday. Where's my daughter?"

"Where are you from?"

"Don't be an idiot. Would I be here if I wasn't from Port Massasauga? What's happening? Why the lockdown? Why—"

"She's fine. She's always like this." Jim. Rodgers must have found him. "Why *are* you here? You know better." He was pissed. He sounded a lot like his mother.

"I didn't know about the lockdown. I was going to the birthday party."

"You should have been sleeping."

While the EMT checked my feet for frostbite, I told him what Abby said. *Five is just enough.*

"She's fine." His tone softened. "All of the kids are fine."

EMTs rolled two gurneys out of the building. They weren't empty. Jim stepped in front of me and blocked my view.

"Not Abby," he said. "She's safe."

"How do you know? Did you see her?"

"Look at me. She is safe. Now, tell me what happened to you."

My EMT—his name tag said *Jed*—pronounced me okay, lucky even, but asked if I wanted to be taken to the hospital.

No. I wasn't going anywhere until I saw Abby.

Someone handed me a hot drink. Tea. Weak, but all I cared about was the warmth. I told Jim where the Jeep was.

"May I have your attention." The principal's voice boomed through a bullhorn. They were releasing the students. Parents who insisted could pick up their children, but they were encouraged to let the students ride the buses, which would make their normal afternoon runs.

"We have to go get Abby," I said.

"I think we need to let her ride the bus. It's her normal routine."

He was right, and I hated him for it. "I need to get home. She can't be alone."

"I'll call my mother. You're a mess."

"No. Normal routine. You said normal routine. I need to be there. Get me there."

"I'll arrange something," he said.

Rodgers took me home in a patrol car. I even convinced him to use the lights and siren. When the bus dropped Abby off, I was still freezing—I felt like I'd never be warm again—but I was clean and dry and, I hoped, not too scary looking.

THE JEEP WAS totaled. Neither the police nor the tow-truck driver found any evidence I hit anyone. They also didn't find my purse or my phone. Somebody cleaned out anything worth stealing, including my boots. I figured it was Blevins.

Jim dealt with calls to the insurance and credit card companies while Abby and I huddled together under a blanket on the couch. Since ASD kids aren't big on physical contact, I should have enjoyed snuggling with my daughter, but although she initiated the cuddling, she remained sullen and withdrawn. I tried to get her to talk about the afternoon, both the lockdown and my accident. All I got out of her was a series of *Idunno's*.

I tried to convince myself the lockdown had nothing to do with Abby or five or anything related to my family. Coincidence. I tightened my hold on Abby, and she squirmed out of my embrace. Snuggles were over, but she stayed next to me on the couch.

Like a good husband, Jim fielded all the incoming calls. Like Macey's. And Evelyn's.

"Mom says maybe now you'll get a more suitable vehicle."

"I liked my Jeep." I liked it so much I drove it for fifteen years, which was what bothered Evelyn.

"That was supposed to make you laugh," he said.

"Didn't work." They didn't even make Cherokees like mine anymore. Maybe I'd find a used one, just to irritate her.

Jim made us hot chocolate, added a little something extra to mine, and joined us under the blanket. Abby kept her distance, but I was grateful for the extra warmth he provided.

As much as I enjoyed the togetherness, I finally suggested Abby go to bed and dragged myself off the couch to go upstairs with her.

"I'll do that," Jim offered.

I shook my head. I needed to see her safely tucked in, but as soon as she fell asleep, I intended to sneak out and talk to him. To find out what exactly happened at the school. Who was on the gurneys. She usually dropped off fast and didn't wake up for a couple of hours. *Please don't make tonight an exception.* I would be back in my usual place before she woke up. It was safe to leave her alone. I hoped.

I settled into the big chair and waited for her to nod off—and tried not to nod off myself. Keeping my eyes open was harder than I expected. Maybe Jim added more than Irish Cream to my cocoa. Maybe I was just exhausted, whether I wanted to admit it or not.

"Mrs. Lamb was screaming," Abby said. "She hurt my ears."

"Why was she screaming?"

"Idunno." She turned her back on me and went silent.

Abby fell asleep, and I went to talk to Jim.

THE SCHOOL'S MAIN office was at the front entrance, separated from the hallway by a glass wall. The receptionist looked up, saw Jack Parisi, the guard, on the floor and a man walking away. She immediately hit the alarm. Jim said the lockdown procedure went according to plan. Teachers and students all did exactly what they were supposed to do. Everything was calm. I had to dig for more information.

"Abby said Mrs. Lamb was screaming."

"Nobody reported screaming," he said.

"Who did they take off in the ambulances?"

"Parisi and Mrs. Lamb."

"Why?"

"Strokes. Heart attacks. I don't know."

"Are they going to be okay?"

"I don't know."

"Why did they both have strokes or heart attacks at the same time?"

"I don't know. I'm not a doctor."

"Did you catch the intruder?"

"No, but the receptionist said it was Blevins. We'll find him."

"What time was this?" Blevins was on Betchel Road. I saw him.

"We got the alarm just before one."

"It wasn't Blevins. He's the reason I ran off the road."

"I know that's what you said, but—"

"There is no way he could have made it from where I saw him to the school in that time." I knew what I saw, and I was adamant.

"The receptionist is positive it was him." He may have intended to sound gentle, but I heard patronizing.

"I know I saw him."

"I have no doubt you think you saw somebody. But if you did, it wasn't Blevins." He channeled his mother. I wanted to slap him.

"Think I saw? *If* I did? Who are you going to believe? Me or some receptionist you don't even know?"

"You've barely slept over the past forty-eight hours. You shouldn't have been driving."

I exploded. I just lost it. Screaming, hollering, tears. I don't even know what I said.

Jim sat and took it all. Stoic, impervious, like a rock. My cornerstone.

When I ran down, he said, "I don't suppose you'll leave Abby alone and come to bed."

It wasn't a question, and it didn't deserve an answer.

"We'll take shifts," he said. "You need to get some sleep."

I was still angry but too worn out to hang on to it. I gave in.

"I'll take the first shift," he said. "You go to bed."

"Two hours. Be sure to wake me up." I wasn't sure I trusted him, but I didn't have the energy left to argue.

I should have set the alarm. He never woke me up.

14.
[ABBY]

Daddy sits in the chair. He is asleep. My mom does not sleep when she sits in my chair.

The Ceiling Man is outside.

I get up and go to my computer, and Sami barks and wakes up Daddy.

"Abby, back in bed," Daddy says.

I go, but I do not lie down.

Sami sits at my feet, and I scratch the top of her head. She likes that.

"Are you going to read?" I ask.

When I wake up, my mom reads *Little Women* to me. She says, "We have read it umpteen times already, but we will read it again. And probably again and again"

Umpteen equals six. The next time we read *Little Women*, umpteen will equal seven. Umpteen is what Ms. Colley calls a *slippery word*.

I hand my book to Daddy. *Little Women* is my special book. It is the same *Little Women* book my mom reads when she is a little girl.

My mom says, "I've had a lot of practice reading this book," but I think Daddy can read it too.

"How about something different," Daddy says.

"No. Finish one thing before you start another. Ms. Colley says it's the rule."

"Far be it from me to argue with Ms. Colley," Daddy says. He is smiling. I think it is a good smile, but maybe it is a being-patient smile. He opens *Little Women*.

"Start at the bookmark," I say.

"I sorta knew that," Daddy says.

The Ceiling Man is quiet.

"Chapter Seven. Amy's Valley of Humiliation," Daddy says.

Chapter Seven is the chapter about pickled limes. I do not think I like pickled limes. I wonder if the Ceiling Man likes them. I do not think pickled limes are red.

"'That boy is a perfect Cyclops, isn't he?' said Amy, one day, as Laurie clattered by on horseback, with a flourish of his whip as he passed." Daddy uses his regular Daddy voice.

"You do not sound like Amy," I say.

The Ceiling Man is listening.

Daddy makes a funny face, but he smiles. I think his smile means good. Good smiles make me smile too.

"'How dare you say so, when he's got both his eyes? And very handsome ones they are, too,' cried Jo, who resented any slighting remarks about her friend." Daddy's voice is high and silly. He does not sound like Jo, but I like his funny voice.

"Stupid book," the Ceiling Man says.

I do not answer him. *Little Women* is not a stupid book. It is one of my favorites. Jo is very brave, and Aunt March is like my Gramma Evelyn.

"'I didn't say anything about his eyes, and I don't see why you need fire up when I admire his riding,'" Daddy reads.

"Daddy. Amy doesn't sound the same as Jo," I say.

"Tell him to put the book down and go to sleep," the Ceiling Man says.

"No. Go away," I say.

"What?" Daddy says. He closes the book, and his smile goes away.

"Not you. I want you to read," I say. My voice sounds funny, but not like Daddy's. It is the voice my mom calls Meltdown Warning Number Six, The Fast Voice.

Daddy opens the book, but he does not look at it. He looks at me. He frowns, and I think I want his smile back.

"You need to look at the book," I say. I want to slow down, but I still use the fast voice.

"Abby, no rocking," Daddy says. "Lay down."

Sometimes, I do not know I am rocking.

"Where is my mom? Amy and Jo are different when she reads." I say.

"She's sleeping. She had a long day. You're stuck with me tonight."

I look at my clock. It says 11:27.

"It is not over yet," I say.

The Ceiling Man is smiling, but his smile is not like Daddy's. The Ceiling Man's smile does not make me want to smile.

The numbers on my clock are red. "I need a new alarm clock," I say.

"Abby, lie down," Daddy says.

Sami lies down, but I don't.

"I'll get in," the Ceiling Man says, "maybe not tonight, but I will get in."

"Abby, you're making me seasick," Daddy says.

"Ms. Colley says that. Not you," I say.

When my mom says, "Abby! Do not ignore me!" it means I am in trouble. When she says, "Jim, are you ignoring me," it means Daddy is in trouble. I do not ignore Daddy. I stop rocking.

"I do not like red ceilings," I say.

"Abby. What red ceilings?" Daddy says.

"Mrs. Lamb fell down," I say.

"That was your fault. Not mine," the Ceiling Man says.

The ambulance people take Mrs. Lamb out on a stretcher. A policeman is with them, but he is not Daddy.

Devon says, "She's okay. They did not cover her face. If they are dead, they cover their faces."

I always cry when Beth dies. I do not like to cry, and I do not like it when Beth dies.

Devon writes *Not Dead* on his list.

"She might be dead," the Ceiling Man says, "and you did it."

Daddy ignores the Ceiling Man. He is not in trouble.

"I didn't," I say.

Daddy stares at me. He is not smiling, but he does not wear his mad face.

I cannot remember what this Daddy-face means, but I do not think I am in trouble. I think he will say, "I like grapes."

He does not. He says, "Abby, tell me what happened."

"Tell him what you did to Mrs. Lamb," the Ceiling Man says.

"Idunno," I say. I am not going to listen to the Ceiling Man anymore. I lie down.

"Abby?" Daddy says.

The clock says 11:34. The long day is not over.

My mom's clock has blue numbers. Blue is better than red. I need a new clock.

"Knock. Knock. Let me in," the Ceiling Man says.

"Do you want me to read?" Daddy says.

If I talk, the Ceiling Man will hear. I nod. A nod means yes.

Daddy reads. "'Oh, my goodness! That little goose means a centaur, and she called him a Cyclops,' exclaimed Jo, with a burst of laughter."

"You like stories? I'll huff and I'll puff and I'll blow your house in," the Ceiling Man says.

"'You needn't be so rude, it's only a lapse of lingy, as Mr. Davis says,' retorted Amy, finishing Jo with her Latin." Daddy does not use his silly voice anymore, but it is okay. I like his regular voice best. I shut my eyes.

The Ceiling Man says something, but I do not listen. He is in the wrong story, and I am ignoring him.

Daddy is a policeman.

"'I just wish I had a little of the money Laurie spends on that horse,' she added, as if to herself, yet hoping her sisters would hear."

Policemen keep people safe.

I only hear Daddy. No more Ceiling Man.

15.
[CAROLE]

My clock read 10:26. AM. I couldn't remember the last time I slept so long or so late. The bed was warm and soft and maybe I'd stay there forever and—

Abby. I slept through my shifts.

Jim was the only person I knew who fell asleep in the dentist's chair. There was no way he stayed awake all night. I dragged myself out of bed.

I found them both in the kitchen.

"You never woke me up," I said.

"And good morning to you, too." Jim was even worse at perky than me, but he handed me a king-sized mug of coffee. I considered forgiving him.

"You needed sleep," he said.

I had, but I wasn't sure how much good it did. I was still groggy, but the coffee might help. All of my joints ached, as if I hadn't moved all night. Despite my seatbelt, when the Jeep rolled, I bounced around just enough to shake things up. I had pains in places I didn't know could hurt. My toenails. My hair. And, I was cold again. Coffee wouldn't help the aches, but it might warm me up.

"How did it go? Did you stay awake?"

"Of course I did," Jim said, insulted I would ask. "Seemed like the usual level of Abby-ness to me. Maybe you should stop worrying."

"Are you kidding me?" If he was attempting to humor me, I wasn't in the mood for it.

"He took a nap, but Sami woke him up when she barked." Abby sat at the table doing one of her word searches. "We ate already. Do you want toast?"

The sullen Abby of the night before was gone, replaced by cheerful, sunny Abby.

"No thanks." I never heard barking. "Why did Sami bark?"

"I wasn't asleep. Just resting my eyes," Jim said.

"You were snoring," Abby said. "Just at me. Maybe the Ceiling Man. We should go to the hospital."

"Huh?" I needed a river of coffee if I was going to keep up with Abby-speak.

"We should visit Mrs. Lamb," she said.

"Not today," I said. "Who is the Ceiling Man?"

"Idunno."

So much for that.

The coffee pot was empty. I suggested Jim make another. Maybe a hot shower would wake me up and soothe my aches and pains.

"Keep an eye on Abby, and see if you can find out who this Ceiling Man is." Jim could fight the *Idunno*. I wasn't up to it.

"If I can stay awake," he said.

Smartass.

Abby lost track of time in the shower. If we didn't stop her, she'd stay in long enough to use all the hot water—and we had a forty-five gallon tank—and then take a good long cold rinse. To avoid water bill induced bankruptcy, we bought her a timer. Ten minute showers were the law in our house, and we were all expected to comply. Jim did. I took my showers when Abby wasn't around.

I took a pre-timer Abby-level shower and hoped she wasn't paying attention. When I got out, moving was a little less painful, and I was a tiny bit warmer. I wouldn't be running any marathons, but it was an improvement. If Abby lectured me on breaking the rules, the shower was worth it. As long as she only did it once or twice—maybe three times—and it didn't become the obsession of the day.

I wanted flannel pajamas and my fuzzy robe but needed to make an effort. Be the Mom. Act like a responsible adult. The idea nearly sent me back to bed. My effort entailed sweats. Still pajamas, but less embarrassing if somebody showed up at the door. Less embarrassing until I added pink fuzzy slippers and an oversized purple wool cardigan. The sweater was older than Abby and looked its age, but was a winner in the warmth and comfort categories. I needed both.

I summoned the courage to stand in front of the mirror and inventory the damage. My black eyes weren't bad, more shadows than shiners. I expected worse. For some reason, my nose was red. I looked like a clown. The kind that inspires nightmares. If anyone came to the door, Jim or Abby would have to answer unless we wanted to scare them off.

Jim had seen crazier, although he'd probably arrested whomever it was. With Abby's fashion sense, she'd love the outfit. I went downstairs.

Rodgers stood in my kitchen.

"Um, hi. We found your purse." He was young and, if I remembered correctly, single, and obviously unsure how to react to my appearance.

Jim kept his mouth clamped shut, but I could tell he was fighting a grin. Or worse.

"Laugh, and Rodgers here will be taking me in for murder."

"Your phone's still there. Everything else is gone." Maybe it was my imagination, but Rodgers professional cop-tone was tainted by a repressed giggle.

"Seriously? They took my Elvis datebook and left the phone?" The purse was waterlogged and ruined, and like Rodgers said, the only thing left inside was my phone. With the shape the purse was in, the phone had to be a goner. No way I could pass water damage off as under warranty. I didn't bother to take it out and check. The datebook was a birthday gift from Abby, and I'd miss it. Sort of.

Abby. She wasn't in the kitchen. Jim left her alone.

"Where's Abby?"

"Oh, good god. It's worse than I thought." My mother-in-law entered the room, followed by Abby.

Jim got the stink eye for not warning me about Evelyn, but his back was turned, so it was a wasted effort. His shoulders shook—I hoped with sobs, not laughter. It would be bad to kill him with another cop watching.

Evelyn carried a box from my favorite bakery.

"Ohhh. Is that a Sandella's box?" I knew it was, but depending on what was in it, I might be willing to make the best of her presence.

"Sticky buns. You should probably limit yourself to one," she said. "They go straight to your hips, and you really can't afford any more of that. Especially—well, I won't say anything else."

Evelyn's talent for the stink eye far exceeded mine. She added a layer of disapproval I had yet to master.

Maybe it was my outfit she took exception to. Or my fright-wig hair. I'd left it that way on purpose. It went with the rest of the ensemble. Evelyn, as usual, was impeccably dressed, every hair shellacked in place, her make-up perfect. I hadn't even considered make-up.

I chose to believe her problem was with my slippers and concentrated on the sticky buns. From Sandella's.

"I like your sweater," Abby said.

Ha. Take that, Evelyn.

I reached for the box.

"You just sit," Evelyn said. "I don't suppose you have any clean plates."

"I will get them. And napkins," Abby said.

Rodgers declined a sticky bun and made his escape. Smart man. Lucky man.

"I thought I might take you out to look at cars this afternoon, but not dressed like that," Evelyn said.

It always tickled me when she spoke to me as if I was a child.

"That can wait." Jim jumped in before I had a chance to answer his mother. "We don't even know what the insurance will pay out on the Jeep."

"Purple is my favorite color," Abby said.

"I sorta like pink." I lifted my foot and waved my fuzzy slipper. Abby giggled. Evelyn stuck her nose in the air. She wasn't eating a bun. Good—more for me.

"If there is any financial difficulty, you know I'm willing to help out. It's not as if you're going to get much for that old thing." Evelyn addressed Jim, not me.

"Have some respect for the dead," I mumbled.

"That's not necessary," Jim said.

I wasn't sure whether he spoke to his mother or me. Maybe I'd end up with a long white Lincoln like hers.

"Gramma's got heated seats," Abby said.

Good point. I still wouldn't drive a Lincoln.

"Well. With *somebody* not working, I'm sure things are a little tight around here," Evelyn said.

Instead of screaming *Hey, lady! Somebody is sitting right here*, I took another sticky bun. Jim could deal with her. She was his freaking mother. I would play nice. The second sticky bun wasn't as warm as the first.

"Excuse me, *somebody* is going to warm this up." Maybe not completely nice.

They all sat in silence, probably working out what to do with the madwoman, while I stuck my plate into the microwave. My purse went off, and everyone except Abby jumped at the sound.

"What in the world is that?" Evelyn said.

R. Crumb and His Cheap Suit Serenaders. "Mysterious Mose." My general *you'll need to look at the caller ID to find out who's calling* ringtone. I was shocked the phone worked, and not only because of the soggy purse.

"I thought you canceled my phone last night," I said to Jim.

"Missed that one."

The caller ID said private caller. I didn't answer. "If it's important, they'll leave a message."

They didn't, but the call roused my curiosity. I used my smartphone as a camera more than as a phone. If it still took calls, there was a chance I could save my pictures. I couldn't resist. I checked.

My photos were still there, along with some I never took.

The school bus in front of our house. Abby getting off the bus. Abby on the front walk. Me meeting her at the door.

16.
[CAROLE]

If not for the rubber case, I would have dropped the phone. I wanted to throw it out the window.

I couldn't say anything in front of Abby. I didn't want to say anything in front of Evelyn.

Across the table, Jim slumped in his chair. He sat up on Abby-duty all night while I slept, and yesterday wasn't easy on either of us.

"What?" He sounded as bad as he looked. We made a fine pair.

His mother noticed too, although it was probably her darling boy she was concerned about. "You two are a mess. Why don't I take Abby for the night?"

Crap. I couldn't exactly say, "As long as you promise to sit up and watch her all night." She'd start campaigning to have me committed.

Abby came to my rescue. "No. I should sleep at my house."

"What? Don't you want to visit your Grandma?" Evelyn was miffed. I thought. It was hard to tell with her, but she usually didn't turn the nose-out-of-joint voice on Abby.

"Yesterday was a little too much excitement for all of us." More than a little. I tried to look pathetic. Not much of a stretch. I definitely sounded pathetic. *Who took those pictures?* "I bet you want to sleep in your own bed." Abby nodded. "Maybe you two can go out this afternoon? And come back for dinner?"

"We can go to a movie! Please, Gramma?" No grandparent, even Evelyn, could resist Abby's excitement.

"I guess we could." Evelyn didn't like doing anything that wasn't her idea, but grandparent-syndrome and Abby's big eyes won out. "You'll need to get dressed. It's far past time for you to be dressed anyway." She treated me to the stink-eye, again.

If I was a bad mother, I wasn't above using it to my advantage. "Maybe you should—"

"I'll go help her find something suitable to wear," Evelyn said. "Otherwise, she may end up dressed like you."

"Good plan." I didn't argue. I wanted them both out of the room.

"Okay. What's going on?" Jim said as soon as they were out of earshot.

I handed him the phone. "The last pictures."

"Who took these?"

"How the hell do I know? Whoever stole my purse."

"When—"

"Yesterday. How did he find us?"

"They took your wallet. Your driver's license."

"It was Blevins."

"Don't start that again."

"I saw him. Oh, god." *My keys.*

Jim didn't say anything.

"I used Abby's key to get into the house yesterday. I don't know where mine are." After Abby lost one house key after another, we hid one in the garage. Back when I still went to work, she used it after school. "He has my keys. He can get into the house."

"I have them. You left them in the Jeep."

Why did Blevins take my purse and not my keys? I stood.

"Where are you going?"

"I don't want to leave the spare in the garage. He knows where we live."

"It's on the counter. You didn't put it back yesterday."

I sat back down. "It is Blevins."

"I'm not going to have this discussion with you."

Jim's refusal to discuss—argue—always worked like Abby's *Idunno*, except it pissed me off. I couldn't fight with someone who refused to fight back.

"I want the locks changed."

"All the keys are accounted for."

"I don't care. I want new locks. And keys."

"Look. I'm tired. You're tired. We're both cranky. If you insist, I'll do it tomorrow. If you want it done today, you'll have to do it yourself." He reached for the last sticky bun.

"That's mine. You had toast."

He backed down. He was stubborn, not stupid.

He put my phone into a zippy-bag. "I don't know that it'll do any good, but there might be prints. I'll run it to the station."

"Not now. You need sleep." I was angry, but I still didn't want him to leave. I wanted to kill him for not believing me about Blevins, but I wanted him home, with me, protecting me. Maybe Evelyn was right. Maybe Abby did inherit her issues from me.

"As soon as I get back."

"Take it tomorrow. If you can't change the locks, you don't need to be driving. Humor me. Do I look like a sane woman?"

"You don't sound like one." Evelyn was back. Yippee.

Jim had his back to me again, but I was sure I heard him snicker.

Abby would be the best dressed kid at the cinema-plex. We'd bought her dress for going to weddings not to the mall.

"We'll do some shopping, have some lunch, then see a movie. *If* there is a suitable one playing," Evelyn said. No worries about Abby picking up any more unsuitable storytelling while she was with her grandmother.

"Gramma says I need new clothes."

She didn't, but I bit my tongue and didn't respond. I'd be nice to Evelyn and save my battles for Jim.

Abby wore ballet flats. The snow was melting, but the weather was still cold and the ground covered in slush. I made her change into more appropriate footwear. Not such a bad mom after all. One point for me. Minus one for Evelyn.

"Be sure to get receipts, and come back here for dinner." I waved them out the door.

"Maybe I'll change and go to Home Depot," I said. How hard could it be to change the back door locks?

"How are you going to get there?"

Oh, yeah. No Jeep. "I'll take your car."

"Not until you get more sleep."

Whether it was heredity or environment, Jim did a fine job of matching his mother's tone. She'd left, and I was in no mood to listen to her voice coming out of her son. He looked and sounded like a smug, condescending jerk, and I geared up to tell him so.

I froze at the sound of the back door opening. Locks didn't do any good if you didn't use them.

Abby stuck her head into the kitchen. "You should ignore him. It is okay. You will not be in trouble," she said and disappeared. The back door slammed. Evelyn revved the Lincoln, and they left.

"I'm not even going to try to work that one out," Jim said.

Neither was I. I ignored him and locked the door.

Jim went to bed. Sami and I curled up on the couch. I nodded off a few times, but when I slept, I dreamt about the photos. I stood at the door. I waited for Abby to get off the bus, but she never did. I tried to find whomever took the pictures. I found him, but he disappeared before I got a good look. Each time, I found him in a different place, and each time he vanished as soon as I found him. I knew it was Blevins.

On my few forays off the couch, Sami stuck to me like Velcro-pup. A walk would do us both good, but I couldn't work up the ambition. In the backyard, she did her business and raced back to the house. I was grateful. I didn't want to be outside either.

After Jim took my phone to the station, I might never see it again. I didn't care about the phone, but I did care about the pictures. I backed them up. All of them, including the mystery photos. I should have worn gloves, but my prints were already all over it, so I didn't bother. If Jim found out, he'd tell me a cop's wife should know better. What he didn't know wouldn't hurt him, and I didn't plan to tell him. I copied the pictures to my laptop without looking at them and went back to the couch.

"Come on, Sami. Time for another nap."

An hour later, I got the laptop back out. I was still staring at the photos when I heard Evelyn's car in the driveway.

I let them in the back door.

"You should have combed your hair and put on real clothes." Abby had spent the afternoon with my mother-in-law.

I ordered pizza for dinner.

"I would have come back earlier and cooked if I'd known you were in that bad of shape," Evelyn said.

While we waited for delivery, Abby showed off her new wardrobe. After Evelyn-directed shopping trips, I always let Abby choose one thing to keep, and the rest were exchanged for clothes more suitable for a seventeen-year old than a sixty-plus-year old. Abby couldn't tell the difference and didn't care, but I did. She unerringly chose to keep the thing I hated most. My money was on the lavender sweatshirt—embroidered butterflies and a built in mock turtleneck. I predicted it would soon meet the bleach bottle in a horrible accident.

Abby explained why each piece was proper attire for a young lady. I made phony oohs and aahs. Jim's approving noises might have been real. Evelyn looked smug. The arrival of the pizza—deluxe, with all the good stuff—rescued me before I said something I shouldn't.

"My favorite!" Faced with pepperoni, mushrooms, and olives, Abby dropped her Evelyn-act.

I hoped Evelyn would decide the pizza was too much for her delicate system and leave, but Abby begged her to stay and grandparent-syndrome prevailed. She acted like she enjoyed her single slice, after she picked the onions off.

Abby went into happy-overload. She doesn't process emotions in the typical way, and overload was usually bad, but when she was really happy, it took over her entire body. Her hands flew to either side of her face, palms forward. She pulled her elbows into her body, scrunched over, and quivered, as if she was trying to draw in all the good feelings around her and keep them inside. Her eyes shone, and her smile was as wide as the Grand Canyon.

I hadn't seen happy-overload in weeks. It was contagious. I basked in her glow, and my chills went away. I was finally warm again.

"Abby, stop that," Evelyn said.

"Let her be," I spoke softly, not wanting Abby to hear, but Evelyn heard me and, for some reason, listened.

We opened a bottle of wine and spent the rest of the evening pretending things were normal. By the time we opened the second bottle, well after Evelyn was gone, I almost believed it.

Jim suggested we take shifts with Abby. "I'm off tomorrow. There's no reason for you not to get some sleep."

"I'll take the first shift this time." Wine tends to make me agreeable. It also makes me sleepy.

I'm in my Jeep, on Betchel Road. Blevins looms in front of me. He has my phone and holds it up to take pictures as I hurtle toward him. I jam my foot on the gas pedal instead of the brake. He is laughing when I hit him.

The impact woke me. The four triple-shots of expresso in under an hour kind of awake. I wanted to jump out of my skin and run laps around the room and bounce off the ceiling. Lights—like I'd looked into the sun or a camera flash, but the wrong shape—danced in my eyes. I didn't know what time it was, and the lights blinded me, blocked out the numbers on Abby's clock. She was asleep. I didn't think I'd been out long enough for her to have woken up.

Sami put her paw on my knee.

"You would have let me know if she woke up, wouldn't you?" I scratched her chin and closed my eyes.

The bright spots didn't go away. I concentrated on the biggest one. A jagged crescent like a backwards *C*, it floated just at the corner of my vision. If I could push it away, make it fade—

"Mom. Mom. It is 12:32." Abby was awake.

"I'm not sleeping." I opened my eyes. She stood right in front of me. I never heard her get out of bed.

"He does not like pizza." She handed me her book. "We should read now."

We'd read *Little Women* so many times, I barely needed the book. As I read, filling in the words I couldn't see from memory, the spots faded, but I read on autopilot until she interrupted me.

"I'm not listening." She sat straight and stiff in her bed, her hands on her ears.

"I thought you loved this book."

"Not you, Mom. You should keep reading."

"I like grapes."

She lay down and closed her eyes. "And bananas. Read. Finish the chapter."

"Yes, ma'am. But I love bananas. One in particular." I did as I was told.

Except, I never woke Jim.

17.
[THE CEILING MAN]

HE LEANED AGAINST THE BUILDING, WATCHED THE SUN RISE, and listened to his stomach growl. His new housing needed food, but the snack cakes and chips available inside the Gas-N-Git held no interest for him.

"Ho Hos are good," Blevins said.

«No. Not what I need.»

Two men stood and chatted by the pumps. They'd filled their tanks before he arrived, and he didn't know who belonged to which car. Not that it mattered. The cars weren't what he was after. Still, the driver of the Prius would no doubt be missed sooner than the driver of the whatever-it-was. A rear bumper held on with a bungee cord was seldom the mark of a solid citizen. Bungee-man would buy him some time.

The girl and her family were solid citizens. He couldn't stop thinking about the brat. If it weren't for her, he'd feed and move on. If it weren't for her, he'd already be gone.

The men's clothing provided no clues. Both wore nearly identical jeans, sheepskin-lined canvas jackets, and work boots—the local uniform.

He nudged Blevins, asked if he knew either of them. No answer.

«First you've got diarrhea of the mouth and now you're missing in action?»

"I'm not listening," Blevins said in perfect imitation of the girl.

"Not until you buy me a Ho Ho."

Irritating.

He focused on the men. Odds were one of them would meet his needs.

"I left with an extra forty in my pocket. They didn't rip me off this time," the short, tubby one said.

"It's a casino. They don't rip you off. You willingly feed them your cash." The scrawny one had a point.

"Yeah, but they're always announcing winners. 'Betty Boopsy won $1000! Joe Ass-wipe won $12,000!' Someday, I wanna hear, 'Congratulations Artie Galpin, winner of millions!'"

The tubby one's name was Artie. Good to know.

"Don't you stick to the penny slots?" Not-Artie laughed. "How much do you think you're gonna win?"

"Screw you. I came home with forty more than I went with. I'm thinking positive," Artie said.

"How much have you lost on other trips? Ever add it all up?"

"Doesn't matter. Forty bucks, man. I'm a freaking winner. Thinking positive. I went there thinking positive, and I came home a winner."

Artie had to belong to the beater. Maybe he'd buy new bungees with his fabulous forty, if he got the chance. The sensible one would belong to the hybrid. Probably had a wife and kids at home. People, so predictable.

Too bad both sounded sober. Drunks were pushovers, but then, so were the stupid.

He reached out and tickled them, just a little.

Artie flinched. No surprise there. Not-Artie didn't move. Didn't completely rule him out, but he'd take more effort. Easy was better.

"You okay?" Not-Artie said.

"I dunno." Artie rubbed the back of his neck. "Thought I felt...eh. Bet it's the stuff the casino pumps into the air. You know, to keep you gambling." He rolled his shoulders and stretched his neck. "I need to head home, get some sleep."

Artie would be easy. Sleepy and stupid was as good as—or better than—drunk.

"Hey, Artie." He spoke from the shadows, his face hidden.

"How-ya-doin?" Artie said.

"Need a ride, man."

"Sure thing. Get in." Artie opened the door to the Prius.

Imagine that. Sometimes, they surprised him. He stepped into the sunlight.

"You know Blevins?" Not-Artie asked.

"Nah. Random act of kindness," Artie said.

"You better hang on to your fat wallet. Guy's an ass."

"I'm thinking positive," Artie said.

Moron. They never knew he played them. They just did as they were told.

"Unless some little girl stops you." Blevins buzzed in his head like a mosquito. "Oh, Mrs. Lamb? Please open the door. Baaaaaa. Baaaaaa."

«*Enough.*» He slammed the door on Blevins.

"Should've bought me a Ho Ho." Blevins voice was muffled and distant. Easy to ignore. He had other things to concentrate on.

"Yeah. Sure. See you Monday." Not-Artie got into the bungie-mo-bile and roared off in a cloud of exhaust.

Monday. They worked together. Artie wasn't wearing a ring. With any luck, no one would miss him before Monday. With any luck, he'd finish the girl and be long gone before Monday.

"Better hurry up," Blevins was back, loud and clear.

«*Enough!*» The cretin went dark, but he didn't know for how long. He'd think positive, like Artie.

"Where ya going?" Artie asked.

"You know Netcher Road?" One of Blevins's hidey-holes.

"Off Workman? With the big pond?"

"Exactly."

They rode in silence until Artie turned onto Netcher.

"All the way to the pond." Car was quiet. He'd give it that. "So, what kind of mileage do you get from this thing?"

"Hasn't lived up to expectations."

"As last words go, those work," the Ceiling Man said.

A SNACK AND two hundred dollars. Not bad. The Prius and the left-over Artie rested at the bottom of the pond. Even if someone missed him, it should take a while to find him.

On Workman Road, he visited the abandoned trailer. Yellow police tape hung in strips on the dented and unlocked door. Whoever broke in was long gone. He wanted to clean up. Blevins's personal habits left a lot to be desired. Should have let him take a shower the last time they were there.

No lights, but the water was hot. He didn't need lights. He needed soap.

The grime rolled off and swirled down the drain. Some remained, embedded in wrinkles and crevices, and he knew he'd carry it as long as he wore Blevins. A drawback of taking only the throw-away people, but worth it. Fewer complications. Nobody missed his pets.

The place was a mess, ransacked, but it appeared the previous visitor was only after cash or drugs and electronics. Wires hung from an empty cabinet. The television was gone, but the day-to-day detritus of the late and unlamented Tits—Blevins did have a way with names—littered the trailer. He found shaving gear and got rid of the beard.

Not exactly a handsome man, to put it mildly. No wonder Blevins went for the cover of chin hair. It wasn't only for lack of shaving opportunity.

"Yeah. Fuck you." Blevins was awake and out of his cage.

«*Eloquent. Back in your crate.*»

The hair was beyond help. He thought about shaving it, but Tits's disposable razors weren't up to the task. Instead, he found a rubber band and pulled it into a ponytail. Slightly less wild man, not quite mellow hippy. Blevins might be recognized, but not with a casual glance. He counted on nobody looking closely, another advantage of using the throw-aways.

Blevins's clothes were so crusty they stood upright in the corner where he'd left them. Time to shop the Tits Discount Store for Redneck Attire.

If the dead man left any heirs, they hadn't claimed his collection of T-shirts with stupid sayings. Understandable. *Half Man, Half Horse* and *It's not a Beer Belly, It's a Gas Tank for a Sex Machine* stayed on the floor. He found a thick flannel shirt and a couple of sweatshirts he was willing to wear. Tits got good marks for keeping up with the laundry. The clothes were clean.

Blevins wasn't a big man, but Tits had been a scrawny guy and the shirts fit. Jeans were a different matter. He considered rolling the cuffs. With Blevins's leather jacket, the look was comical. His standards were low, but they were still standards.

In the open junk drawer—there was always a junk drawer—he found a pair of scissors and cut two inches off the pant legs. Raggedy, but better than looking like an extra in an amateur production of *Grease*. In the same drawer, he found a Swiss Army knife and pocketed it. Might come in handy.

He searched the trailer for anything else useful. No interest in the cans of beans or the spoiled food in the fridge. Not with a bellyful of Artie. If Tits left behind any cash, it was gone.

No electricity meant no heat. As much as he'd like to stay, bodies were high maintenance, and his was cold. The state of the trailer offended him. Standards. The girl was enough of a mess. He didn't have the time or inclination to deal with any more chaos. He emptied the contents of Blevins's backpack onto the floor, stuffed in the extra shirts, and prepared to leave.

The cash from the mother's purse and Artie's casino jackpot were more than enough for one of the no-tell-motels on the edge of town. If he even needed the cash. He'd get a room. Warm up. Sleep all day. Work on his girl problem later.

Girl problem. He liked it. Sounded so human. So insignificant. So easily solved. Thinking positive, just like Artie.

Time to get rid of any sign he—or Blevins—was there. No heat, but hot water. The gas was still on. Might as well go the easy route. Clear the entire mess and save someone the trouble of cleaning. He blew out the pilot on the ancient stovetop and turned all the burners to high. The pilot in the oven, he left on.

By the time the trailer blew, the Ceiling Man was long gone.

THE EDGE-O-TOWN MOTEL. Aptly named, both literally and metaphorically. A ribbon of Christmas bells jingled when he opened the door.

"Whaddaya want?" The Sunday morning desk clerk looked like

he'd been on an all-night bender for a week. He didn't bother to turn away from his television.

"I need a room."

"Blevins, out." The clerk jumped to his feet. Hands on hips, he stood behind the desk and glared.

"He hates me," Blevins said.

«*Understandable.*» "I have cash."

"Whadja do?" Win the lottery? Wouldn't a recognized ya all cleaned up, 'cept you still sound like a hillbilly asshole."

"Are you going to give me a room or what?"

"Boss says you're eighty-sixed. Not allowed in. He'd fire my ass just for letting you stand here and talk to me."

"Guy's a dickwad," Blevins said. "Why don't you do your thing on him?"

«*Patience.*» "Don't tell him. Like I said, cash." Blevins had a point. The clerk was an even bigger loser than Artie. Under other circumstances, he'd make a fine snack. Maybe later. He didn't know how long he'd need the room. Best keep the imbecile around. His replacement might have, what was it people said—a mind of his own. In the meantime, no use parting with his cash.

He reached out and pushed, harder than he needed to.

The clerk jumped, like he'd received a low voltage shock, and rubbed the back of his neck. He swayed, slack-jawed and drooling.

Cretin.

"I like that. Hurt him good," Blevins said.

«*Not today.*» "Give me a room."

The clerk shook himself. "Blevins?"

«*The key. Now.*»

"Back corner. 46D. Towels are five bucks extra." Puppet-boy handed him a key but made no move for the guest register.

"Give me a stack."

The bells clanked on his way out the door.

"Cool. You never gave him any money," Blevins said.

«*I know.*»

18.
[CAROLE]

ABBY AND JIM MADE WAFFLES. THE TOASTER KIND, ACCOMPANIED by microwaved bacon. What Jim lacked in cooking skills, he made up for in effort or at least intention.

"You should still take it easy," Abby said. "You had an accident."

She had a point. I still ached from head to toe. My vision was back to normal, no weird spots, but my head hurt. Not bad, but pain nibbled around the edges and threatened to close in.

"Maple syrup fixes everything," Abby said.

"It's the secret to my culinary prowess," Jim said.

"It is a wonderful thing." I poured far more than my share over my stack of waffles and bacon. I had a lot to fix. For an instant breakfast, it looked and smelled delicious. "How are your handyman skills?"

"Why?"

"Because one of us is going to change the locks today, or else I'm calling the locksmith. At Sunday rates." I took a bite of my breakfast. "This is really good."

"Don't talk with your mouth full," Abby said. "It is Uncle Kyle's maple syrup."

Kyle. Nancy. The kids.

When Kyle tapped his maple trees, we knew spring wasn't far off. Sugaring was his hobby, not a business, and he only made enough syrup for a small circle of family and friends. I was grateful to be among them. Some years, the syrup was better than others. Last year, for the first time, all of the kids were old enough to help, and the results were stellar. We were on our last jar.

I pushed my plate away. Breakfast was ruined. "Maybe I will call the locksmith. I want a new deadbolt."

"I'll do it this afternoon," Jim said.

"This morning. As soon as the store opens."

"Don't you think you're over-reacting? Maybe a little?" Jim went to the key hooks. "All the keys are accounted for. Look. Mine. Yours... where's the one from the garage?"

"I put it back," Abby said. "It was on the counter. Someone did not put it back where it belongs."

"When?" It didn't make any real difference, as long as it was still where it belonged, but I needed to know.

"When Gramma and me came home. When you ordered the pizza."

"Go get it. Bring it in." Last night. If he saw Abby take it out... *please, let it be on its hook.*

"Why?"

"Because I said so."

"I'm not dressed."

"I don't care. Put on your coat and boots and go get the key. Take Sami with you."

"Daddy already took Sami out."

"Abby! Quit arguing and do it."

"Abby, listen to your mother." Jim's stern-dad voice felt like interference and didn't help either my mood or my headache, but she listened to him. No backtalk. She stomped to the back door and returned with her boots.

"Humor me, kiddo." I tried to sound a little more like the good-witch than the wicked one I felt like.

"Sami, come!" Abby stuck out her lower lip and gave me an evil-teenager look.

Sometimes it was hard to tell whether she was giving me adolescent crap or just being Abby. Sometimes, it was easy.

"Boom." She said and stomped off in a cloud of teenage attitude.

"I'll go help her with the leash," Jim said. "Sami, come." The two of them followed Abby to the door.

"Walk Sami around the yard exactly six times, get the key from the garage, and come back in," Jim said.

Abby didn't answer. She was probably pissed at both of us.

Jim came back and promised to take care of the locks as soon as he got the supplies.

"I wonder if Kyle's doing syrup this year? It's almost tapping season, and he has no one to help him." I dumped my uneaten breakfast into the garbage and watched Abby through the window. Sami stuck so close to her, she tripped. She'd be in a fine mood when she came in. "I want the new locks by tonight."

"I *said* I'd take care of it. What reason are you giving Abby for not keeping a new key in the garage?"

Good question. One I couldn't answer. She deserved an explanation. The garage key was *her* key. *Well, there's this creepy guy who might be watching us and I don't want him to have a key to the house* wasn't an option, at least not a good one.

"I don't know. You figure it out. You two can discuss it while you go to the store and change the locks. I'm going to bed. My head hurts, and the smell of that syrup is making me sick."

By the time I woke up, the back door had shiny new locks. The new deadbolt only locked—and more important, unlocked—from the inside.

"I thought you were more worried about when we're home than when we're not," Jim said.

"Thank you."

Whatever he told Abby about her key, she accepted it. When he put the new keys on our keychains and hung the spare on the key rack, she said, "It is okay, Mom. You should feel safe."

Maybe he told her I was a little crazy. Best not to ask.

"Your phone is in jail now," she said. "No more worrying about it."

I understood exactly what she meant. A little crazy came naturally to me.

MONDAY MORNING, WE returned to our familiar drill. Peanut butter toast and coffee. Small talk from Abby and Jim. Grunts from me.

When the bus arrived, I walked Abby to the curb. Okay, I followed her out the door before I realized what I was doing. As we walked, I looked for someone—Blevins—watching us. As far as I could tell, the street was empty.

We reached the bus, and Abby stopped. "Mom. Do not do that again. I am seventeen. Not five."

Although I'd never wished for a typical daughter, I was sure that at that moment, Abby wanted a normal mother more than anything else in the world. She got on the bus, indignation personified. I smiled and waved at the driver. He laughed. Nothing like a little mother-daughter humiliation to start the day.

The rest of the week settled back to routine. Our new routine, anyway.

I sat vigil in Abby's room all night. In the morning, she went to school, and I resisted following her to the bus. Instead, I stood in the doorway and kept an eye on her until she was seated and the doors were closed. Jim hitched a ride to work with Rodgers and left me his car. I went to bed.

I always thought *slept hard* was a ridiculous phrase, not to mention inaccurate. Sleep was soft and comforting. I slept hard, a deep and dreamless sleep, and if the barely disturbed blankets were any evidence, a motionless sleep, but not a restful one.

The aches in my body faded, but my head still wasn't right. The pain left, replaced by lightheadedness, a pressure at the top of my head, like my brain pushed at the top of my skull and wanted to open a door and make its escape. Moving too fast made me dizzy. Not room spinning, stomach lurching dizzy, more like my rebellious brain changed direction and tried to get out my forehead or the back of my skull—which depended on which direction I moved—and threatened to topple me over. Kind of like a hangover, which was unfair. I hadn't had a drink since pizza and wine night.

I knew I ought to see the doctor, but didn't want to deal with it. Instead, I took the easy route and self-diagnosed. Too much comfort food and not enough exercise, both things I could fix on my own. If that didn't work, I would think about calling Dr. Yates.

Whenever Abby or Jim asked how I felt, I smiled and said, "Way better."

Jim might have believed me, but Abby didn't. More than once, I caught her staring at me.

"Don't stare at your mother," I said. "She's boring."

"You should ignore him," she said.

You should ignore him and *I'm not listening* replaced red ceilings and hungry men in Abby-speak. I still didn't have a clue what she meant, but considered it an improvement.

Jim worried I wasn't getting enough sleep. I lied and assured him the sleep I was getting was good and left me feeling bright and chipper. I may have snapped at him. He looked as doubtful as Abby.

He brought home a flash drive. "The stuff from your phone, I thought you might want some of the pictures."

The mystery photos weren't on the drive, and I didn't tell him about my own back-up. At least once a day, I got out my laptop and examined them. An Abby-level obsession, but justified. No matter how long I stared at them, they told me nothing.

Midweek, I left the house for the first time since the day of the accident and the lockdown. Twice, I thought I saw Blevins. The first time, he loitered outside the grocery store. The second, he crossed the street in front of me at a red light. Both times, it turned out to be somebody else, but, I thought, the same man each time. He was the right build and had a Blevins-like air about him, but was beardless and generally cleaner. And quieter. The Blevins I knew caused a scene wherever he went. When I saw his not-quite-double outside the store, he just lurked. Blevins always demanded handouts. If there was anyone who didn't need a doppelgänger, it was Blevins.

I looked at new cars, but wasn't enamored with anything I saw. No use rushing into anything. A car was a long-term relationship. I still mourned the loss of my Jeep and after a decade of no car payments, wasn't thrilled at the prospect of reacquiring one. Sooner or later, I would suck it up and choose a car. Or, keep driving Jim's.

The snow was gone, and it was past time for Sami to get over her nonsense about walks. Between the weather, her resistance, and all of the other recent madness, I couldn't remember the last time I'd taken her on a real walk. She needed the exercise, and frankly, so did I. A walk would clear my head. The fresh air would invigorate me.

Or something like that.

We made it all the way to the corner before she planted her butt on the ground and refused to move in any direction except home. Some trainers say to wait it out. The owner must outlast the dog and show her who's boss. Those trainers live in warmer climes. Sami shivered, and she had a fur coat. After fifteen minutes, I was frozen and the dog won.

"We'll try again tomorrow," I said.

She wagged her butt and turned her big Aussie eyes on me. I didn't know whether she was telling me *Okay, I'll do better tomorrow* or *Fine, woman, just get me home now*, but the way she rocketed into the house when I opened the back door made me think it was the latter.

On Friday, the school called. Abby was in meltdown, and I needed to go get her. The office secretary made the call. The situation was serious. If Ms. Colley didn't call me herself, she was with Abby and couldn't take the time.

The one day Jim didn't leave me his car, and I needed it. I called the neighbors. I knew it was Livvy's quilting-club day, but Pete was retired, usually home, and an all around good guy. He'd drive me to the school.

No answer. Not many people I knew were available during the daytime. Unlike me, they went to work. I considered calling Nancy, but didn't want to bother her. In truth, I wasn't yet ready to spend time with her, and after not seeing her since the funerals, I couldn't call her just because *I* needed help.

No choice. As much as I hated to do it, I called Evelyn. She said she'd be right over.

19.
[ABBY]

THE CLOCK SAYS 1:56.

Ms. Short collects our spelling tests. She is our substitute aide because Mrs. Lamb is sick, but Ms. Short is not short. She is tall and young. Mrs. Lamb is short and old. Twyla does not like Ms. Short, but I like her. She is pretty and has an indoor voice. Ms. Short does not hurt my ears.

No party today. It is an ordinary Friday, except for no Mrs. Lamb.

Ms. Colley tells us to go to the Quiet Corner. She uses her soft voice, but I think it is a bad voice.

"But we are not loud," I say.

Devon checks his list. "Two o'clock is Math. We do not do math in the Quiet Corner," he says.

Today is now an unusual day.

Ms. Short does not join us in the Quiet Corner. She straightens up the room. It is Friday and the room must be neat for the weekend. It is on Devon's list.

"I think I should help Ms. Short," I say.

"Abby, join us in the Quiet Corner," Ms. Colley says. Maybe her soft voice is a sad voice. Sad is bad too.

"I have something to tell you," she says. Her voice does not hurt my ears, but my throat and my chest are funny and tight. I do not like this Ms. Colley-voice.

I hope she will tell us a story. She should tell us a math story about three girls and two boys and three apples and happy ever after. I want to ask her to tell us a story, but my words are stuck in my chest.

"Mrs. Lamb will not be coming back to school. She passed away last night," she says.

"That means she's dead," Devon says. He writes *Dead* on his list.

Twyla does not say anything. She never says anything. She stands up and walks away.

"Twyla, sit down," Ms. Colley says, but Twyla ignores her. She takes her hat and scarf from the cupboard. Mrs. Lamb made them, and I do not like red anymore.

The policeman does not keep Mrs. Lamb safe. Mrs. Lamb's policeman is not my dad.

"Why is she passed away?" I push my words through my throat, and they scratch all the way out.

"Dead," Devon says.

"She had a stroke." Ms. Colley's face is very still. Her mouth frowns. A frown equals sad. Or mad. Maybe Ms. Colley is mad at me.

The Ceiling Man says I hurt Mrs. Lamb. It is not my fault.

"That means her brain blew up," Devon says. He writes *Stroke* on his list.

"Not exactly," Ms. Colley says. "Remember when we studied how our blood moves through our bodies?"

Twyla wraps her red scarf around her neck. The scarf goes around two times. The ends hang in front of her. Two ends. It is too warm in our room to wear a red scarf.

When I stroke Gramma's cat, she purrs.

Twyla strokes one end of her scarf.

"Circulation," I say.

"Veins and arteries," Devon says. He writes *Veins and Arteries* on his list. Devon gets *A*'s in Science.

Twyla's hand moves up and down. Up and down. Her left hand on her red scarf. I count. One stroke. Two strokes. Three. Four. I count on down but not on up. A stroke is down.

Mrs. Lamb is on the floor. The floor is down.

"One of the blood vessels in Mrs. Lamb's head sprang a leak," Ms. Colley says.

"Was it a vein or an artery?" Devon says.

"I don't know," Ms. Colley says. "The doctors tried to help her, but they couldn't. She went to sleep and never woke up. We will miss her," she says.

Fivesixseveneight.

"A head filled with red," Devon says. "I am a poet and I know it." He laughs and writes *Poet* on his list.

I do not think he is funny.

Nine. Ten.

Maybe I do stroke Mrs. Lamb. The Ceiling Man says maybe I did it.

Mrs. Lamb screams and nobody tells her to stop and it hurts.

"Abby, you are making me seasick," Ms. Colley says.

"Now the family must plan a funeral," Devon says. He writes *Funeral* on his list. When Devon writes it on his list it is true.

Mrs. Lamb is dead.

"We should go," I say, but no one hears me. My chest and throat are in a knot and my words are trapped and cannot come out.

Twyla is wrapped in red. She puts on her hat.

"Abby, hush. You're hurting our ears," Ms. Colley says.

Stella-cat does not scream when I stroke her.

Twyla does not talk but her head is full of pictures.

Mrs. Lamb is on the floor.

"Red head. Hands on ears," I say, and the words are not stuck in my chest.

"Uh-oh," Devon says. "Meltdown alert." He writes on his list, but I do not know what he writes.

Twyla's head is red. My head fills with red. Mrs. Lamb's head explodes.

I do not do it.

I search for the Ceiling Man. He is asleep.

"What did you do to Mrs. Lamb?" I say. I think maybe I am shouting.

"Use your indoor voice." The Ceiling Man is awake. He smiles, but I do not think he is happy.

I am not happy.

"You hurt Mrs. Lamb's head," I say.

"You did that."

"No. You hit her head. I did not see you, but you did." Someone else is here. I cannot find him, but he is laughing. I think he is in a box and should not laugh.

"Little Bunny Foo Foo..." The Ceiling Man is singing.

Gramma Evelyn says, "Hate is a very strong word."

"Hopping through the forest..."

Gramma says, "Do not say *hate*."

"Scooping up the field mice and bopping them on the head."

"Stop." I hate Little Bunny Foo Foo.

"Indoor voice, indoor voice, Little Bunny."

The Ceiling Man's smile makes me want to cry. It is not a good smile, and I do not want to talk to him anymore.

The other man talks, but I cannot understand him. I think maybe he wants me to let him out of his box but I cannot because I do not know where his box is.

"Abby, do you need to go home?" Ms. Colley says.

The clock says 2:07. The bus leaves in thirty-three minutes and if I am not in my seat it leaves without me. My mom does not have a car. Her car is wrecked and she should get a new one.

"Do you know where your mother is?" the Ceiling Man says.

My mom is not at work. She does not go to work anymore.

I cannot breathe. I am wrapped in a blanket. It is heavy and scratchy and I hate it.

Gramma says, "Don't say *hate*."

"I bet I can find her," the Ceiling Man says. "Your grandmother too."

"Unnnggh." When I make that noise, my mom says, "Do not grunt at me," but I cannot stop it. It just comes out.

The blanket stinks. It smells like dirt and pennies.

"Unnnggh," I say.

"Call her mother," Ms. Colley says.

"I'll call her," the Ceiling Man says, but I can barely hear him. The other man laughs. The red is gone and my head is full of night.

"ABBY. ABBY." My mom is here. She makes her voice soft because she knows loud hurts my ears.

"Abby. Breathe." My mom is very quiet and far away, and I am not sure she is really here.

"The blanket is gone," I say. I can breathe now.

20.
[CAROLE]

WHEN A CHILD GOES APE-CRAZY IN THE MIDDLE OF A STORE, people turn their noses up and act as if the parents are criminally negligent. It gets extra fun when strangers give parenting advice or offer lessons in discipline.

Abby's tantrums—or what we thought were tantrums—started when she was three. They were somehow a little more than the typical toddler tantrum. We couldn't communicate with or comfort her, and attempts to touch or talk to her made things worse.

She talked late, and we thought her lack of communication skills frustrated her. We tried working on her words. We tried discipline. We tried gentle New Age-y parenting techniques. My library of How To Be a Better Parent Books made me suspect some of her cute quirks, like her obsession with keys and shaking them near the corner of her eyes, could be a sign her tantrums were something other than bad temper.

We visited doctors and psychologists. For years, all we got was, "Well, it's not *fill in the blank with anything and everything a kid could be tested for, including autism.*"

One egotistical bastard told us that since *he* couldn't find anything, maybe we should look into parenting classes. We never went back to him. We'd already been to parenting classes.

When she was finally diagnosed, there was an element of relief, but the diagnosis didn't explain everything.

The verdict on Abby was PDD-NOS.

The first three letters stand for Pervasive Development Disorder, another term for Autism, but it's the last three that are important. Not Otherwise Specified.

Abby met many markers for conditions on the Autism Spectrum, but she didn't meet enough markers on any single condition to qualify for the label.

Her symptoms simply add up to *Abby*.

When she was in junior high, she showed me a picture of the cover of Pink Floyd's *The Dark Side of the Moon*.

"That is a spectrum," she said.

"It is," I said.

"What color am I?"

It took a second to make the connection and understand what she was asking. "All of them," I said.

"I like that."

For the next few weeks, she told people, "I am a rainbow."

Most thought she was being sweet. I knew she was being literal.

Having a diagnosis gave us something to work with. We learned a few coping skills, as did Abby. As she got older, we recognized melt-down triggers.

One is memory overload. She remembered *everything*. At seventeen, she could tell us the date and reason for the only day of school she missed in third grade, but she lacked the memory filters most people have. To her, past and present were often the same. I suspected her obsession with clocks was an effort to control something she couldn't process.

When she was fifteen, I walked into the bathroom after she'd showered and found her dirty clothes and wet towels in the middle of the floor. I told her to pick up her mess. Later, when I asked if she'd done it, she said yes.

The next time I went into the bathroom, I found the clothes and towels still on the floor. I called her. I made her pick them up. I yelled at her for lying to me.

"I lied to Ms. Colley," she said.

"What?"

"She asked me if I washed my cup. I said yes."

"And you didn't?"

"No."

"No more of that, okay?" I was ready to drop the subject, but Abby wasn't.

"I lied to Gramma."

She'd told her grandmother no, she didn't eat the cookies when she did. At least, that's what I thought she said. She talked so fast she was hard to understand.

"I lie to Livvy."

The tense change was another sign we were headed for trouble.

"I lie to Tracy."

Tracy was her after-school sitter when she was nine.

She continued, and soon we were back to kindergarten. With each confession, all lies in answer to yes or no questions, she grew more agitated. She relived each remembered sin. An avalanche of memories buried her, and we headed for a meltdown.

I managed to distract her. We baked cookies or did something else she enjoyed, something that required her to concentrate on what she was doing. I didn't remember what, but if I asked Abby, she would. Over the next few hours, she confessed to more minor transgressions as if they were acts of evil. Most were news to me or, as far as I was concerned, long forgotten trivialities. The meltdown was averted, an accomplishment I do remember.

Memory overload was a trigger I understood. It's bad enough when one or two things one would rather forget come back unbidden. An unrestrained and out of context flood of memories would be unbearable.

Sensory overload was another trigger, and one I could only imagine. After one trip to the ballpark, we never took Abby to another baseball game. The noise, the action, the lights, the crowd—her surroundings burned her like a hot iron. We left before the end of the first inning.

I kept an Unofficial Meltdown Warning List. Some signs were easy to spot. The Fast Voice—just what it sounded like. Contraction Failure—contractions in speech didn't come naturally to Abby. They were a learned skill, and when she stopped using them, it was a bad sign.

Time Shift—past tense was another learned conversation skill, and when she spoke solely in the present tense, the memory avalanche was on its way. Talking in Circles—she stopped referring to people and things directly and referred to them by relationship. Jim became *your husband* and Stella, *the cat of your husband's mother*. The Grunt—if she grunted at me once, she was mildly pissed, usually at me. More than once and I needed to prepare for a meltdown. There were more. It was a long list and hard to keep track, but Jim and I tried, for her sake and ours.

The triggers we could watch for and—maybe—protect her from were the good ones. The ones we didn't see coming, when life up and smacked her in the head, were the ones that broke my heart.

FOR ANYONE WHO considered speed limits and stop signs more than a vague suggestion, the drive from Evelyn's house to mine took twenty minutes. Fifteen minutes after I hung up the phone, she pulled into my driveway and honked. I grabbed my coat and ran.

The ride to the school explained how she made it so quickly. I never knew Evelyn—or the Lincoln—could move so fast.

"You're going to get a ticket," I said.

"Eh. My son's a cop."

I couldn't tell if she was joking.

We hit the school at the height of after-school traffic. School buses, students' cars, parents—getting through the throng and finding a parking place took as long as the drive. Just as I opened my mouth to suggest I get out and walk, she zipped into a spot. The two students she nearly mowed down used a few words I doubted she'd ever heard.

I suggested she wait in the car.

"How long will you be?"

"It depends on what shape Abby's in." As far as I knew, the last time Evelyn saw a serious meltdown, Abby was four or five and it looked like a temper tantrum.

"How bad can it be? I mean, I know they called you, but—really. She's a good girl."

"Remember when she was little, and she screamed and cried and wouldn't let us near her?"

"She doesn't do that anymore."

"Not often, but it could be like that. Or, she might be a big ball of misery. Or anger. I might be able to talk her out of it. We might have to just wait it out. She might already be out of it, at least enough to walk to the car. I'll know when I see her. Maybe."

"But she's a good girl."

"Doesn't have a thing to do with it."

"I'll come with you."

Yippee.

We checked in at the office. Ms. Colley met us at the classroom door and filled us in. Poor Mrs. Lamb, but I was concerned about my daughter. Abby sat on the floor in the Quiet Corner, her arms wrapped around her drawn-up knees. She rocked at double speed, but it was the sound that got me. Her high-pitched wail hurt my ears. A banshee's keen, desolate and cold.

"I just want to give her a hug," Evelyn said.

"NO. We can't touch her." The words came out sharper than intended, but I didn't have time to explain meltdown etiquette. I left her with Ms. Colley and went to my daughter.

"ABBY." HER NAME came out more a breath than a whisper, and she didn't respond.

"Abby." A little louder, barely a whisper. I thought she responded.

Wishful thinking. Her wail continued.

I said her name again, and the wailing stopped. She still rocked, her eyes were still closed, but the silence came as a respite, for me if not for Abby.

Evelyn said something, and Ms. Colley shushed her. I glanced at Ms. Colley. She nodded and ushered Evelyn from the room. Abby jumped at the sound of the door closing, a good sign—*reaction to environmental stimuli*. She was on her way back.

"Abby, breathe." My favorite aunt's slogan was "Breathe. It'll get you through anything." She was long gone, but her words stuck with me. They brought me—and Abby—through many tough times. I wanted to join Abby on the floor and curl up in a ball, but I stayed as still as I could and repeated her name and reminded her to breathe, over and over, until she opened her eyes and looked at me. No eye contact, but a step in the right direction.

"Hey, kiddo. Welcome back. Breathe."

She said something about a blanket. I didn't get it, but I didn't care. Stinky blankets were better than red ceilings or worse.

"Do you want to go home now?"

She got up without a word.

Ms. Colley and a tall woman I didn't know waited in the hall. Abby slumped, head down, drained. Still no eye contact, but Ms. Colley understood. Evelyn didn't. She swooped, arms out for a hug. Abby jumped back and hit the lockers, a wounded and cornered animal.

"Don't take it personally," I said. "It'll be days before anyone gets a hug.

Evelyn stayed uncharacteristically quiet.

The tall woman turned out to be Mrs. Lamb's substitute.

"Leave it to my daughter to break you in," I said. If she turned out to be the permanent replacement, at least she knew what she was getting into. She handed me Abby's coat and book bag, and I held the coat out to Abby.

She shook her head and whispered, "Scratchy."

I thanked Ms. Colley and the new aide. On our way to the door, I suggested Evelyn get the car and pick us up. "She won't put her coat on."

"But it's freezing! The car will be cold. Abby, put your coat on."

Abby either didn't hear her or ignored her.

"Remember when she was little and kept squirming out of her Dr. Denton's?" As a toddler, night after night Abby shed the one-piece footed pajamas like a snakeskin. In retrospect, it was an early sign of her ASD. At the time, Jim and I found it hilarious. "It's like that. We're lucky she's still dressed."

Evelyn put the Lincoln's heat on full furnace, and we rode home in silence. I snuck peeks at Abby. She'd found a piece of paper and methodically shredded it. I hoped it wasn't anything important, but if it was, Evelyn shouldn't have left it in the backseat.

I hadn't yet heard a word of criticism from my mother-in-law. Maybe I just wasn't listening.

As we pulled in the driveway, it hit me. "Crap," I said.

"What now?"

"I don't have my keys." I ran out so fast I forgot to grab them or my purse. "We're going to have to go find Jim and get his." First week with no spare, and I locked myself out.

"I have one," Evelyn said.

"What? Why do you—"

"Jim gave it to me. He was worried *Abby* might lock herself out."

There it was. Implied criticism. Evelyn's superpower.

"If I am locked out, I go to Pete and Livvy's and call Gramma," Abby said.

"May I have the key? Please?" I couldn't mask the irritation in my voice. I didn't want Evelyn to have the ability to let herself into my house whenever she felt like it. The new locks were meant to keep out invaders. As for Jim not bothering to tell me she had a key, I'd deal with that later, when I had time to be pissed.

"I'll unlock the door for you." She had the key, and she wasn't giving it up.

Sami barked while Evelyn unlocked the door. Abby put her hands over her ears and sang, more off-key than usual, "To Grandmother's house we goooooo."

"Oh, honey. Do you want to come home with me?" Both the *honey* and the sugared tone meant she was inviting Abby, and I wasn't included.

"No." Abby went in, and Sami quit barking. At least she was talking.

"Thank you." I did appreciate Evelyn's help and wanted her to know.

"Anything for Abby."

We stood awkwardly outside the door. I was afraid she expected to be invited in. Not that she needed an invite. If I went in, she'd follow. Even if I locked her out, she had a key.

"Well, if you don't need anything else..."

"Just quiet. And rest."

"I'll run to the store for you, or make dinner—"

"We're good."

She got the message.

As she got into her car, I said, "Thanks again. I really do appreciate your help."

"Like I said. Anything for *Abby*." Her emphasis on the last word might have been my imagination. Probably not.

I called Jim and asked him to pick up take-out on his way home.

"Anything special?"

"I'll leave it up to you." I didn't want to make decisions anymore than I wanted to cook.

He did well, spaghetti with marinara and all the sides from one of my favorite restaurants. I considered my resolution to eat better and stuck to the salad. The croutons and dressing were delicious.

While we ate, I filled him in on the day. Abby hadn't spoken since we came in the door, but with her there, I used code words. Incident. Rough time. Level Red.

"No red." Abby covered her plate with a napkin. Red sauce seeped through and stained the white paper. "Not hungry." She pushed away her plate.

"How about some salad? I'll trade you."

"Not hungry. I should take my shower now."

"Set your timer." I fought the urge to follow her upstairs. Showers were the only time I left her alone, and the only time I had to talk to Jim without her around.

"How was your day?"

"Uneventful, especially compared to yours."

"Your mother was very helpful. I should do something nice for her. Maybe I'll bake her a cake."

"She's diabetic."

"Oh, that's right. Maybe I'll just give her a key to my house. Oh, wait. She already has one."

"I hear that turned out to be a good thing."

Evelyn must have called him. Screw the salad. I took an extra piece of garlic bread.

"Couldn't you have just left a spare with Pete and Livvy?"

"Abby wanted me to leave it with her grandmother. It's Abby's key."

I reached for Abby's uneaten dinner. No sense letting it go to waste.

"I need to take care of my car problem."

"Tomorrow, if you can make up your mind what you want."

"To grandmother's house we go." Abby sang in the shower, tuneless but loud.

The next morning, we went car shopping.

21.
[CAROLE]

Someone watches. I can't find him, but he is here. His stare burns holes in my skin.

Abby is almost to the bus.

Hurry. Hurry.

She runs down the sidewalk, and the bus driver opens the doors.

Abby disappears.

She doesn't get on the bus. She is just—gone.

Blevins grins at me from the driver's seat. "Hey! Good trick! Where'd she go?"

I try to scream and run but can't move. Cold. Wet. Whimpering.

Abby's crying. Where is she...

I woke up. Sami nuzzled my hand with her cold nose. The insistent whine came from her.

Abby was awake too. She sat up and stared at me.

"Time to read." Other than her flat speech, all evidence of the meltdown was gone.

I scratched Sami's chin and whispered, "Thanks, pup." I shouldn't have fallen asleep, but it was good to know she was on sentry duty. She quit whimpering, but remained tense and ready to pounce. "Relax," I told her. "No squirrels here unless you count Abby and me."

We read until Abby fell back to sleep. I managed to stay awake for the rest of the night, with Sami curled up at—or on—my feet. By morning, my head ached, but I drove Abby to school. If she wouldn't let me walk her to the bus, she wasn't getting on it.

She sulked. She loved the school bus. When she was younger, her favorite toys were yellow school buses. She still had a dozen in different sizes and styles and refused to give them up. They lined a shelf in her room, and she counted them every night before bed.

I tried to convince her I wanted to take my new Jeep for a spin.

"It's my new toy," I said. "I want to play with it."

She didn't buy it.

I chatted and made small talk for the entire drive. All I got in return was a string of *Idunno's*.

At the school, the drop-off line was long, but I refused to let her out until we were as close to the entrance as I could get.

"Have a good day," I said.

"Are you and Sami going for a walk?" Her first complete sentence since we left the house.

"Maybe." If my head quit hurting.

"Stay away from the forest."

"What forest?"

"Idunno."

The car behind us honked, and she jumped out. I watched her all the way to the door. She opened it and disappeared inside. I sat there until the driver behind me laid on his horn.

A walk was a good idea. Fresh air. Exercise. First, I needed sleep— and for the blasted headache to go away.

EVEN WITHOUT OPENING my eyes, I knew sunshine flooded the room. The warm glow through my eyelids made me appreciate Abby's new dislike for red. I peeked at the clock. Afternoon sunshine. Late afternoon. I forgot to set the alarm.

Something was missing. My headache was gone, even the nagging bit around the edges that had plagued me for days. I felt good. Chipper. No need to see the doctor. My efforts to eat better and get a little exercise paid off.

Although I'd slept longer than I meant to—good thing it wasn't a cloudy day—I had just enough time to walk Sami before I picked up Abby. She wasn't riding the bus in the afternoon anymore than she was in the morning.

Sami didn't fight the leash. She trotted by my side out the driveway and down the sidewalk like the well-trained dog she was. We made it around the corner, down another block, and turned onto Acorn Avenue.

Stay away from the forest.

Port Massasauga retained bits of its farm-land origins. Small stands of trees dotted residential areas. Hardly forests, but one of my favorite things about the city. On Acorn Avenue, rather than oaks, the copse was filled with pines and stayed green and lush throughout the winter. It was beautiful.

Stay away from the forest. It was just another random Abby-ism, but my heart beat faster as we neared the trees. By my side, Sami growled and went to alert. We drew even with the trees, and she burst into her deep warning bark. I stopped, and she leapt, nearly jerking the leash from my hand. Squirrels. The pines must have held legions of squirrels.

"Sami, sit." The well-trained dog was gone. She jumped and strained at the leash. She'd pull my arm off, or at the very least dislocate my shoulder.

Stay away from the forest. Abby's voice, dead serious, filled my head as if she was standing next to me.

"Get a grip." I spoke to both myself and the dog.

«*Okay.*»

I didn't expect an answer and couldn't tell where it came from. Sami and I were alone, except for the one grey squirrel that shot from the pines and raced across the street. Sami paid no attention and continued barking at the trees.

"Sami—" Nausea hit. Bright lights danced behind my dark sunglasses, half-blinding me. "—Heel." I turned toward home and lost my balance but caught myself before I fell. Sami quit barking and went back to growling.

"Go away. You're impossible." The spots didn't listen, but Sami answered with a clipped bark. Agonizing pain shot through my temples. Home seemed very far away.

"I hope you have a hidden talent as a seeing-eye dog." More like a four-legged homing pigeon, but she got me home. By the time I unlocked the back door, the spots were gone, but not the sick stomach or the full-force headache. As much as I wanted to, I couldn't go back to bed. School let out in fifteen minutes.

I didn't trust myself behind the wheel. I called Ms. Colley and told her to put Abby on the bus.

Cold and miserable, I stood at the curb and waited. I wore the giant wrap-around post-cataract surgery sunglasses Evelyn had given Abby, but the frozen afternoon sunshine still burned my eyes. When the bus arrived, both my head and stomach protested the smell of exhaust.

The driver opened the doors and grinned at me from his perch. "Nice sunglasses," he said.

I heard *good trick*.

Abby brushed past me without a word.

ABBY DIDN'T SPEAK to me the rest of the day, but her body language told me how much she loathed my over-protective mom-at-the-curb act. When I asked about her day, she grunted. When I told her not to grunt at me, she looked a hair's breadth away from sticking her tongue out. I wasn't sure whether I wanted to laugh or smack her, but both were bad ideas and took too much effort.

Every time I thought I felt better, another wave of pain and nausea engulfed me. I considered asking Jim to take shifts on nighttime Abby duty but was afraid to ask. He'd dropped heavy hints the night watches were unnecessary, and I was in no shape to tackle that discussion. Or set off an argument.

Didn't matter. He called and said he was working over and didn't know when he'd be home.

"Did something happen?" I asked. The fear I'd kept buried since Abby's meltdown bubbled to the surface.

"Nah. Not much. Some guy hasn't shown up for work for a while, and his mother and sister filed a missing persons report."

It sounded like much to me. "When did he disappear?" Not last Friday. Please, not last Friday. Not while Abby rocked.

"Week, week and a half ago. His car's gone. He just took off, but we have to ask questions. And do paperwork. Lots and lots of paperwork."

Jim hated paperwork, but his nonchalance about the missing man meant he wasn't telling me the whole story. I wished him luck with the paperwork and hung up without interrogating him. Maybe it was my imagination, or the headache. There was no connection between the meltdown and the missing man. No connection between a stranger's disappearance and blankets and ceilings.

"Daddy will be late tonight. We're on our own for dinner." My stomach heaved at the thought of food. Abby was on her own.

"We should have mac and cheese," she said.

"Not tonight. It's a cereal night. I don't feel like cooking." She could have cereal. I didn't plan to eat.

"I will make the mac and cheese myself."

"I said no. Get yourself a bowl of cereal or make a sandwich. I think there's sliced cheese in the fridge."

"I'll make tuna sandwiches." Her version of compromise—she didn't do exactly what I told her to do, but offered something close.

"Clean up after yourself." She always made a mess, and I wasn't up to cleaning the kitchen anymore than cooking. "I'll wait and eat with Daddy." A lie, but a good excuse for not eating with her. Abby didn't do well around illness. If Jim or I had the slightest cold, she went into high-stress mode until we stopped coughing and blowing our noses. If I told her I didn't want dinner, she'd think I was ready for hospitalization.

The stink of tuna drifted in from the kitchen. I gagged. Abby made as much noise as she could, banging bowls and slamming the fridge door. I pulled my afghan over my head and took shallow breaths. It helped a little with the lights and the smell, but not the noise. I never dreamt plastic bowls could be so loud.

"Here you go." Abby pulled the blanket off my head, dropped it on the floor, and held out a tuna-on-toast sandwich like a peace offering.

I retched, but swallowed the rising bile and thanked her. She was back with her own sandwich before I could force myself to take a bite.

"What is wrong?"

"I'm not very hungry. I'll eat later."

"Are you sick?"

"Just tired."

"Eat your sandwich. It will make you feel better." Her words came fast, not meltdown level, but on their way.

"I'll taste it, but I'm really not hungry. I'll wait for your dad and eat with him." I took a tiny bite, which I'm sure was delicious. All I tasted was vomit.

"You are sick. I told you to stay away from the forest."

Fireworks shot off in my head.

"Abby, tell me about the forest." Acorn Avenue. The headache started at the forest.

"You should listen. You should not go there." She shouted, and her anger was contagious.

"Tell me what you are talking about." My screech was a sledgehammer to the side of my head.

"I tell you to stay away from the forest. You do not listen."

"Abby, please—"

"I should take my shower now." She stomped away.

"Abby!" My rage was out of proportion to the situation, but I couldn't control it. Fighting it hurt worse than letting it out.

"Be sure to set your timer." Cold and mean, I was the Wicked Witch of the West.

She stopped at the bottom of the stairs. "I like Ms. Colley better. You should listen." On her way up, she hit every stair as hard as she could.

The slam of the bathroom door was excruciating.

The Ms. Colley comment was typical upset-Abby and didn't bother me. The forest comments haunted me, but I couldn't think about them. The roar of the shower sounded like Niagara Falls, and even looking at the sandwich sickened me. I could get rid of the sandwich and tell Abby I ate it.

The whine of the garbage disposal and the reek of tuna were too much. I finally vomited. I swayed and grabbed the edge of the sink. The room darkened and spun, and the sledgehammer turned to a jackhammer. *I need to sit down before I fall down.*

The living room was a million miles away. So was the kitchen table. I lowered myself to the floor. *Breathe. Breathe.*

Abby shouldn't see me like this. If Jim walked in and found me on the floor, it wouldn't do him any good either. Or me.

My mother suffered from migraines. A bad one took her down for a week, sometimes more. At her worst, she couldn't stand light, sound, or smell. Often, she threw up. Sick headaches, my grandmother called them. I'd never had one, but if this was a migraine, my grandmother nailed it.

The shower stopped. Blissful silence, until Abby stomped to her room. It sounded like she was bowling right above my head.

As bad as my mother's migraines were, I never found her curled up on the kitchen floor. I pressed my fingers into my temples as hard as I could stand, something I'd seen her do. When I was an obnoxious teen, I saw the gesture as an over-dramatic bid for sympathy, but it worked. The pounding dulled. I owed my mother an apology.

Abby was still upstairs. She was either really pissed or didn't want anything to do with me, but I couldn't leave her alone. I grabbed the counter and pulled myself up. Quick moves were bad. I clung to the counter and gasped for air. The room steadied. When I could move without falling over, I made my way upstairs one slow step at a time.

Abby lay in bed, her back to the open door.

"Hey," I said.

She was either already asleep or ignoring me.

The bathroom light made me long for my sunglasses. I searched for something stronger than Tylenol and found a bottle of Vicodin. Jim's, from the dentist. Mr. Stoic had barely touched them, if he'd taken any.

I swallowed two and hoped they'd stay down long enough to help. Just in case they didn't, I grabbed the wastebasket on the way out. I wasn't cleaning up any messes, not even my own.

Sami sprawled at Abby's feet. She wasn't allowed on the bed but didn't bother to jump off when she saw me. I didn't bother to scold her.

Abby's new clock projected the time on the ceiling. When I bought it, I thought she'd love it. All she said was "Blue is better than red."

Only six. Too early for her to be in bed. Too early for me to be in the chair. I settled in and pulled a blanket over my head, glad Jim wasn't around to see us. My cocoon and the pills helped. My headache receded, and as long as I didn't move, my stomach behaved.

I don't know how, but I was awake when Jim got home. The numbers on the ceiling said 11:58. Six hours was a long stretch of sleep for

Abby, but deep, steady breathing, both hers and Sami's, reassured me.

Jim stuck his head into the room.

"Abby made sandwiches. There's tuna salad in the fridge," I said.

"Already ate. You sound terrible."

"Long day."

"Come to bed. Abby will be fine."

"I'm good here."

"Are you sure you're okay? You don't sound it."

"Headache. I'll be fine."

"Maybe you should see the doctor."

"Shhhh. You'll wake Abby."

"We need to talk about this. It's getting ridiculous."

"Not tonight."

"The situation is out of hand. You're a mess."

"We'll talk soon. I promise." Under the blanket, I crossed my fingers.

He went to bed, and my headache returned. It had a sound track. A laugh track. It sounded like Blevins.

22.
[ABBY]

DADDY IS HOME, AND I AM GLAD. DADDY IS A POLICEMAN. Policemen keep people safe. He talks to my mom, and I think he is angry but will still keep us safe. My mom's head is angry. Everyone is angry, and I should be asleep.

"Is my Little Bunny upset?" the Ceiling Man says.

I pretend to be asleep. I do not answer him. I am not a bunny.

"Tell your mom hello for me. Maybe I should tell her myself," the Ceiling Man says.

I ignore him.

"Oh, Mommy..."

I cannot pretend. I do not want him to hurt my mom. I open my eyes.

My mom sits in her chair. Her eyes are closed and she rubs her head and rocks. Temples. She rubs her temples. Temples are on the side of your head, and temples are churches. I hate slippery words.

Gramma says, "Hate is a very strong word."

I do not like slippery words.

I think maybe the Ceiling Man hurts my mom's head, but I do not ask him. Maybe if I do not talk to him he will go away.

"Little Bunny Foo Foo..."

My mom should listen to me. She should stay away from the forest. I do not think she knows she is rocking. Sometimes, I do not know I am rocking.

"Hopping through the forest..."

Bunnies do not talk except in stories. I do not talk, but I am not a bunny and I do not think I am in a story.

If my mom hears the Ceiling Man, I do not think she will like him and I think she will be angry. Everyone is angry tonight.

"I'm your mom's new best friend," the Ceiling Man says.

Aunt Nancy is my mom's friend. Twyla is my best friend. I do not think the Ceiling Man is anybody's friend. Maybe the man in the box, but I do not think he is a nice friend.

My mom does not know I am awake. Her head hurts. I do not think she should read. I get my music and put my earphones on. No more listening to the Ceiling Man. No more Bunny Foo Foo.

When I listen to my music, I sing and I am happy. When I sing, my mom puts her hands over her ears and laughs and says *oh Abby my ears*, but I think she is happy too.

My mom puts her hands over her ears but she does not laugh. I do not sing. I am quiet.

"Quiet like a mouse," the Ceiling Man says, but I ignore him.

"Go downstairs," he says. "Let me in. I'll make Mommy feel better."

The Ceiling Man does not make me feel good. I think he is a liar. Liars are bad.

"Go away," I whisper. My mom's head hurts and I must be quiet.

"Help me out, my Little Bunny Foo Foo."

I am not Bunny Foo Foo. I turn my music up loud. It hurts my ears, but I ignore it.

"Maybe you're a piglet? Little Pig, Little Pig, let me in."

It is not nice to call a person a pig.

Devon calls Mrs. Lamb a pig. He thinks he is funny. He says, "The lamb is a pig is a horse is a cow." Ms. Colley sends him to the Quiet Corner, and he writes *A lamb is not a pig* on his list.

Mrs. Lamb is dead. Devon's list says so.

The Ceiling Man's friend laughs. He is in his box, but I can hear him. "A little girl," he says.

I am not a little girl. I am not a little pig. I am not a little bunny. I am Abby.

"Let me in, Little Abby-Bunny-Piglet."

My music sings, "You can't come in."

"You can't come in." I think it but I do not say it because I am quiet and I do not go downstairs and let the Ceiling Man in.

You can't come in. I like this song. It is one of my mom's favorites and sometimes we sing it together.

"I'll get Mommy to let me in," the Ceiling Man says.

"Stay away from my mom." My words are in my head not my mouth. I stay shushed because my mom's head hurts.

The Ceiling Man hears me. "Are you going to stop me? Like you did with Mrs.Lamb? We know how that turned out."

Twyla does not talk, but sometimes she talks to me. She does not use her mouth, but I know what she says.

"I like red," the Ceiling Man says. "Maybe I should be friends with Twyla."

"You hurt Mrs. Lamb," I say without my mouth.

"You hurt her. You'll hurt Mommy too."

My mom is making me seasick.

"Go away," I say. The Ceiling Man does not listen.

"Little Pig, Little Pig, let me come in."

I am not a little pig.

"Twyla needs a red ceiling," he says.

Twyla does not need words. Her head is full of pictures. I need words, but sometimes I cannot find them.

"I'll huff and I'll puff and I'll blow your house down," the Ceiling Man says.

I do not listen to him. I listen to my music.

You can't come in. The same song sings over and over. It is on Repeat, but I do not make it stop.

"I am coming in," the Ceiling Man says. "You can't stop me."

"You can't come in." I close my eyes tight and sing in my head but my mom does not sing with me.

"I know better songs," the Ceiling Man says.

Sami is growling and I am rocking. The Ceiling Man is laughing.

"You can't come in," I say with my mouth.

Sami is barking and I open my eyes. My mom is not in her chair. The Ceiling Man is quiet.

Sami barks her mean bark but I do not think she is barking at me.

"Tell that dog to shut up," the Ceiling Man says.

I do not think he likes Sami and I want him to be afraid. I do not tell Sami to shut up.

"I hate fucking dogs," the man in the box says.

Gramma says, "Don't say *hate*."

Fuck is worse than hate. Gramma would not like the Ceiling Man.

"Stay here," Daddy says.

"Be careful," my mom says.

"You can't come in," my music says.

My mom sits on my bed. "Abby," she says.

"You can't come in," I say.

Sami's barking is outside my room and outside my house. I think she is with my dad. I do not want her to be with the Ceiling Man.

I take off my ear-buds but do not turn off my music.

"You can't come in," my music says.

"Where's your book?" my mom says.

My mom's head hurts. She should not read.

"To Grandmother's house we go," the Ceiling Man sings.

"Don't worry, Daddy will keep us safe." I find my words and use my mouth.

"Did you hear something?" my mom says.

"Now, *that's* a good song," the Ceiling Man says.

"Idunno." I do not know how to tell my mom about the Ceiling Man.

"Oh, Mommy, let me introduce myself," the Ceiling Man says.

My mom closes her eyes and puts her hands on her head and rocks.

Policemen catch bad guys. Daddy should catch the Ceiling Man.

"A little girl and a fucking dog," the man in the box says.

My mom should not rock.

I think the Ceiling Man should go to jail and never come back.

I hate the Ceiling Man.

23.
[CAROLE]

KNOCKING. IN MY HEAD. SMALL EXPLOSIONS. PAIN.

You can't come in. You can't come in.

"Carole. Carole. Are you all right?" Jim's voice.

"He is gone now," Abby said.

My head cleared, and I opened my eyes.

"Are you okay?" Jim said.

"Someone was outside, trying to get in," I said.

"I didn't find anyone."

I remembered waking him up, telling him I heard someone outside, and making him go check. I remembered sitting down with Abby. "Don't worry, Daddy will keep us safe," she said, and the pain in my head exploded. After that, everything was blank.

"You can't come in." Abby's ear-buds lay on the bed, the volume on the iPod turned up high enough they might as well have been speakers. I picked it up and shut it off.

"Carole?" Jim's tone demanded an explanation.

"There was someone trying to get into the house," I said.

"I couldn't find anybody or anything. It was the orange cat. Or the teenagers next door. Are you okay?"

"I'm fine." If I told him I heard someone climbing the side of the house, he'd think I was insane. Or find out—somehow—that I took his Vicodin. He wouldn't approve. "But I *did* hear something."

"Maybe you were dreaming."

"She wasn't," Abby said.

"Did you hear something?" her father asked.

"Idunno."

You can't come in. The iPod was off, but the song lingered.

"You're right," I said. "Probably the kids next door."

"Why don't you come to bed." Not a question. A command.

"I'm good here." I got off the bed and went back to my chair.

"It's okay," Abby said. "We can all sleep now."

ALTHOUGH ABBY GAVE me permission to sleep, I had no problem staying awake. Any drowsiness from the painkiller was gone. I didn't know why I blacked out on Abby's bed but blamed the migraine. The migraine was gone, so I didn't worry about it. Instead, I sat alert and listened for the intruder to return. No matter what Jim said, I knew what I heard.

By morning, I felt great. Wide awake. Chipper. Better than I had since well before I rolled the Jeep. Before I started spending my nights in Abby's room.

Until Abby handed me my toast. At the smell of peanut butter, my stomach heaved.

"Are you okay?" Abby asked.

"I'm fine." Jim's scowl dared me to prove it. I took a bite of toast—and I was fine. I hadn't eaten anything since yesterday's toast, twenty-four hours ago. "Hungry is all. I need my breakfast. And more coffee."

"And a good night's sleep," Jim said.

When I said I would drive Abby to school again, her only comment was "Sami should go with us."

At the school, we waited in line for drop-off. I would never again mock over-protective parents.

"What will you do today?" Abby asked.

"I really don't know yet."

"When you go anywhere, take Sami."

"I don't know that we'll go for a walk." It was snowing again. Not much, but enough to make me wimp out on a walk.

"Take her even when you go in the car."

In the backseat, Sami woofed.

"Well, if you both insist." I tried to make a joke out of it.

"We do." Abby wasn't joking.

I NEEDED SLEEP, but saw no point in completely wasting a good day. We hadn't had a family night in too long. If I pulled one together, maybe Jim would stop giving me the evil eye.

The only thing Abby liked better than mac and cheese was pesto. On the way home from the school, I stopped at the Farmer's Market. Fresh basil, three-cheese tortellini, pine nuts, sun-dried tomatoes. I planned to do it up right. I looked forward to it. I hadn't looked forward to anything for weeks. Months. Cooking was an excellent place to start.

I stood in the checkout line and worked out a plan. A good dinner, then we would all curl up on the couch and watch a movie. Something feel-good and sappy. Something to make Abby smile. Something to get Jim off my back.

"Jeez. Somebody's upset," the cashier said.

"What?"

"Don't you hear that?"

Lost in my thoughts, I hadn't. Barking. It sounded like Sami.

"Oh. Guess so." I didn't admit the noise was probably my dog.

As soon as I left the store, the barking ceased. Sami stood in the driver's seat and snarled, her teeth bared, but as soon as she saw me, she wagged her butt and jumped into the backseat. A cat. She was reacting to a cat. No panic. I would hang on to my good day even if it killed me.

Sami didn't get the good day memo. When we got home, I opened the Jeep door, and she shot out and took off. I stuck the groceries in the house, grabbed her leash, and went to find her. She was over her orneriness about leaving the house or the yard, but I didn't think she'd go far.

I found her behind the house, nosing around in the flowerbed.

"Sami, come."

Even a well-trained dog practices selective hearing at times.

Weeks of fighting to get her outside, and I would have to fight to get her in. Kids and dogs were supposed to be at the top of the list of

Things That Make Life Better. I wanted to have a talk with whomever made that list.

She was in my lavender bed. *Lavendula Grosso.* Giant lavender. The huge plants looked dead in the winter, but retained their shape. Two were trampled flat.

Maybe Jim did it while searching for my prowler. Maybe it was an animal. A neighborhood dog on the loose.

Maybe it wasn't.

My hands shook. I couldn't manage to snap Sami's leash to her collar, but I didn't need it. She glued herself to my leg. I tripped over her twice before we made it to the back door.

I will put the groceries away. I will sleep. I will pick up Abby. I will make a nice night for my family. I will stick to my plan. I repeated my mantra while I put away the groceries. I'd just fallen into a rhythm when Sami barked and I dropped the bag of tortellini. *What now?*

The mailman. Sami always barked at the mailman.

Canine conditioning. Human approaches domain. Dog barks. Human leaves. Domain is safe. Success. Yay. Doggy happiness.

"Maybe I'll try barking, but you should shut up," I said. "My nerves can't take much more."

She wagged her rump.

Sifting through the mail killed any remnant of my good mood. Unpaid bills. Since I paid them all online, anything sent the old-fashioned way was automatically bad news. Final notices and cut-off threats. Cooking wasn't the only thing I'd ignored.

Jim would be pissed. I was pissed at myself.

The phone bill was printed in red. Letters and words spun into a blur of crimson. My ears rang, and my chest constricted. I couldn't breathe. The room went red. I couldn't think beyond the pain in my chest and the tingling in my arms. The room spun and I sank to the floor.

The red faded and the iron band around my chest let go. I struggled for air, but I was sobbing, not suffocating. The sensible part of my brain told me I was over-reacting. A panic attack. Over stupid bills. The sensible was overruled by the emotional.

Still shaking, I went online. I made phone calls. The woman at the gas company asked if I was all right. I took care of each bill and fed it to the paper shredder. Jim didn't need to know.

Buried in the bills was a postcard from the dentist. Abby and I had appointments for check-ups and cleanings. I shredded the card too. I couldn't deal with Abby obsessing about the dentist for the next two weeks. The red confetti that was once the phone bill topped the shredder bin. I bagged it all and took out the trash. Not because I was afraid Jim would see it. Because I didn't want to look at it.

It was noon. I'd spent more time on hold with all the customer service departments than I realized. I needed to pick Abby up at 2:40.

I slept two hours. In my dreams, Abby vanished again and again, but I woke up still pain free.

I left early and took Sami. I wanted to be first in the parental pick-up line. I wanted to get out of the car and meet her at the door, but when I showed up ten minutes before anyone else, the guy on traffic duty looked suspicious enough.

Abby and Twyla came out together. I recognized Twyla by her coat. She was a tiny thing, and her puffy red anorak appeared to wear her instead of the other way around. The hood was up, so even her face disappeared.

Abby was barely in the car before she said, "Did we get a postcard from the dentist?"

"*What?*"

"Twyla has a dentist appointment. Mine is always two weeks after hers."

"Oh." A logical explanation. The kind of information Abby recorded and filed away. "Not yet." I lied. She'd never know.

"We should get it tomorrow."

If I told her about the shredded card, she'd retrieve and reassemble the scraps.

"Twyla looks like Little Red Riding Hood." Time for a subject change.

"I should call Gramma Evelyn."

"Why?"

"She should not let the wolf in."

When I was young, I saw a live-action movie version of Little Red

Riding Hood and developed nightmares. No matter how hard my parents tried to convince me it was only a dream, every night I saw the wolf crouched on my bedroom floor, ready to leap into my bed and swallow me. I slept on the top of a set of bunk beds, but he could make the jump and I would be gone in an instant. Not letting the wolf in sounded like a good idea.

"Okay," I said. The conversation made a certain amount of Abby-sense, but I didn't want to talk about wolves, fairytale or otherwise. The movie, and the nightmares, left such a mark on me that as an adult I hunted it down. It was surreal and scary for a children's film, but the wolf turned out to be a man in a wolf suit. A really bad wolf suit. His nose fell off in one scene.

Memories hold more power than reality.

My wolf lived on in my head. Real, he opened his huge mouth and showed his teeth, ready to devour Gramma, Red, a little girl huddled under her blankets on the top bunk, and anyone else who came his way.

"How do you feel about pesto for dinner?" I said.

"He can't blow our house down."

"With a salad, so we can pretend to be healthy."

"Our house is strong."

"And maybe garlic bread. With cheese. Who cares about healthy?"

"We have two chimneys."

"Abby, do you know you're a banana?"

"But we don't build a fire in our fireplace."

"It's okay, Abby. I love bananas. A lot."

"Gramma should not let the wolf in."

"I like grapes." I should have let her obsess over the dentist. Sometimes, I still dreamt about the wolf.

24.
[THE CEILING MAN]

HE WAVED AT CHUCKLES AS HE PASSED THE OFFICE. HIS NEW buddy worked the shit-shifts, midnights and Sundays. The name tag said Charlie, but he called the idiot Chuckles. Chuckles called him Mr. Blevins. His inner-Blevins got a kick out of that. He'd almost grown fond of Chuckles. If he had to dump Blevins before he blew town, Chuckles was a possibility.

"Hey!" Blevins said.

« Back to your cage. »

Chuckles would undoubtedly be more docile than Blevins but probably had a deeper paper trail. A job, no matter how menial, made him a semi-functional member of society, half-wit or not. He was cleaner than Blevins. He certainly kept the room clean. As an unofficial guest of the management, maid service was out of the question—if the Edge-O-Town even had maids—but Chuckles was obliging.

"Too bad the little girl's not," Blevins said.

« Chuckles is looking better and better. »

The brat had talent. She was him a lifetime ago—a dozen lifetimes ago—except she was too stupid to know what she had. Not one of his past watchers ever confronted him. She managed it across distance. When she showed up at the motel, he assumed she'd located him and was nearby, maybe in the parking lot. When he realized she was across town, still at school, he was shocked—and impressed. He needed proximity. Face to face was best, but he could work from outside a room or even a building, as long as he was close. A conversation across two miles was beyond him. A damaged human brat should not hold more talent than he had. Wisdom said get rid of her, but he had bigger plans. He would use her. He had the talent. He had the skills. He had the tools, including her mother. The first step was breaking her. It would be a pleasure.

"You know that's a fucking Christmas song," Blevins said. "You're a little late."

He was humming and hadn't realized it.

«*Everybody gets a present tonight.*»

Not necessarily one they wanted, but it was no deposit, no return. He wanted the brat to watch him unwrap Grandma.

«*Over the river and through the woods, now Grandmother's cap I spy.*»

The brat's strength would be her downfall.

BLEVINS LED HIM to the house. He despised relying on his host for anything, but the quick images in the brat's head at the mention of *Grandmother's house* didn't tell him where it was. Blevins and his stupid bicycle had been all over town.

"I'm a fucking guidebook," Blevins said. "Bet Chuckles couldn't help."

The tidy exterior impressed him, well maintained, no broken branches or leftover fall leaves littering the grounds, and surrounded by perfectly trimmed and symmetrical evergreen shrubs. Grandma was a woman after his heart, if he'd had a heart of his own. The place was too large for one old woman, but the brat gave him the impression Grandma lived alone.

The morning snow had melted by afternoon, but frozen grass crackled under his feet as he circled the house, sent out gentle feelers, and searched for the woman. He located her—second story, back. Asleep.

«*Oh, Grandma, what a big house you have.*»

She shook him off, a bad dream she refused to acknowledge.

«*Wake up. Let me in.*»

She snored on.

"Having problems?" Blevins said. "Maybe you should make some real noise."

«Subtlety.» Waking the neighbors was a bad idea.

"What's that?"

He tried to picture her, but all he had were images from the brat, all soft and fuzzy. A cartoon version of a grandmother, not a real woman, but Blevins recognized her.

"I know her. She's a bitch. She ain't gonna listen to you."

«We'll see.»

The shrubbery was mulched with round white stones. He grabbed a handful and tossed one at a second story window. It bounced off the frame with a soft thud.

"You're gonna hafta put more oomph in it. With my arm, you ought be able to shatter it good. I used to play ball, you know."

«I'm sure you were the Cy Young of the indigent.»

The second rock hit the same spot as the first, its thud a little louder. A light came on, and a silhouette filled the window.

«Let me in.»

The shadow behind the curtains didn't move, but her fright whetted his appetite.

The brat should show up soon. He'd dropped enough hints. With her talent, she had to know what he planned. She might have talent, but he had experience and skills.

«Let me in.»

He threw a third stone. The curtains parted, and Grandma's face appeared. He prodded. Growing fear, but not submission.

"Thought you said old and scared was a piece of cake?" Blevins said. "She's listening to you about as good as the kid does."

«Go downstairs. Unlock the door.» He threw one last stone at the window frame, hard.

"Good throw. Bad aim. Break the fucking window," Blevins said.

«Unlock the door. Let me in.» A frisson. She was weakening.

He sent her a picture. A ceiling, splattered and dripping with red. His memory. The brat's memory.

"Go away. I'm calling the police." The quiver in the old woman's words undercut her attempt at authority.

"She's a pigheaded bitch, just like her granddaughter," Blevins said.

«Do not say bitch. A bitch is a dog not a person.»

The girl. Excellent.

«Welcome to the party, Little Piggy.»

Grandma disappeared from the window. He reached out and tracked her, but she remained on the second floor.

«Go downstairs. Unlock the door.»

«No,» the brat said.

«Don't answer for Gramma. It's not polite.»

«You should leave now. The Woodsman will come.»

«I'm rewriting the story just for you, my Little Piggy.»

"The police are on their way." He heard, felt, savored Grandma's fear. His hunger surged.

«Daddy is the Woodsman.» No fear from the brat, just confidence. Security.

«Let me in.»

NO. The word echoed through his skull, but he couldn't tell whether it came from the brat or the woman. He needed to feed.

"Fucking sirens," Blevins said.

He was ravenous and running out of time.

«The Woodsman saves the Grandmother.» Smug. The brat was smug.

The sirens grew louder.

"They're close," Blevins said. "We're gonna get caught."

Hunger fought with common sense, but the imbecile was correct. He left.

SENSE MAY HAVE overcome his hunger, but it didn't kill it. Once awakened, his craving burned. He didn't want to feed. He needed to. Not the nourishment. He longed for the kill.

"I know where there's a fucking smorgasbord," Blevins said.

«The brat. Her family.» He wanted them, but it wasn't the time. Neither the brat nor her father would let him in. Sooner or later, the mother would, but she wasn't yet there.

"Invisible people. Nobody will know you were there."

«Show me.»

Blevins directed him to a wooded gulf, the remains of Port Massasauga's dying river. The two men huddled inside a makeshift shelter would have made fine carnival geeks, back in the day. Their brains eaten away by cheap booze, they never knew what hit them. Chickens would have been more fun. Taking them satisfied neither his hunger nor his rage, but at least his belly was full.

25.
[CAROLE]

THE PHONE RANG. THE LANDLINE. MIDDLE OF THE NIGHT CALLS were never good news.

Jim answered it on the second ring. His deep murmur, but not his words, carried through the walls. The conversation was short. I knew he'd hung up because the phone rang a second time. Two midnight calls.

Abby sat up and leaned forward, her eyes open but unfocussed. I strained to understand Jim's side of the conversation but couldn't.

"No." Abby started rocking.

"Abby, you're making me seasick."

She blinked and stilled.

"Do you want to read?" I said.

"No."

"Are you okay?"

"Daddy is the Woodsman."

"Carole." Jim, dressed, stood in the doorway and motioned me into the hall.

"Something's going on at Mom's," he said.

"What?"

"I don't know. The first call was from her, but she didn't make a whole lot of sense."

"The second call?"

"Jan in the Sheriff's dispatch. Mom called them. They sent a car."

Evelyn lived in the township, but Jan used to work for the city and knew Jim. It was good of her to call him. "Did she say anything?"

"Just that Mom sounded confused. Jan tried to keep her on the line, but she hung up."

"Be careful," I said. He didn't need to tell me where he was going.

"Gramma did not let the wolf in," Abby said.

Grapes, but not really. Abby had obsessed over Red and Grandma and the wolf all evening. I regretted mentioning the story. I should've given her the dentist's postcard.

"Abby, there is no wolf. It's just a story." The same line my parents used on me. It didn't work on Abby any better than it had on me.

"He cannot huff and puff," she said.

"Different story, kiddo. How about some *Little Women*?" No wolves there.

"Daddy is the Woodsman."

I opened the book. Even if she didn't need the distraction, I did.

She didn't fall asleep, but she stayed quiet and listened. We were still reading when Jim returned.

"Everything okay?" I said.

He nodded. I wanted details but couldn't ask in front of Abby.

"No red ceiling. No Ceiling Man," Abby said.

"Who is the Ceiling Man?" Jim said.

"He is angry, but he is gone."

"Abby, tell me who he is."

"Gramma did not let the wolf in, and I am glad."

"Abby, who is the wolf? Is he the Ceiling Man?" Not a Dad-command. A cop-command.

"Idunno."

JIM HUNG AROUND while I drove Abby to school and when I returned, filled me in on what happened at Evelyn's. When she thought she heard a prowler, her first reaction was to call her golden boy. No surprise there. He told her to call 911.

By the time the sheriffs arrived, the prowler was gone. If there even was a prowler. Jim was noncommittal about whether or not the cops found any sign of one. I got the impression there was a chance she'd imagined the whole thing.

Or not. I remembered my trampled lavender.

"She said he kept screaming at her to let him in, but none of the neighbors heard anything," he said.

"Maybe she had a nightmare." I knew how real nightmares could be.

"She kept talking woodsmen and wolves and red ceilings. She sounded a lot like Abby. Worse."

Jim's grandmother suffered from dementia in her last years. Even though I liked her much better than Evelyn, the thought of Jim's mother going the same route worried me. Maybe more than it did him. He had a son's worry. I worried about putting up with her. She was demented enough already.

"I'll go see her this afternoon." I could play the good daughter-in-law, after I got some sleep.

"Call first."

Maybe she wouldn't want to see me, and I could sleep longer. I called as soon as he left.

"It was nothing." Her voice contradicted her words. She sounded like a frightened old woman, not the Mighty Mighty Evil-lyn.

"I thought that after I pick up Abby, we'd stop by and visit." If she didn't want to deal with me, she always enjoyed seeing Abby.

"I won't be here," she said. "I'm going to spend the day at the Senior Center."

"That'll be nice."

"The girl who's been in charge since you left is very good. She listens to my suggestions."

Less little old lady, more Evil-lyn. I should have slept before I called her.

"That's good to know." I pulled up the syrup voice. "Would you like to come over for dinner?" For Jim. I would deal with her for Jim.

"No. I wouldn't want to put you out."

"It's no problem. We have to eat anyway." The syrup thinned.

"I'm going to call my son and have him stop and check my locks on his way home."

Because that's not putting anybody out. Syrup. She was obviously more upset than she was willing to let on to me.

"He's good with locks," I said. "If you change your mind about dinner, come home with him. One of us can run you home later."

"I need to go," she said.

"Evelyn, if you need anything, call me."

"I wasn't dreaming, you know. There *was* someone out there."

"I'm sure there was."

"Don't humor me."

"I wasn't. I believe—"

"I looked out the window. I saw him. He was there, on the ground, screaming at me. He wanted me to let him into my house. He wanted to...hurt me."

I half expected her to say *eat me*. It all sounded too much like my childhood wolf nightmare. Part of me felt sorry for her. Most of me hoped it didn't go on for months. I understood how my parents felt.

"I didn't let him in," she said.

Gramma did not let the wolf in. I never told Abby about my nightmares. "Are you sure you're okay? I'll come drive you to the Center if you want."

"I'm fine. I am perfectly capable of driving myself. I'm going to spend the day with my friends."

And I definitely wasn't counted among her friends. "Be sure to call Jim. He'll have no problem stopping by."

"Of course not. He's my son."

Our almost-sharing time was over.

"Call me if you need anything," I said.

"I will."

We said polite good-byes and hung up. I went to bed.

"HE'S ANGRY," ABBY *says.*

"Who? Tell me who!" Furious, I reach for her, but she moves beyond my reach. "You can't come in!"

"No red." She is unperturbed.

"What do you mean?" My rage boils. I want to shake her, to make her answer, but she eludes my grasp.

Far away, Evelyn's high pitched scream echoes, on and on.

"Daddy is the Woodsman," Abby says.

"Abby!" I lunge...

I awoke with my headache back and barely enough time to make it to the school—and a truck load of guilt. It was only a dream, but the desire to hurt my daughter not only felt real, it lingered.

ABBY DIDN'T HELP my guilt. She settled into the front seat and shot me the teenage *I hate adults* look. When I asked her how her day went, she grunted. Every time I glanced at her, I found her staring at me.

"Don't stare at your mother. She's boring."

She grunted.

Crazy-mom wearing pajamas and post-cataract grandma glasses wasn't boring. Humiliating, maybe, but I couldn't shake the suspicion she knew about my dream and hated me for it. I dropped my attempts at small talk and let her glare.

We pulled into our driveway, and the pain in my head exploded. I clutched the steering wheel, took deep breaths, and waited for it to pass. Willed it to pass.

"It is okay, Mom. He cannot get in."

I couldn't find the words to ask what she meant. Didn't trust myself to ask, but I wanted to know, needed to know.

"I will not let him get in." Abby's whispered nonsense rang in my ears and my head.

"Who?" I forced out the single word.

"Idunno."

I gripped the steering wheel and choked back the urge to grab her and shake her and wring the answer out of her. *Breathe. Breathe.* I pictured the pain—and my anger—crashing over me, waves battering the shoreline and ebbing with the outgoing tide. *Breathe.* The rage drained and the pain receded, not completely, but enough to pull myself together. I was no longer drowning.

I handed my keys to Abby. "Here. You can unlock."

Inside, I made a beeline for the Vicodin. Not many left. I took one and hid the bottle in my make-up bag. If Jim noticed the missing bottle, I could tell him I threw it away. If he noticed the diminishing number of pills, I couldn't tell him I was tossing them out one at a time.

Abby stood at the bathroom door and held out an envelope with my name on it.

"Permission slip?"

She shook her head. "Ms. Colley sends you a note." She stared at her feet and waited while I read it.

She fell asleep in class not once, but three times in a day, which was three more than her total in the two years she'd been in Ms. Colley's class. The teacher downplayed it, but the underlying message was *What's going on? Are things all right at home?*

"Abby, do you feel okay?

"Huh."

"That's not an answer. Are you getting sick?" Anger, unbidden, colored my words, and she stiffened.

"Idunno."

Shame blotted out my anger. The leftovers of my stupid nightmare made me act like a shrew. I would never hurt her.

I still felt guilty.

"Mac and cheese for dinner?" A peace offering. A *mea culpa* for a dream Abby didn't, couldn't, know about. If nothing else, comfort food would be good for our souls, if not our bodies.

She answered with a big, loopy Abby-grin.

"Do you have homework? Get it done, and we'll get cooking." As long as she had enough to keep her busy until the Vicodin took effect and didn't ask for help, we'd be good.

By the time she said, "All done," the pain faded to its familiar nibble around the edges, and I could function. I should have checked her work, but it was either that or cook. I wasn't up for both, and guilt-infused comfort food was the higher priority.

"Let's be chefs," I said.

Mac and cheese was one of the first things Abby and I started making as a team, and we had it down to a science. We each knew our roles. We didn't need a recipe. When I needed an ingredient, Abby handed it to me. We were a well-oiled mac and cheese making machine.

We were both off our games.

"What's this?" I held up the jar of mayo she handed me.

"Sour cream," she said.

"Try again, kiddo."

I put the casserole in the oven, set the timer and said, "Should be ready when Daddy gets home."

"You need to turn the oven on," she said.

"Ooops."

"I think we are both bananas," she said.

"I think you're right."

Despite our mutual air-headedness, dinner didn't turn out bad. Abby and Jim took seconds. I forced myself to finish one serving. Compared to the anticipation, the real thing was blah. I blamed it on my headache. Or the Vicodin.

"Were you out of onion powder?" Jim asked.

"Ooops," Abby said. "We are bananas."

I forgot. So did Abby. At least we caught the mayo and the oven.

"How was your mom?" I said.

"Okay. Worn out. I don't think she ever went back to sleep last night."

"I did call her."

"I heard."

"She sounded shaken."

"She says she's fine."

He never believed *me* when I said I was fine.

"Gramma did not let the wolf in," Abby said.

I tensed, expecting him to question her about the wolf.

Instead, he said, "I like grapes" and took a third helping of dinner.

EVELYN WASN'T THE only one worn out. We skipped the movie part of my plan and called it an early night. Jim went to bed before Abby was out of the shower and didn't argue about me spending the night in her room. Good. My headache was back, and I didn't need him asking, "Are you okay?"

There were four pills left. I downed three.

The few times Abby had taken serious painkillers, they made her goofy. And sleepy.

« *Give her one.* »

A single Vicodin would knock her out. I wouldn't have to worry about her waking up.

I couldn't drug my daughter just so I could get some rest.

« Give her one. »

If she was falling asleep in school, a full night's sleep would be good for her. We'd both be better off for it.

« Give her one. »

I filled a water cup.

"Here. Take this." I handed the last pill to Abby.

"Why?"

"Because I'm the Mom and I said so."

She took it.

26.
[ABBY]

"ABBY, ABBY. WAKE UP." MY MOM SHAKES ME. I DO NOT LIKE HER hand on my shoulder, and I think she should not shake me.

"No," I say.

"Abby, come on. We have to go." My mom grabs my arm and squeezes, and I cannot get away.

The Ceiling Man is laughing. "Your mom is mine, Little Bunny," he says.

"No."

"Time to come see me."

"Go away," I say.

I think maybe my mom is asleep, but she is standing up. People should lie down when they are asleep. She pulls and pulls. I do not want to get out of my bed.

"Leave us alone," I say and the Ceiling Man laughs.

My mom is quiet but her fingernails are sharp and I think they might cut my arm and I think she needs to let go.

"I'm hungry," the Ceiling Man says. "If she hurts you, I'll punish her for you. She'll never hurt you again. Promise."

Sami's mean bark hurts my ears. My mom pulls and I am on the floor. The blue numbers on my ceiling say 2:11, but blue is better than red. I think I need my dad. I think I need the Woodsman.

"Get up. Come on," my mom says.

Sami barks and growls. I see her teeth. I think I need to scream but my scream is stuck.

"What the hell is going on?" Daddy turns on my light.

The Woodsman is here, but I cannot answer him. My words are stuck in my chest and I cannot even say *Idunno*. My mom is hurting my arm. Sami is hurting my ears. The light is hurting my eyes. My words are hurting my chest, and I cannot breathe.

My mom would not hurt me if she is awake. I think she is asleep and it is the Ceiling Man.

"Your mom is mine," the Ceiling Man says.

I do not think he has a mom and I do not think he should have mine.

"We'll share, Little Bunny."

I am a banana. My mom loves bananas. A lot.

"Bananas bruise easy," the Ceiling Man says.

"Daddy will stop you," I say but not with my mouth because my mouth does not work. Daddy is a policeman. He catches bad guys. He is shaking my mom and she is shaking my arm.

"Carole, wake up!" Daddy yells and hurts my ears. My mom lets me go. Daddy is the Woodsman.

"Abby, are you okay?" Daddy says. My mom does not say anything.

"I am not a little bunny," I say. My words are not stuck anymore and I use my mouth, but I do not think Daddy hears me.

"Shit," the Ceiling Man says.

"What the hell did you think you were doing?" Daddy is yelling but I do not think he is yelling at me.

"It is not my mom's fault," I say. "It is the Ceiling Man." Nobody is listening to me.

The Ceiling Man laughs. "I'm listening," he says.

My arm hurts. There is yelling and barking and my ears hurt. It is the Ceiling Man's fault and I think I am angry.

"Unnnggh," I say.

"Now see what you did?" Daddy says. He should use his soft voice but he does not.

I cannot breathe. My arm hurts and my eyes burn and I should hurt the Ceiling Man.

I am crying. I hate crying and I cannot stop.

"Sami, hush," Daddy says. Sami barks and does not stop.

"He is here," I say. "He should go away and leave us alone."

"Who?" Daddy says.

I look for the Ceiling Man. His friend is laughing too.

"You are a bad man," I say.

"Abby. Who are you talking to?" Daddy should stop hurting my ears.

My head fills with red and I do not like red. I push the Ceiling Man and he falls down.

"Whoa. How did she do that?" the Ceiling Man's friend says.

Nobody is laughing anymore.

"I'll huff and I'll puff and I'll blow your house in," the Ceiling Man says.

"No you won't," I say.

"Abby!" Daddy does not stop yelling.

The blanket is stinky and I do not want it on me but I cannot push it off. I scream and the red disappears. The Ceiling Man is gone.

I am not a little bunny.

"ABBY, BREATHE." My mom's face is wet and her words are trembly but she does not hurt my ears.

"Don't you think you've done enough damage?" Daddy hurts my ears.

"Lower your voice," my mom says.

"He is gone now," I say. I get off the floor and into my bed. "No blankets," I say.

"You go to bed. I'll stay here," Daddy says. He does not hurt my ears.

"I am in bed," I say.

"No," my mom says.

My dad frowns. I do not think it is a sad frown. I think he is Mad Dad. He leaves my room.

"Abby, I am so sorry," my mom says. Her face is wet and she is whispering.

"I am a banana," I say. My mom loves bananas.

Daddy is back. He carries his pillow and a blanket and puts them on the floor and sits down.

"No blankets," I say.

"I guess we'll all spend the night here," Mad Dad says.

Daddy is the Woodsman.

My window rattles and my mom jumps, but it is only the wind. The Ceiling Man is gone.

"Our house is strong," I say.

"YOU ARE *NOT* driving this morning." Daddy does not hurt my ears but I think maybe he is still Mad Dad.

My mom is quiet. Her elbows are on the table, and her head is in her hands. I think her head hurts.

Gramma says, "No elbows on the table." I do not think I should remind my mom about elbows.

I will ride the bus to school.

I get out the peanut butter and put two slices of bread in the toaster.

"Abby will take the bus home too," Daddy says. "I'll call my mother. She can come over this afternoon and stay with both of you."

"I don't need a babysitter," my mom says. I barely hear her. I do not know if Daddy hears her.

Mad Dad did not give my mom her coffee and I think she needs it. The sunflower mug is my favorite. Sunflowers make my mom happy. There is no red on the sunflower mug. I only put coffee in it. No milk. No sugar. Daddy puts milk in his coffee. Gramma Evelyn does not put anything in her coffee. My mom and Gramma are alike.

"No elbows on the table," I say and put my mom's coffee on the table.

"Thank you, honey," she says. She takes her elbows off the table. Her mouth smiles, but I do not think she is happy.

Smiles should not be slippery.

Daddy watches us. I think he is still Mad Dad. Devon should write *Mad Dad goes away* on his list.

"Bananas bruise easy," I say.

"Abby, let me see your arm," Daddy says. He looks at both of my arms all the way up to my shoulders. "No bruises here," he says. "This banana's all good." He does not look at my mom. He tries to give me a hug but I do not want one.

"Where are you going?" my mom says.

"Daddy says I can ride the bus."

"Wait in the porch," my mom says.

I think she wants to cry. I think her head hurts. I should tell Daddy it is not my mom's fault.

"Sunflowers make you happy," I say.

Devon rides the bus. I will tell Devon to write *No more Mad Dad* on his list. When Devon writes it on his list, it is final.

"It's awfully windy," Daddy says. "Why don't you wait inside?"

"It huffs and it puffs," I say.

"But it won't blow our house in," Daddy says.

"The Ceiling Man did it," I say.

"Abby, who is the Ceiling Man?" Daddy says.

"Idunno."

I do not know who he is. I only know he is.

27.
[THE CEILING MAN]

"THAT WHOLE FAMILY IS FUCKING NUTS," BLEVINS SAID. "Especially the dog."

Nuts was the wrong word. Nuts, he could control. Mom was close to nuts, and she was his. She would have brought him the brat, if not for the dog. And Daddy.

"Told you I hate fucking dogs," Blevins said.

Time to return to Plan A. Get rid of the brat. Make that Plan A Plus. Mommy, Daddy, and the dog were goners too.

He hoped they enjoyed their last day. He was fed up, but not fed, and there wouldn't be enough left of the brat and her parents for a snack, let alone a meal. Not one he wanted, any way. Once they were gone, he'd pay Grandma another visit. Maybe he'd drop in on Twyla too. One for the road.

"I know what you're gonna do," Blevins said. "Can we bring marshmallows?"

28.
[CAROLE]

I DIDN'T REMEMBER ANY OF IT. I ONLY KNEW WHAT JIM TOLD ME.

I hurt Abby.

It was the Vicodin. I shouldn't have taken three. They were gone. It wouldn't happen again.

I drugged Abby.

"It's okay, Mom. It is not your fault," she said.

My headache was gone, and I missed it. The pain might have blocked out the self-loathing.

After Abby left for school, Jim went to the living room and called Evelyn. From the kitchen, I couldn't make out his words, but the tone was nothing like the cold, controlled voice he'd used on me all morning.

"You get some sleep. Mom will be here before Abby gets home." For me, he brought back the ice.

"If I'm still asleep, she can let herself in."

"Don't push me."

I didn't mean it the way he took it. "Look—"

"No. No more discussion. We'll talk tonight." He spoke to the cupboards. He wouldn't look at me.

I shut up. Anything I said would be a spark to the powder keg. It wasn't like I had any words to make things better. I hurt my daughter.

And she forgave me.

I held myself together until he left, but when the door slammed behind him, the tears flowed.

I CRIED MYSELF to sleep, but the sleep didn't last. I tossed and turned and tried to remember what I'd done. I'd settled into my chair and wrapped myself in my blanket, but after that, nothing until Jim shouted at me and...

I hurt my daughter.

When Sami barked, I dragged myself out of bed and to the window. Evelyn was in the driveway. As much as I wanted to go back to bed, I had to face her sometime. I had no idea what Jim told her, but I deserved anything she dished out.

By the time I made it downstairs, she was already in the kitchen. Sami had no problem with Evelyn letting herself in. Her butt was going a mile a minute while Evelyn petted her and cooed.

"Now I know where Jim gets it," I said.

She jumped. "I didn't hear you come down. I knocked, but—"

"It's okay." I poured a cup of cold coffee and stuck it in the microwave.

"I'll make fresh."

"This is fine."

"You look..."

I knew what I looked like. I didn't need her to tell me. Red nose, swollen eyes, I didn't cry pretty. But, whatever she had to say, I deserved it. Whatever Jim told her, I deserved it.

She switched tracks. "Have you eaten?"

"Abby made toast this morning." My eyes burned, and I blinked away the tears. Not in front of Evelyn.

"I brought vegetable soup."

I sat at the table, watched her heat up a bowl, and wondered why she was being nice to me. Jim must not have told her, at least not everything. Maybe he did, and she thought she was getting rid of me.

The soup was delicious.

Evelyn and I waited for Abby in the sun porch. With Evelyn watching, I couldn't bring myself to go out and stand at the curb.

Abby was sweet and forgiving in the morning, but she'd had all day to dwell on what happened. Had she told Ms. Colley? *Mommy tried to hurt me.*

Evelyn yammered away, but she was background noise.

"Is that okay?" she said.

"I'm sorry. I was daydreaming."

"I said I would make dinner before I leave. Anything in particular you would like?"

The bus pulled up. "Ask Abby," I said.

Abby walked right past her grandmother and gave me a big hug. A real one. Not one of her lean in for a split second and jump away duty-hugs. "It was not your fault," she whispered before she let go.

She couldn't have made me feel worse if she'd tried. It was all I could do not to fall apart in front of Evelyn.

I curled up on the couch and listened to Abby and Evelyn laughing in the kitchen. I wanted to join them—even Evelyn—cooking, having fun, being a family. Instead, I pulled the afghan over my head and tried to shut them out.

When Jim came in, the giggles increased. I could almost hear the hugs.

"Smells wonderful," he said. "Let me get changed and I'll help."

By the time he passed through the living room, I was sitting up, blanket off my head, trying to look human.

"How was your day?" I asked.

"Quiet." He still wouldn't look at me.

When he came back downstairs, I didn't try talking to him. He didn't speak to me, either.

I SHOULD HAVE enjoyed dinner, and not because it was delicious. Evelyn made her Extra Special Deviled Eggs, one of her holiday dinner staples. She didn't know, but Jim hated them. When we were first married, she gave me the recipe and told me they were one of his favorite things.

The first time I made them, he took one bite and looked at me like I had two heads.

"Please. Never again. They're disgusting," he said.

"Did I mess up the recipe?"

"No, they taste just like Mom's. I can't stand them."

"She said you loved them."

"I never told her."

I never made them again, but I enjoyed watching him find ways to pretend to eat them whenever Evelyn did. I wondered why she'd made them that night. It wasn't a holiday. Maybe Abby requested them.

Jim slipped one off his plate and passed it to Sami. The dog loved eggs.

He saw me grin.

"Pass the eggs, Mom." He took one and stuffed the whole thing into his mouth.

My smile, weak to start with, died. Evelyn would eventually leave, and Abby would go to her shower.

When Jim and I were alone, things would get ugly.

29.
[ABBY]

My timer says, "Beeeeep beeeeep beeeeep."

I turn off the water and get out of the shower. It is the only way to make my timer shush.

Mom and Daddy are fighting. They do not know I hear them.

"I can't deal with this anymore," Daddy says. "What the hell did you think you were doing last night?"

"I don't know," my mom says.

It is not my mom's fault.

"Where were you going? You could have hurt her."

"I said I don't know. I don't remember anything."

"You need to see the doctor," Daddy says, "and you need to get some sleep. Real sleep."

"I'm getting enough sleep," my mom says.

I do not think she is telling the truth. Lying is bad, but my mom is not bad. Maybe she is not lying. Maybe she does not know she should get more sleep. If she does not know, maybe it is not a lie.

"I asked Mom to keep coming over in the afternoons," Daddy says.

"What did you tell her? *My wife's a little crazy? Hang out and make sure she doesn't hurt the kid?*"

My mom is not crazy. It is the Ceiling Man's fault.

My mom would not hurt me. She loves bananas.

The Ceiling Man says, "Bananas bruise easy."

My mom loves grapes too. I do not know if grapes bruise easy, but I should ask her if I can be a grape. I do not think I should be a banana anymore.

If I tell my mom and Daddy I can hear them fighting, they will stop. I think I need to listen.

I cannot hear what Daddy says. His voice is very low and very soft and I think that means he is very angry.

"How can I stop?" my mom says. "Haven't you noticed how scatter-brained and full-strength-Abby she's been lately? Ms. Colley says she's out of it in school too."

"Has it dawned on you that she's picking that up from you?" Daddy's voice is not so soft but I think it is still angry. It is Mad Dad time. *No more Mad Dad* is not on Devon's list. I will tell him again.

"I'm fine," my mom says.

"Is that why you forgot to pay the bills?"

My mom does not say anything.

"Didn't think I knew about that, did you? Were you planning on telling me?" Mad Dad says.

"I took care of it," my mom says.

"You need to stop obsessing over Abby and start paying attention to real things. And get some sleep. This isn't good for any of us," Daddy says.

"Can't deal with a crazy wife along with a crazy mother and daughter?"

"That about sums it up," Mad Dad says.

My mom does not answer. They are both quiet, but I think the quiet is still fighting.

They do not know I hear them. I should tell them so they will stop fighting.

I think I must listen.

"I'm sorry," Daddy says. He is not Mad Dad now.

"You said it," my mom says.

"Promise you will see the doctor," Daddy says.

"It's on the list," my mom says.

Devon should write it on his list. He should write:

    1. Abby's mom sees the doctor.

    2. The doctor says Abby's mom is just fine.

When Devon writes it on his list, it is final.

"Tomorrow," Daddy says. "Call her first thing tomorrow."

My mom needs to call the dentist. It is time for my check-up and I did not get a postcard. I will remind her tomorrow and she will call the dentist and the doctor and we will all be just fine.

"I will. I promise," my mom says.

"And get some sleep."

"I'll add it to my list."

My mom has a list. I do not have a list.

Devon says, "The list is my thing. I am the List Maker." He will write my list in his notebook. "Because I am a Good Guy," he says. "*Devon is a Good Guy* is on my list."

Devon should write:

3. Abby's mom sleeps.

"Abby? Are you still in the bathroom? What are you doing in there?" My mom's voice is full of extra happy. That means she is pretending. When my mom uses her extra happy voice, Daddy says, "Uh-oh. Perky. We're in trouble, kid."

I do not want to be in trouble.

My towel is still on the bar. My pajamas are on the floor. I forgot to get dry and get dressed. I do not need my towel. I am dripped dry.

"Abby? Answer me." My mom rattles the door, but it is locked.

"Abby?" She does not sound happy. Not even pretend happy.

"I am getting dressed." I pick up my pajamas.

"What's taking you so long?"

"Idunno."

Devon should write:

4. And they all live happy ever after. But not pretend happy.

THE NIGHT IS quiet. The Ceiling Man is not here.

Daddy says my mom *must sleep.*

It is quiet. I think my mom is safe.

Daddy is in his sleeping bag on my floor.

Daddy says, "I am not leaving you alone with her." My mom looks like she will cry, but she does not.

I let my mom go to sleep. I will sleep too. I think we will all be better after we get some sleep.

I am glad the Woodsman is here.

"Beeeeep. Beeeeep. Beeeeep." I am not in the shower. I am in bed. My ceiling clock says 2:45.

"Beeeeep. Beeeeep. Beeeeep." I am not in the shower and my timer should not say *beeeeep*.

Sami is barking and the *beeeeep* hurts my ears. My timer is not beeping. It is the smoke alarm.

Sometimes the smoke alarm goes off when Daddy cooks. It is 2:45 AM and Daddy is not cooking.

The ceiling clock has blue numbers. Blue is better than red. No more red ceilings.

The Ceiling Man is here.

My mom is asleep in my chair.

Daddy says, "Carole, you must get some sleep." I think it is time for my mom to wake up even if it is 2:45 AM.

Daddy is not cooking. We are on fire.

"Abby, take Sami and go outside," Daddy says.

"Mom. Mom. Mom." My mom does not hear me.

The smoke alarm screams. Sami barks. My ears hurt.

"Mom. Mom." Her eyes are closed and she does not move but her chest goes up and down.

"Your wife does not wake up. She should wake up now," I say.

"Take Sami and go outside," Daddy says. "Just like we practiced."

The Ceiling Man is laughing and my ears hurt.

"Abby. Don't just stand there. Go. Now. I'll get Mom," Daddy says.

I cannot go downstairs.

"Fire," I say.

"Remember what we practiced."

"Downstairs," I say. "We cannot go downstairs. The fire is waiting downstairs."

Daddy's face is funny and I do not know what his funny face means. He shuts my door and puts his sleeping bag in front of the crack at the bottom of the door.

I do not remember practicing this.

"Abby, remember what we wrote on the emergency list?"

Devon makes lists. I do not make lists. Daddy makes special lists. I close my eyes and I see Daddy's Emergency List.

"Number Seven. If Abby cannot go down the stairs, she must go out her bedroom window and on to the porch roof," I say.

My mom is not awake. She cannot go out my window.

Daddy opens my window. "Out," he says. "I'll take Mom."

Beeeeeping. Barking. Laughing. I put my hands over my ears.

I cannot wake up my mom.

"Abby! Look at me!" Daddy is yelling and I do not want him to be Mad Dad. I did not make the fire.

I do not keep my mom awake, but it is not my fault. Daddy says, "You need sleep," and my mom says, "I'm fine."

We are not fine. We are on fire.

"The Ceiling Man did it," I say.

30.
[ABBY]

"ABBY!" DADDY HURTS MY EARS. "GO OUT YOUR WINDOW. WAIT for me on the roof."

My feet are bare.

"I will catch my death of cold," I say. I sound like Gramma Evelyn.

I shove my feet into my blue sneakers, but I do not untie them first and the backs squish under my heel. My mom hates it when I squish my shoes. It is one of her Pet Peeves. She says, "You are ruining those sneakers and hurting my head."

I am not hurting my mom's head and she should wake up.

My clock says 2:48. I think it is broken.

"More than three minutes," I say. "Your wife should wake up."

"I'll get your mom. Put this on and go!"

Daddy holds my Port Massasauga High School Fighting Falcons sweatshirt. It is red and black but mostly red.

"No," I say. "Your wife must wake up."

"Abby! Out!"

I look at the ceiling. No numbers.

"My clock is broken," I say. "I did not let the wolf in."

"Abby. Look at me. The electricity is out. You need to go to the porch roof now."

Sami is barking at my mom but my mom does not wake up.

"What about Sami?" I say.

"I'll put her out right behind you. Go!"

Daddy is yelling. Sami is barking. The Ceiling Man is laughing. My ears hurt and my eyes burn.

"Put shoes on your wife," I say. I do not want her to catch her death of cold.

"Abby, go!"

"Put shoes on your wife," I say. "Do not squish the heels. She does not like that."

Daddy puts my pink sneakers on my mom's feet. He does not untie them first but her feet go right in. No squished heels and I am glad. I do not want her head to hurt. My pink sneakers look like clown feet on my mom.

"She needs a red nose," the Ceiling Man says.

"No red. I am ignoring you," I say.

"ABBY!" Daddy is Mad Dad and he scares me.

I go out the window. It is cold and the Ceiling Man is outside but he is not on the roof.

Mr. Pete is in my yard. Fire drills mean I leave my house and go across the street to Mr. Pete's house. I am on the roof and I cannot go to Mr. Pete's house. Mr. Pete is at my house.

The Ceiling Man is at my house but I cannot see him. He is not in my front yard with Mr. Pete.

I will not jump. The Fire Drill list does not say *Mr. Pete goes to Abby's House*. It does not say *Abby jumps*. Devon should write a new Fire Drill List. My mom should wake up. I cannot jump off my roof.

"Abby, are you okay?" Mr. Pete says. He yells too. Everybody yells and my ears hurt and we are on fire and I am not okay.

"My mom will not wake up," I say.

"Where are your mom and dad?" Mr. Pete says.

"Idunno."

"Abby, put this on." Daddy throws my sweatshirt at me and it slides down the roof and falls off.

"Your mom is next," the Ceiling Man says.

"I cannot jump," I say. My mom should wake up now and say "Abby, do you know you are a banana?"

"I'm going to go get a ladder. Stay right there," Mr. Pete says.

"Stay away from the Ceiling Man," I say, but I do not think Mr. Pete hears me. He is running away.

I am on the porch roof and I cannot run away.

Daddy borrows Mr. Pete's tools. Daddy says, "Pete has all the cool tools."

My sweatshirt is red and it falls all the way to the ground. I do not want to fall all the way to the ground. I do not stay right there. I crawl back to my window.

"I cannot jump," I say.

My mom is still asleep. She is over Daddy's shoulder. "Abby, out of the way," he says.

"Do not throw your wife." I do not want my mom to be like my red sweatshirt. I do not want to be like my red sweatshirt.

"Is a ladder a tool?" I say.

The Ceiling Man is laughing. His laugh is a red laugh.

Sirens scream and I put my hands on my ears. My eyes are watery.

"If you move, he'll throw your mom," the Ceiling Man says. "She'll be broken."

My face is wet. Maybe I am crying and I do not want to cry.

My mom says, "Breathe, Abby. Breathe." My mom should wake up and say *Abby, breathe.*

"Breathe, Abby. Breathe," I say.

"Abby, move!" Daddy should not yell. My mom does not yell when she says *Abby, breathe.*

"Don't do it. He'll throw your mom off the roof," the Ceiling Man says.

"Do not throw your wife," I say.

"I'm not going to throw your mother, but you need to move." Daddy talks soft and slow. I think he is trying to be patient but he is not doing a very good job of it.

"You told your wife she *must sleep*," I say.

"She'll be broken. And red," the Ceiling Man says.

"Abby. You must get out of the way so I can get your mom out of the house. *Then* we will wake her up." Daddy tries to hide Mad Dad, but I think Mad Dad is here.

"I cannot jump," I say.

"Move so I can get out and then we will get down," Mad Dad says.

"Mrs. Livvy's husband has all the cool tools," I say.

"Abby, come on." Mr. Pete is on his ladder.

"Is a ladder a cool tool?"

Daddy's mouth moves. I do not know if he is Mad Dad. The sirens are too loud. My ears hurt and I cannot hear him. The sirens stop, and I think the firemen are here.

"I hate red," I say.

"Shit," the Ceiling Man says. He is angry and full of red. His red is filling me up, and I smell dirt and pennies.

"No." I push the Ceiling Man away, and he laughs.

"Abby, go with the fireman," Daddy says. Mr. Pete is gone, and a fireman is on the ladder. He is yellow, not red.

"Is a ladder a tool?" I say.

The Ceiling Man's red is loud and he is full of red and fire and thunder. He stinks and I hate him. I push him hard and I think I will fall and I do not want to be crumbled on the ground like my sweatshirt. I hang on to the windowsill.

My house sounds like Gramma Evelyn's fireplace but does not smell good. My eyes burn and I think they are full of tears.

Arms are around my waist and I do not like to be touched and maybe it is the Ceiling Man. I should say *stop do not touch me* but my words are stuck and maybe lost.

"Come on, honey. Let go." The arms are on a fireman. He is not the Ceiling Man. I do not fall to the ground. I am not my sweatshirt.

"Abby, let go." Daddy does not yell. He whispers, but he is serious.

I cannot make my hands let go of the windowsill. My fingers hurt and I think my hands are bleeding. Daddy talks. I think he is talking to the fireman, but I do not know what he says. My crying fills my ears.

The Ceiling Man wants to fill my head but I do not let him in.

"I do not like red. I do not like to be touched." My words are not lost.

"Come on, honey. We'll go down the ladder, and I won't let you fall," the fireman says.

The Ceiling Man is full of black, not red. "We're not finished." He whispers like Daddy, but his voice is scratchy and not soft.

"Abby, the fireman will help you down the ladder," Daddy says and he is not Mad Dad. "Go with him."

Daddy is a policeman. He helps people and keeps them safe. Firemen are like policemen.

"Do not throw my mom," I say. I take my hands off of the windowsill and they are not bleeding.

The fireman carries me down the ladder, and I cannot look at my sweatshirt on the ground. I cannot breathe. One of my shoes falls off.

My mom says, "Abby! Those are sneakers, not clogs. Untie them before you put them on!"

"My mom hates it when I do not untie my sneakers," I say.

"Shhhhhhhh," the fireman says. I think maybe I am screaming.

"I need Sami," I say.

"I'll get her. I promise," the fireman says.

"My mom should wake up now."

"We'll get her too."

"Daddy is the Woodsman," I say. The fireman does not answer.

"The Ceiling Man is full of red and fire," I say.

"It'll be okay, honey," the fireman says.

I hope he is right. Maybe he is a Woodsman too.

THE MAN IN the ambulance says I am *Oooo-kay* and I am *Breathing just fine*.

He is wrong. I am not *Oooo-kay* and there is too much noise and too much touching and I am not *breathing just fine*.

"My mom needs to be okay," I say. I am not crying but my eyes are burning. My mom is inside the ambulance and I do not know if she is *breathing just fine*. I do not think she is awake.

"We'll take good care of her," he says. His shirt says *Jason*. His name is Jason and he does not call me honey.

"Abby, come with me," Daddy says.

"Good-bye, Jason. My mom should wake up."

SAMI IS OFF the roof and stuck to my leg.

My mom says, "She is doing her Velcro-pup act." My mom is in the ambulance. She should wake up and Sami should Velcro-pup my mom too.

My house is filled with fire and I stand across the street. The fire in Gramma Evelyn's fireplace smells good and warm and cozy. The fire in my house smells bad and it makes my nose burn and my eyes water. Too many people are here and they are watching my house and I do not know if it makes their noses burn. I cannot see my dad and I cannot breathe.

"We're not finished, Little Bunny," the Ceiling Man says and he is gone.

Sami growls. I do not have her leash. It is burnt up in my house.

I think the Ceiling Man is still here. He does not talk to me, but I think he is watching my house burn down and I think he is angry. I do not want to talk to him so I do not look for him.

"Look after Abby," Daddy says.

"I'll take good care of her," Mrs. Livvy says.

"Daddy is the Woodsman," I say.

I have both my shoes. I untie them and put them on my feet properly. My mom should wake up and see that my shoes are put on properly.

Mrs. Livvy puts a blanket on my shoulders. It is not scratchy and it smells like purple flowers. Lavender. The flowers are called lavender and they grow by my house in the summer and I think they are all burnt up.

Mr. Pete ties a rope to Sami's collar and gives me the other end. "I don't have a leash, but this should do the trick," he says.

"My mom should wake up now," I say.

"She'll be fine, honey." Mrs. Livvy sounds like the fireman. She tries to hug me but I do not let her. Our house is on fire and it stinks and hurts my ears and there are too many people and my ears are screaming. I am rocking and I cannot stop.

My mom should wake up and say, "Abby, you are making me seasick." I will let her hug me even if it hurts and Sami will Velcro-pup her and my mom will be okay.

"I hate the Ceiling Man," I say.

"Shhhhhh," Mrs. Livvy says.

"Mom, Mom, Mom, Mom," I say, but I do not say it with my mouth and Mrs. Livvy does not hear me. My mom should wake up.

31.
[CAROLE]

"Mom, Mom, Mom, Mom."

Abby calls for me, but drowning in red and noise, I can't find her.

"Mom, Mom, Mom, Mom."

She's close—somewhere above me, just out of my reach. I kick my feet, try to surface, but the red sucks me back.

"Mom, Mom, Mom, Mom."

I open my mouth to call to her. The red fills my mouth, fills my lungs, chokes me. I can't fight. I stop struggling and sink. The red turns to black, and I know it will take me.

"Mom, Mom, Mom, Mom. You should wake up now."

A dream. A nightmare. If I open my eyes...

"Mom. Mom, Mom." *Abby is my lifeline. I won't give in.* "Mom." *I search for her call. If I find it, I can pull myself from the mire.*

«*Lady Bird, Lady Bird, fly away home...*»

Not Abby.

«*Your house is on fire and your child shall burn...*»

I knew the raspy, laughing voice, but couldn't place it.

Plastic clung to my face. I clawed at it, ripped it off. *Smoke.* Something was burning. *Ohmygodthehouseisonfire.* The black disappeared, replaced by blazing red.

"Ma'am. You need to leave the oxygen mask on."

"Abby." Why weren't the smoke alarms screeching? I needed to get up. I needed to get Abby. I needed to wake Jim—

"Shhhhh. Ma'am, lay back. You need to stay calm."

Someone held me down. I fought, grappled with hands, arms. I had no strength.

"Mom, Mom, Mom."

I heaved against the searing red, and it released me. I opened my eyes.

A man loomed over me. A uniform. An EMT.

«No place to hide, Lady Bird. She'll burn.»

"Why would you say that!"

"Ma'am, calm down." A smooth Johnny Cash voice. The EMT hadn't sung the nursery rhyme.

"My daughter. I need to—"

"She's fine. She's with your neighbor. Livvy?"

I wasn't in Abby's room. The EMT brought the oxygen mask back toward my face. I slapped him away.

"You're not Jed," I said.

"Excuse me?"

"My EMT. His name is Jed." *At the school. Ages ago.* I wasn't at the school. I was home, in— "Abby. Where's Abby?"

"Ma'am, I'm Jason. Your daughter's fine. Checked her over myself."

"Why?"

"Just a precaution. She's fine and she's safe. Right now, I need to look you over and make sure you're fine too. Do you know how long you were unconscious?"

"I don't even know what time it is. I need to find Abby. Abby always knows what time it is." I swung my legs over the side of the bed. Cot. Gurney? The room spun. Not a room. An ambulance.

"Ma'am. Do you know where you are?"

"Why am I in an ambulance?"

"Did you take anything? A sedative? A painkiller? Prescription or over-the counter?" A note of accusation crept into Jason's deep voice.

The Vicodin. Not tonight. Last night. I shook my head.

"Are you having any trouble breathing? Tightness in your chest?"

Both, but I wasn't about to tell him. He came at me with the damned mask again. I let him put it on me, then ripped it off and threw it back at him. "I'm fine. I need to get to my daughter."

"We checked her out. She's fine. She wouldn't wear the oxygen mask either."

"Why did she need oxygen?" My ears rang. My throat constricted. *Breathe. Breathe.* If I hyperventilated, Jason would never let me go.

"Just a precaution. What was the last thing you remember before going unconscious? Did you hit your head? Get hit by something to knock you out?"

The last thing I remembered was Jim refusing to leave me alone with Abby.

"Screw this," I said. "I'm going to find my daughter."

Jason followed me out the door.

OUTSIDE, THE SCENE was surreal. Hoses snaked across the yard, and firemen shouted to each other. Yellow tape divided our yard from the street. Warm light bathed the crowd beyond the tape. They'd trampled Pete's flower beds. He would be pissed. The rubberneckers had to be neighbors—who else would be there in the middle of the night—but I didn't recognize any of them, and I didn't see Abby.

Your house is on fire and your child shall burn. No. Jason saw her. She was fine.

The fire crackled behind me, and even standing in the street, the heat engulfed me. I kept my back to the house. I couldn't look at it. Not yet.

Where is Abby?

Blevins stood at the edge of the crowd, almost in the shadows. He raised his squared hands to his eyes and mimicked taking a picture. A muffled boom came from the house. I jumped, and he was gone.

"ABBY!" The scream felt like ground glass in my throat, and the acrid smell of burning wood and plastic made me miss the oxygen mask.

Lights from the fire trucks strobed across the crowd, and the sea of faces flashed red.

Abby hates red.

My eyes watered, and I started hacking. Jason grabbed my arm. I shook him off.

"Ma'am, You really should stay and let us check you over."

The blood pressure cuff was still on my arm. I tore it off and handed it to Jason. "Abby hates red. Help me find her or go back to your truck."

"I told you, she's fine. I'm more worried about you. Please, come back to the ambulance. Let's make sure you're all right. Then we'll look for her."

"Help me find my daughter. Then, maybe." I had no intention of going back with him. I stumbled. Jason caught me before I fell.

"You really need to come back and let us check you over."

"It's the shoes." Abby's shoes. "They're too big. ABBY!"

"Mom!"

Abby and Sami stood next to Livvy. I tried to run and ended up face down in the mud. *Stupid shoes*. Before I managed to get up, Sami was there wagging her butt.

Jason pulled me up, and I was face to face with my daughter.

"Mr. Pete's rope did not work," she said. "Sami got away from me."

I broke all the rules of Abby-contact and without asking, grabbed her in a bear-hug. She didn't fight. She hugged back. It was the longest and tightest embrace I'd had since she was two.

"Breathe, Mom. Breathe," she said.

When she let go, I forced myself to back off. She was wrapped in one of Livvy's handmade quilts, and I'd left a muddy body print on it.

"I ruined your quilt." For some reason, it seemed important. Livvy was proud of her quilts.

"It's okay," Livvy said. "Abby was freezing, and I grabbed the first thing I saw."

"Thank you."

Abby lifted the quilt, and I joined her under it.

"If you need anything, you know where to find me." Jason gave up on me and left.

"Be careful," Abby said.

THE FIREFIGHTERS POURED water on the house. Through the house. The roof was gone. Flames shot out the windows—or what was left of them. My home of fifteen years was little more than a shell. I couldn't imagine anything inside was salvageable.

With a loud crack, the attic collapsed in a shower of embers. The crowd behind me gasped like they were at some kind of freakish fireworks display.

I would smack the first one who let loose with an *oooo-aaaah*.

I thought about all the things I planned to grab if we ever had a fire. Books. Photos. Abby's school buses. *I bet Jim didn't save anything.*

"Daddy saved you," Abby said.

I must have spoken aloud. I didn't mean to.

"Daddy is the Woodsman."

I'd barely given Jim a thought since I'd come to in the ambulance. I felt guilty, but not as guilty as I should have—and I should have felt guilty about that too, but couldn't summon up the energy. Abby was safe and with me, and that was all that mattered.

"Where's Jim?" I asked Livvy.

She nodded toward where he leaned against a police car. One of the men with him was a uniformed cop I didn't know. The other looked vaguely familiar. Jim glanced over and I waved. He didn't wave back, but he headed in my direction, accompanied by the man I almost recognized.

Our hug was brief. I wanted to cling to him, like Abby attached herself to me, but he stiffened and backed away.

His *You okay?* was perfunctory. I matched my *I think so* to his tone.

Sami got a warmer greeting than I did.

"You remember George?" Jim said.

I did remember George. He was the fire department cop—the Fire Marshall.

"Why are you here?" I said.

"I just need to ask you a few questions."

"Maybe Livvy should take Abby in the house," Jim said.

"No." Abby and I spoke at the same time. I wasn't letting her out of my sight.

"It's okay," George said. "I need to talk to you both. Where were you when you first became aware of the fire?"

"In the ambulance." Stupid question. Jim must have told him I was asleep.

"Abby? How about you?" George used the classic speak-gently-to-the-handicapped voice. I didn't like him.

"Idunno," she said.

"Could the oven or a burner have been left on after cooking?"

"I don't know. I didn't cook," I said.

"Abby, honey? Were you in the kitchen?" He spoke slowly and paused between each word.

Abby shrugged. Condescension wouldn't get him anywhere with her.

"Have you noticed any electrical or wiring problems?"

"No."

"The Ceiling Man," Abby mumbled.

"What was that, honey? Speak up. Was there a problem with a ceiling fan?"

"Idunno."

"We don't have any ceiling fans," I said. "Didn't have any."

"Oh. Anybody bothering you or hanging around the house?" He addressed me and ignored Abby.

Jim's face was wooden. We'd lost our home, and he was playing cop.

"Blevins was here when I was looking for Abby."

"Who?" George glanced at Jim.

"You know, the moron on the bike. The one who breaks windows."

"Have you had problems with him before?" He used the patronizing tone on me.

"He ran me off the road, but Jim doesn't believe me. And somebody was outside the house in the middle of the night last week, but he doesn't believe that either." I sounded like a pouty five-year-old. I didn't care.

"The. Ceiling. Man." Abby enunciated each word.

I wondered if George knew he was being mocked.

"Who?" George managed to make the single word condescending. He didn't get it.

"Idunno." Abby pulled the quilt tighter around the two of us. "I need to go inside Mrs. Livvy's house now. My mom does too."

I completely agreed, but before I had a chance to say so, we were interrupted.

A single voice, but not a lone scream—the shrieks went on and on. They cut above the noise of the burning house and running fire trucks and silenced the crowd.

Abby winced and covered her ears. "We need to go in now," she said.

George and the cop who stayed by the car took off running. Jim hesitated. I told him to go, and he did.

"Nononononono." Abby verged on meltdown. I didn't know how she'd held out so long. I didn't know how I had.

"We need to take her inside," I told Livvy. The screams didn't stop. By the time we made it to the back door, they were joined by more sirens.

"Fire trucks have red lights, but police cars have blue lights," Abby said.

THE HOUSE WAS warm, but Abby refused to give up the quilt. I recognized it. Livvy searched for years to find the pattern, an unusual one called Virginia Snowball, and spent even longer collecting 1930's replica fabrics, all to recreate the quilt she had on her bed as a child. Her great-grandmother made the original from feed-sacks, and both Livvy and her mother loved it and used it until it wore out. Livvy sold or gave away most of her creations, but the Snowball quilt she made for herself.

"I made it to be used, washed, and used some more. Just like the first one was," she'd said. She even let her grandkids drag it around outside. She called it her comfort quilt.

It was in worse shape than the grandkids ever left it. Besides my muddy body-print, Abby and I had both trampled all over the bottom. On her way across the yard, Abby dragged it through the grass and mud. Inside, she left a trail of brown and green between the back door and the kitchen table. The floor would come clean. I wasn't so sure about the quilt.

The sirens quit. Livvy's kitchen was at the back of the house, insulated from the madness outside. Abby rocked, and I didn't stop her. Her lips moved in silent conversation. I wondered who she spoke to and what she said. Did she see red ceilings? I pushed the thought away. The rocking was a comfort—one I'd denied her for too long—and she needed it. The familiar rhythm of her movement comforted me too. The warm kitchen, the hot, sweet tea, the Mighty Samsonite curled up on my feet—despite the situation, I was calmer than I'd been in weeks.

Or, maybe I was just exhausted. I knew that across the street my home was if not gone, close to it. Sooner or later, Jim would show up and tell me something else terrible had happened. I hoped for later. I wanted to stay in my cocoon as long as possible. Denial is a comfortable place.

Livvy and I didn't talk. We sat and watched Abby rock. And waited.

It wasn't Jim who brought us the news. It was Pete.

"I think we all need something stronger than tea." He pulled a bottle of bourbon from the cupboard.

"It is the Ceiling Man," Abby whispered.

I was the only one close enough to hear her. I held my mug out to Pete.

Jason the EMT was dead. He never made it back to the ambulance.

One of the onlookers got bored and decided to go home. She tripped over him, just beyond the light of the fire. He was still warm. His throat was ripped out. His belly was open and he'd been eviscerated.

When she found him, we all heard her screams. Nobody heard a peep when he died.

32.
[THE CEILING MAN]

"You weren't very hungry," Blevins said.

«*Shut up.*»

Hunger wasn't the issue. Anger was the issue. He had the mother in his grasp until the idiot EMT woke her up.

It wasn't really the EMT. It was the damned girl, but Jason the EMT wouldn't be waking anybody else.

He put on a good show for the girl, but he never sensed fear. If she felt anything, it was—he couldn't tell. Disgust, maybe. Or distain.

"I hate red," she said and disappeared.

She shouldn't be able to come and go as she pleased. He was in control. He was always in control.

"Ha," Blevins said.

If he had more time, he'd have left less of Jason for that screaming idiot to trip over. He hated to waste food.

Chuckles had left him fresh towels and done his laundry. *The Edge-O-Town Motel—Port Massasauga's Luxury Accommodations.* He'd recommend them to all his friends, if he had any.

The smell of smoke clung to him.

"Not another fucking shower. You're killing me."

He took a cue from the girl and ignored Blevins. She had a few things right.

As the hot water streamed over him, he searched for the girl. He tracked her down right away. Too fast. Whatever their connection was, it was growing stronger.

She was with her mother—physically. He wasn't sure where she really was. Usually, her head was full of pictures that flashed by so fast he couldn't keep up with them. Usually, he didn't bother to try. Instead of her crazy picture show, nothingness surrounded him.

«*How's your Mommy, Little Piggy?*»

The only answer was quiet, a sense of peace. It'd been a long time since he was on a boat, but he smelled ocean. The hypnotic rhythm of waves lulled him almost to—*No.* He'd located her but hadn't found *her*.

«*Knock, knock, Little Piggy.*»

"Leave my mom alone. Leave my mom alone."

«*Oh, Little Pig, Little Pig, let me come in.*»

"Leave my mom alone. Leave my mom alone."

«*I huffed and I puffed and your house is gone, Little Piggy.*»

"Leave my mom alone. Leave my mom alone. Leave my mom alone." She didn't break rhythm.

Annoying.

"Jesus. Can't the little retard say anything else?" Blevins said.

«*Shut up.*»

"Leave my mom alone. Leave my mom alone."

He saw it. Bricks. The little brat was building a wall. Each *Leave my mom alone* was a perfectly placed yellow brick.

"She fucking hates red, you know." Blevins snickered.

He didn't know how long she'd been at it, but the wall rose between him and the mother and almost blocked the woman from sight.

It wasn't real.

«*Oh, Little Piggy. Do you think I can't knock down your silly little wall?*»

"Leave my mom alone. Leave my mom alone." She didn't break stride. If anything, she sounded surer, stronger.

«*Little Pig, Little Pig, watch this.*» He pushed.

«*Fuck!*» Pain seared his palms and shot up his arms.

He checked his hands—Blevins's hands—expecting to find them red and blistered. Not a mark on them.

"I didn't feel a thing," Blevins said.

"Leave my mom alone. Leave my mom alone." She picked up speed.

"Try it again," Blevins said. "It was kinda fun."

«Shut. Up.»

Shit. She wasn't building a wall around her mother.

"Leave my mom alone. Leave my mom alone. Leave my mom alone."

Her wall rose around him. He pulled out. The mist vanished and left him staring at the yellow tiles of the bathroom wall. Between the tiles, mildew blossomed red. He grinned. As a metaphor, a sordid shower stall in a cheap dive wasn't bad.

"He huffed and he puffed, but he couldn't blow the brick wall down. Did da widdle girl beat you again?"

«Shut up or you'll be gone too.»

"Why don't we just leave? Why's the damn retard so important?"

«There is no we.»

"I'm thinking you fucking need me."

«No, I really don't. There's plenty more just like you out there.»

He didn't have time to go house-hunting. Not until he figured out the girl. Or got rid of her. He didn't know which he wanted more, but if he had to choose one, it was the latter.

"Why not both?"

«Good plan. Then maybe I'll get rid of you.»

He dried off and flopped on the bed. Sunlight filtered through the cheap curtains, and he closed his eyes. The night wore him out. Or else Blevins was wearing out faster than he expected. Whichever, he was tired. And hungry. He should have made a to-go package from the EMT.

"I know a couple more guys we can eat."

«I told you. There is no we.»

He wouldn't sleep. He picked up the remote and clicked on the television. If nothing else, it would keep Blevins distracted for at least a little while.

33.
[CAROLE]

Pete and Livvy offered us a place to stay for as long as we needed. Their house had enough room for visiting grandchildren, but little room for long-term guests. I wanted to keep them as friends. Sharing close quarters with my family for any length of time would put a strain on any relationship.

Most of the motels were twenty-five miles away, at the interstate exit. The only one in or close to town was the Edge-O-Town, and it was a dump. On the bright side, if word got out a city cop was staying there at least half their long-term residents would flee. Port Massasauga had a couple of bed and breakfasts, but I couldn't remember their names and didn't know if they were open year-round.

I asked Livvy for the phone book. Later, at a more reasonable hour—when the half of Port Massasauga's population not outside watching my house burn was awake—I'd call the bed and breakfasts and find us a place to stay.

Jim joined us as the sun came up. "I called my mother," he said. "She's on her way to get you and Abby."

So much for the bed and breakfasts.

Evelyn's house was built for a large family. It was too big even when Jim was growing up and it held only the two of them. We'd tried to get her to sell it and move to a smaller place—well, Jim had. I suspected she held on to it in the hope he would leave me and come home to her, with Abby in tow. She had enough room to open a bed and breakfast of her own, but strangers in her house would drive her around the bend. Further around the bend. There was plenty of room for Abby and Jim, but I didn't think a house large enough to hold both Evelyn and me existed.

"Is she going to take us to a motel? The Sleep Inn by the freeway is supposed to be cheap but nice." Fat chance, but I had to ask.

"Don't be ridiculous," Jim said.

Pete and Livvy disappeared. They might have wanted to give us family time, or maybe Jim scared them away. He looked rough and sounded worse.

"I need to go to school," Abby said.

"I think you can miss a day." He used the Mad Dad voice and didn't look at Abby when he spoke.

I knew he was worn out, but his snarl at Abby bothered me more than his snapping at me. She hadn't done anything.

"She doesn't want to mess up her perfect attendance," I said.

"I need to go to school."

"You don't have any clothes. You can miss one day." His phone rang.

For the first time it registered that, while Abby and I were in our pajamas, he was dressed. I thought in the same clothes he'd worn the night before, but my memory was hazy.

He pulled the phone out of his pocket and answered it.

"Mom wants to know if she should bring anything."

"How do you have your phone?"

"I grabbed it before I left."

"Did you grab mine?"

"I was busy grabbing you."

"Oh." I felt about two inches tall. "Can she bring Abby some clothes?"

"I need to go to school," Abby said.

Jim looked at us both like we were from another galaxy and went out the back door, still talking to his mother.

Maybe he could stay with his mother and Abby and I could go to a motel. The Edge-O-Town was looking pretty good.

EVELYN BUSTLED IN brimming with helpful concern. Abby fended off her hug, and she didn't push it. I gave her credit for backing off.

"Did you bring me clothes? I need to go to school," Abby said.

"We'll worry about that later," Evelyn said.

"I need to go to school," Abby said.

The Fast Voice. Missing school could be the thing that broke her.

"I'll get you there," I said. "You might be late, but you'll get there."

"Not too late." Not as fast, but still near the red zone.

Evelyn thanked Livvy for taking such good care of us, as if we were a couple of toddlers retrieved from an elderly aunt. I resisted sticking my thumb in my mouth.

"It's what friends do." Livvy politely deflected Evelyn's gushing. Pete was nowhere to be seen. I got the impression neither of them was too fond of my mother-in-law.

"Gather yourselves up so we can get going. Jim's joining us for breakfast." Evelyn was in charge.

Abby picked up Sami's rope leash. Livvy's quilt fell from her shoulders. "Let's go."

Evelyn looked taken aback. She might like Sami, but I didn't think she'd thought about actually having a dog in her house. She kept quiet, the second point she earned in the space of a few minutes.

Abby picked up the quilt and settled it around her shoulders.

"We should go now. I am late for school."

"Why don't you leave that dirty old quilt here?" Both points vanished, and Evelyn moved back to the deficit column. "We'll get you a clean blanket once we get to my house."

"No." Abby gripped the quilt. Sami ducked under it and stuck her nose out between the folds.

"Let her take it. She needs it," I said. "I'll wash it and bring it back as soon as I get a chance." The latter was directed at Livvy.

"No hurry," she said. "It's Abby's for as long as she needs it."

EVELYN DID LAY out a good breakfast. Pancakes, eggs, bacon, home fries—a heart attack on a plate breakfast, the best kind. I didn't think I would be able to eat, but when she set a heaping plate in front of me, I dug in. So did Jim. Sami didn't join us. She curled up in the corner and nursed her scratched nose, courtesy of Evelyn's cat. If we stayed with Evelyn long, I'd probably end up joining her.

Abby barely touched her food.

"I need to go to school," she said.

"Why don't you stay with me today? I could use the company," Evelyn said.

"I need to go to school. I am late."

"Do you think you can find her something to wear?" I figured Evelyn would jump at her big chance to truly dress Abby like herself.

Jim stayed out of the conversation.

"I suppose. Abby, you need to take a shower." Not as thrilled as I expected.

We all smelled like smoke. It was a wonder Evelyn let us into her pristine house.

"I took one last night. I am late for school."

"We had a long night," I said. "You need to be clean before you put on clean clothes."

She pointed at the clock on the stove. "It is 9:07. I am late for school."

"Abby! Take a shower or you don't go. No arguing." Mad Dad met Angry Cop. Abby cringed.

"Go on. Listen to your dad. Take a shower, get dressed, and we'll get you to school," I said.

"I need to go to school." She left the kitchen.

Evelyn followed. "I'll find her something to wear."

Once we were alone, I wanted to ask Jim about the fire. What happened? How did I end up in the ambulance?

I wanted to ask him about Jason the EMT.

He didn't give me the chance.

"What did you take last night?" Full strength Mad Dad, but directed at me.

"What are you talking about?"

"You were dead to the world. What did you take?"

"Nothing."

"Don't lie to me."

"I'm not. Why would you say that?"

"There has to be some reason you wouldn't wake up."

"I swear I didn't take anything." Even to my own ears, I sounded guilty. *If he remembers the Vicodin, he can't check the medicine cabinet for it.* I was guilty.

"What were you doing downstairs before we settled in?"

"What do you mean?"

"You were the last one downstairs."

"No. You were. You were checking the doors when I went up."

"You went back down after I came up. Why?"

"I did not." *He's interrogating me.*

"You did. What did you do?"

He thinks I started the fire.

"I don't know. I don't remember going downstairs." *I didn't, did I?*

"Think. I brought my sleeping bag into Abby's room. We had... words."

"You said you wouldn't leave me alone with her."

"And you went downstairs."

"No I didn't. I sat in the chair and fell asleep." A vague memory of getting up from Abby's chair stirred. Was it real or the power of suggestion?

"You went downstairs. What did you do?"

"I don't remember." He had his phone. "What about you?"

"What do you mean?"

"You're dressed. You have your phone, and I don't know what else."

"What's your point?"

"Were you expecting something? Did you *know* you'd need to leave?"

"You need to see the doctor."

"I already said I would."

Mr. Boy Scout Policeman always slept with his keys, phone, and wallet on the nightstand. There was no reason he shouldn't have had them all next to him on Abby's floor, but why was he dressed? Off duty, he kept his gun in a lockbox, on the top shelf of our bedroom closet. I was afraid to ask if he had that too. *Did he know the fire was coming?*

"We should go now." Abby wore an ugly sweater and green pants, both two sizes too big. Her hair was wet, but at least it was combed.

"She wouldn't let me dry her hair," Evelyn said.

"Gramma's clothes almost fit. I need to go to school."

I asked to borrow Evelyn's car.

"No," Jim said. Evelyn didn't get a chance to answer.

"It is 9:31. I am late. We need to go now," Abby said.

"I'll take her. There are clean towels in the bathroom for you both. Carole, I put out a robe for you, we'll do something about clothes when I get back. Jim, I don't know what you're going to wear." Evelyn stuffed Livvy's quilt into a black garbage bag.

"What are you doing?" Not a calm question—I overreacted.

"I'll drop this off at the laundromat. Maybe they can save it. At the very least, it'll smell better."

"I am late. We do not have time to go to the laundromat," Abby said.

"First you, then the quilt," Evelyn said.

She's enjoying this. "I need to talk to Ms. Colley. Explain what's going on," I said. Someone needed to explain it to me.

"I'll talk to her," Evelyn put on her coat and handed another to Abby. "Put this on. It's cold," she said.

"I'll get your car out of the garage," Jim said. Evelyn handed him her keys, and he left without a coat.

WHEN HE CAME back, his phone was in his hand. "I made a doctor appointment for you this morning."

"I told you I'd make one myself."

"Yeah, well. You're going today. Eleven thirty. I practically begged to get you in."

"Did you tell Kristi how pathetic I am?" Kristi was the dragon at the office desk.

"I talked to Dr. Yates."

To get through Kristi to the doctor must have taken a good story.

"I don't have my car," I said.

"Mom will take you. You're in no shape to drive," he said in the same voice—a combination of soothing and stern—he used on Abby on her bad days.

"Can't you take me?" I didn't stick my lower lip out, but my whine said more than my words.

"Roberts is coming to get me. I'm going back to the house. I have to meet the insurance adjuster, among other things."

"Don't you think I should be with you for that?"

"I'll handle it. You are going to the doctor."

"I don't have anything to wear."

"Mom will lend you something."

"Oh, goody."

"Stop. You can go in your pajamas for all I care, but you *will* see the doctor today."

I resigned myself to going to the doctor. With Evelyn. Wearing her clothes.

A car honked in the driveway. "I'm going back to the house," Jim said.

34.
[CAROLE]

EVELYN HAD GOOD TASTE IN BATHROBES—I'D GIVE HER THAT—but as comforting as the fluffy goodness was, all I wanted was Livvy's quilt. Maybe my longing for the quilt was misplaced emotion. Maybe it felt like home, the home I no longer had, because I wasn't as upset about losing the house and fifteen years of souvenirs of my life as I should have been. Instead, I was serene, calm. The world was bright and shiny.

Jim's childhood bedroom was a shrine to Evelyn's golden boy—baseball trophies lined the shelves, posters of bands and ballplayers on the walls, and twin beds. I wouldn't have been surprised to find superhero sheets, but when I peeked I found plain white linens. Crisp, clean, fresh smelling linens, as if she knew we were coming.

I sat on one of the beds and tried to force myself to feel *something*. Anything. The constant panic of the last weeks was gone. So were my home and a decade and a half of my life. If I didn't know better, I would have thought I was drugged. My mind acknowledged reality, but my emotions didn't. *Maybe it's better this way.*

I never heard Evelyn come in.

"Abby can sleep in here. It's her room when she visits. You and Jim can have your choice of the spare rooms. Or take both of them."

"I was just—thinking." I didn't know how long I'd sat. *A blank spot.* Maybe I did go back downstairs the night before and didn't remember. Even the thought of blackouts didn't disturb my weird serenity. I stopped worrying about my little bubble of denial. It wasn't a bad place to be.

"Abby said you wear a twelve, but I wasn't sure what to get you so I just got these." She handed me two Walmart bags.

Sweats. Green sweats. One set in light green, one in dark. I looked like death in any shade of green, but at least they were clean. She even got me underwear.

"Um, I didn't know what size, so I just—here." She handed me another bag.

Sports bra. It would work.

"Thank you," I said.

"I bought everyone new pajamas too. We'll just throw the smoky ones away."

"We should try to wash Abby's. They're her favorites."

"Jim called," Evelyn said. "If we are going to get to your appointment on time, don't you think you should—"

"I'll get dressed."

With Evelyn as my babysitter—jailer— I wasn't getting out of the doctor. I'd have to make the best of it.

"I didn't get shoes. If Abby's right about your size, I have some you can wear."

There wasn't any best of it. No, there was. Evelyn still irritated me. My sanity wasn't completely gone.

My blood pressure was up a little, but all things considered, even Dr. Yates didn't find that surprising. When she asked if I was getting enough sleep, I lied. *Enough* is a relative term.

I did tell her about my headaches, and that my mother and probably my grandmother suffered from migraines.

"My mother had migraines but never knew that's what they were," she said. "She used to hold her coffee cup against the side of her head. It wasn't until I was in med school that I realized what her *sick headaches* were."

"My grandmother called hers sick headaches. Good description."

"They're often hereditary. I got lucky and missed them."

"I thought I had."

"Have you noticed any common elements before your headaches? Particular foods? Perfumes or other strong fumes? Bright or flickering lights?"

"Not that I noticed, but I really wasn't paying attention."

"Stress? For some people, not enough sleep is a trigger."

"I told you, I'm sleeping fine. Different schedule maybe, but fine. As for stress, my house burnt down. I'm staying with my mother-in-law. I'm wearing ugly green sweats. And that's just the last twelve hours." I left out Jason the EMT. She'd probably heard about him by now. I didn't mention how oddly unstressed I was.

"That's acute stress. How about chronic—ongoing—stress?"

"Nothing out of the ordinary." Another lie.

"Do you have a headache now?"

"No." I didn't tell her I felt better than I had in weeks.

"You appear to be handling the current situation well. Has it all sunk in yet?"

"I'm coping." I didn't need Dr. Yates to tell me the crash was going to be a bitch.

"How about blackouts, loss of memory?"

"Not that I recall."

She didn't laugh. "I need you to stand against the wall. Good. Now touch your nose with the index finger of your left hand."

"I feel ridiculous," I said but did it.

"Just a couple of simple neurological tests. It's best to start with simple. Now, do the same thing with your right finger."

Exactly why I liked Dr. Yates. No crazy tests unless they were absolutely necessary. I touched my nose.

"You're in pretty good shape. Especially considering the night you had. I think we should do a sleep study, but we'll wait on that. In your current circumstances, I don't think the results would be accurate."

"Hardly," I said.

"With your family history, the headaches are probably migraines, but we need to do some tests, make sure. Especially since you never had them until after your accident."

I never mentioned rolling the Jeep. She and Jim must have had quite the talk.

"What kind of tests?"

"Blood work. An MRI."

"Do we have to do needles? I hate needles."

At that, she laughed. "Can't avoid it with the blood work. I'll order the MRI without contrast and spare you that needle. You'll just have to stay still and let them take a few pictures of your brain. I know your life is crazy right now..."

You have no idea.

"...but I want this done as soon as possible."

"Why the rush?"

"From what I understand, you've been through a lot in a short time. It's unusual, but not unheard of, for hereditary migraines to make their first appearance at your age. You probably should have been checked out after your accident. Since you weren't, we'll do it now. Make sure the headaches are migraines and not something else."

"How about next week?"

"I'm sure you've eaten today?"

"Yeah."

"You need to fast, so the blood work will have to wait until tomorrow. I'll have Kristi see if she can get you in for the MRI this afternoon. She can get you in faster than if you call."

Dr. Yates was serious. I didn't see any way to get out of it. Especially with Evelyn as my babysitter.

KRISTI MANAGED TO get me in for the MRI, at a private radiology office, right away. "The hospital didn't have room for you. They're nicer at Basset & Thompkins anyway." She lowered her voice for the last part.

"Go directly to the office and they'll fit you in as soon as possible. They're in the strip mall right across from the hospital." She handed me papers. "I got it preauthorized with your insurance company. Since you don't have your card or anything, I thought that would make it easier for you."

I cursed her efficiency. I'd hoped to use the fact that my insurance card—and everything else in my purse—was ashes as an excuse to delay Dr. Yates's tests.

"I'm not sure we have time for this today." I knew I didn't want to deal with it.

"I didn't have any plans for this afternoon," Evelyn said.

With Evil-lyn the Prison Guard listening to every word, there was no escape.

Good thing Evelyn didn't have plans. *As soon as possible* didn't mean the same thing as *soon*. We sat and flipped through magazines for hours.

"Abby would look nice in this." Evelyn showed me a picture of a young model in an old lady pantsuit.

"You'd look even better in it." I didn't think she caught the sarcasm.

"Not my color. Could be yours." Maybe she did.

A technician entered the waiting area and called another patient back.

"If we don't get a chance to eat soon, I'll be able to get that blood work done now." My head hurt—just a little, around the edges. *From skipping lunch. Not a migraine.*

"Maybe when I pick Abby up from school, I'll take her shopping. You can come along too, if you're up to it," Evelyn said.

"We'll see." Abby needed clothes, we all did, but I wasn't sure about letting her go alone with Evelyn. If I went shopping with Evelyn, my headache would turn into one of *those* headaches. Dr. Yates said stress could be a trigger.

We both went back to our magazines.

The technician called another patient. Again. Sooner or later, my *as soon as possible* had to come. My headache grew.

The waiting area didn't have a clock. I figured it was a psychological ploy. They didn't want us to know how long we sat there.

"What time is it?"

Evelyn looked at her watch.

"Oh! I need to go get Abby. Will you be okay here alone?"

"How much trouble can I get into?" It wasn't like I could run away. She had the car keys. And the car.

As soon as she left, the technician called my name.

"Are you wearing any metal? Earrings? Other jewelry?" The tech handed me a hospital gown. There were worse things than green sweats.

"No."

"Put this on. You can leave your clothes in the dressing room." She unlocked a door and pointed me in.

I closed the door of the tiny room, and the walls closed in. The floor shifted, tilted, and tipped me into the red. I couldn't breathe. The red turned black, and I was lost.

35.
[ABBY]

At 1:45 we take out our geography books, but we do not open them. Ms. Colley is talking. She puts a map of Europe on the wall.

"Spain is the fifth largest country in Europe," Ms. Colley says.

Spain is green on Ms. Colley's map.

"Spain is on the Iberian Peninsula." Ms. Colley changes pictures. The flag of Spain is red and yellow. I do not like red.

"Yellow looks like fire," I say.

Devon writes *Abby's house was yellow* on his list.

"Orange too," I say.

"Abby, hush," Ms. Colley says.

"No more house for you," Devon says.

Twyla pounds her fist on her desk.

"The Ceiling Man did it," I say.

Devon writes *The Ceiling Man did it* on his list.

"Class, pay attention." Ms. Colley is talking about Spain. We are not listening. Spain is in Europe.

"Abby is wearing her grandmother's clothes," Devon says.

"They are all I have. My clothes burnt up too."

Devon writes *Abby needs new clothes and a new house* on his list.

Twyla pounds both fists on her desk. I think she is sad. I think it is because my house is burnt down. Maybe she is afraid her house will burn down too.

"It is okay, Twyla. Your house is made of bricks," I say.

"I give up," Ms. Colley says. "Abby, do you want to tell us about what happened?"

It is 1:57. It is time for Geography. My house burning down is not Geography. I think Ms. Colley is being flexible.

"Sami and I were on the porch roof. It was not like the Fire Drill List," I say.

"I'll write you a new Fire Drill List," Devon says.

"Thank you. The old one is all burnt up."

Twyla pulls on my sleeve. I do not think she likes Gramma Evelyn's clothes.

"Twyla, back to your seat," Ms. Colley says.

"It is okay," I say. "When I get new clothes they will fit."

Devon makes good lists. He should make the new Fire Drill List better than the old one.

Twyla does not go back to her seat.

"Write *This is just a drill. There is no fire.*"

When Devon writes it on his list, it is final.

"Do not mess with the list," Devon says.

Twyla pulls my sleeve again. She gives me her red hat and scarf. Her birthday hat and scarf.

The Ceiling Man comes to Twyla's birthday party, but I do not let him in. Mrs. Lamb wants to let him in, but I do not let her. Mrs. Lamb is dead.

"Twyla, that's very nice of you," Ms. Colley says. "Abby, I think Twyla is concerned because you lost all of your clothes."

Devon writes *Everything is lost* on his list.

Mrs. Lamb knits hats and scarves. I hate red. Mrs. Lamb cannot make me a purple hat and scarf. She is dead.

"Abby, you should say *Thank You*," Ms. Colley says.

"I will make a new list," Devon says. "One. Spain is big. Two. No more fires. Three. Always say *Thank You*."

Mrs. Livvy makes quilts. I hope Mrs. Livvy's quilt is not ruined. Maybe she will make a new one. It is her comfort quilt. Mrs. Livvy says, "Everybody needs a little comfort sometimes."

Comfort is not red.

"Abby, go back to your seat," Ms. Colley says.

Twyla's hat and scarf are red. Mrs. Lamb is dead. I think Jason the EMT is dead too. I think he is red. Dead rhymes with red. I hate red.

I drop Twyla's hat and scarf in the wastebasket.

"Abby, what are you doing?" Ms. Colley says.

A big jar of blue paint sits on the counter. Art class is in the morning and I am late. Ms. Colley says, "Oh, Abby, you missed art! We're just about to clean up. But I'm glad you made it to school." She sets the paint on the counter and talks to Gramma Evelyn. She forgets to put the paint away.

Art class is my favorite. I should not be late. My house is gone.

Tempera paint is for art class. Blue is for the sky. Blue is better than red. Sky is better than dead. Blue does not rhyme with red. I open the jar and pour the blue paint in the wastebasket.

"Four. Abby is in big trouble," Devon says.

The blue tempera paint covers Twyla's hat and scarf. I cannot see the red anymore.

"Abby! Stop!" Ms. Colley says.

Twyla is mad. I know she is mad because she screams. She does not talk, but sometimes she screams. Sometimes she screams scared. Sometimes she screams mad. She screams her mad scream.

"No more fucking red," I say.

I think Twyla should scream scared.

"Abby!" Ms. Colley does not sound like she is being flexible.

"I will take a time out," I say.

THERE IS A red pillow in the Quiet Corner. I throw it and it hits Ms. Short. I do not care when she yells.

"Be flexible," I say.

Devon laughs. I do not know why there is so much red.

"Abby said *fucking red*," Devon says. "Abby is in big fucking trouble. I will write it on my fucking list."

"Everybody hush," Ms. Colley says. "Sit at your desks and put your heads down. We will all take a quiet moment."

Devon laughs. Twyla screams. I think they are ignoring Ms. Colley.

I ignore everybody. They hurt my ears.

Ms. Colley cannot call my mom. My mom's phone is all burnt up.

It is 2:09. I will stay in time out for twenty-one minutes. 2:30 means go home.

The bus driver says, "If you are not in your seat at 2:40, I'm leaving without you."

I am not in my seat at 2:40 any more. I do not ride the bus any more.

My mom does not have her car. My mom cannot pick me up.

The Ceiling Man laughs. I do not want him near my mom. I think Gramma Evelyn will pick me up.

Daddy is the Woodsman. My mom does not burn up.

I do not want to hear the Ceiling Man. I do not want him near my mom.

The Ceiling Man laughs. I cannot ignore him. I look for the Ceiling Man. I do not want him near my mom.

"She's baaaaaack," says the Ceiling Man's friend. He is in his box but I hear him anyway.

I hear everybody. They are all in my ears and in my head. They hurt my ears. I think they will hurt my head too.

The Ceiling Man ignores his friend. I ignore him too. He should stay in his box and shut up.

I cannot ignore the Ceiling Man.

"Stay away from my mom."

"Your wall is crumbling, Little Piggy."

My wall has a hole where the Ceiling Man tried to push it down. It is a small hole.

"Leave my mom alone." I can fix the wall. It is a small hole and I will not let it grow.

"It won't work," the Ceiling Man says. "I found her. She's mine, Little Piggy. Then, you. Maybe I'll visit little Miss Twyla too."

Twyla screams. She is far away and I cannot tell if she is scared or mad. I think she should be scared.

"Leave my mom alone."

The hole is small. I can fix it.

I think maybe Twyla needs a wall too. I do not know if I can make two walls. One wall is very hard.

"A red wall," the Ceiling Man says.

Devon laughs.

My head is full of noise and red. I must fix my mom's wall. No more red.

"Leave my mom alone. Leave my mom alone."

"ABBY, ABBY, ABBY." Gramma Evelyn is here. She whispers.

Gramma Evelyn never whispers. I am wrong. Never is zero. Gramma whispers now and that is one time not zero, but she does not say *breathe*.

"The wall is almost fixed," I say. "Almost is not good enough."

"I'll huff and I'll puff, Little Piggy. I'll get Grandma too."

"Too many stories," I say.

"Time to go," Gramma says.

"I need to fix the wall."

"We need to go get your mom," Gramma says.

"Okay." I say. "I will fix the wall and my mom will be safe."

"What are you talking about?" Gramma says. I do not know if she is scared or tired or mad. Her voice is slippery.

"Idunno."

Everyone is gone except Ms. Colley. The room is quiet, but my head is not quiet. The Ceiling Man laughs.

"Leave my mom alone."

"...appointment with the psychologist," Ms. Colley says.

I do not hear what Gramma says. She is whispering.

"No more never," I say.

Gramma has my coat. It is not my coat. I do not have a coat. Gramma Evelyn has her coat that I am borrowing. My coat is burnt up.

"We need to go get my mom," I say and put on Gramma Evelyn's coat.

The Ceiling Man laughs.

"And Mrs. Livvy's quilt." Mrs. Livvy says it is a comfort quilt. I think I need a comfort quilt. I think my mom does too.

"We will," Gramma says.

I think her slippery voice means she needs a comfort quilt too.

"Little Piggy, Little Piggy, I'm going to get in," the Ceiling Man says.

"Leave my mom alone."

"Oh, honey," Gramma says, but she does not say oh-honey-what and I do not ask.

I must fix the wall.

36.
[CAROLE]

Pounding. Not my head. The door.

"Ma'am? Are you okay in there?"

"What?"

"Are you okay? You've been in there a while. You need to put on the gown so we can get this taken care of."

I wore the thin gown, but I couldn't remember putting it on. Another blackout. Another hole in my memory. *You went downstairs.* Had I? Why would Jim say that if it wasn't true? My hands shook. For the first time since the fire, I *felt* something. Fear. What had I done?

"Ma'am?"

I couldn't find the words to answer her. *Breathe. Breathe.* When I opened the door, the tech's expression shifted from annoyed to perky.

"No need to worry," she said. "All you have to do is lie still. In here." She led me into the MRI room.

One foot in front of the other, with each step I concentrated on building a façade, locking my fear inside. The tech dealt with medical fears all the time. She didn't know that I hurt my daughter. That maybe I'd come close to killing my family and myself.

"Up on the table, please. Lie on your back. Arms at your sides."

I can do this. I stretched out and willed both my trembling body and my racing mind to still.

My attempt at composure failed when the tech approached me with what looked like a giant hypodermic. The room blurred and my head throbbed, but the red stayed away.

I wrapped both of my arms around my chest. "Dr. Yates said no dye. No needles."

"I'll check again, but I don't think that's what the orders say."

"Do that."

I could get dressed and leave.

The tech returned. "Orders say contrast. If you want, you can talk to your doctor and try another time."

She didn't say *with an appointment*, but the message was there.

"Let's just get it over with," I said. The pressure in my head increased. I wondered if it would show on the MRI, if it was physical or mental. Either way, the pain was real.

It probably wasn't intentional that it took her six tries to hit a vein. Maybe it was. I couldn't look at her or the needle. I closed my eyes and fought the headache and the red.

"Stay still."

Breathe. Breathe.

"Ma'am? Carole? We're finished. You can get up now."

I must have dozed off. Or passed out. Or something. Another blank spot, but my headache along with everything else—panic, worry, fear—was gone. I'd returned to numb. The tech could have come at me with a six-foot needle, and I wouldn't have cared.

Instead she said, "All done. You can go get dressed."

"What's it look like in there?"

"All I can confirm is that, yes, you do have a brain." A rote response. She probably made the same joke every day. "Your doctor will call you as soon as she looks them over."

I got dressed without another panic attack or blackout or whatever it was.

In the waiting room, Evelyn flipped through another magazine. Abby sat beside her and rocked. She held her hands at chin level and fluttered her fingers. Her lips moved as if she was deep in conversation, but she was silent.

"I'm all done," I said.

"I don't think we're going shopping today," Evelyn said.

The magazine she held vibrated. Her voice shook as much as her hands.

189

"Hi Mom." Abby returned from wherever she'd been.

"Shopping can wait until tomorrow," I said. Somebody flipped my off switch, and exhaustion settled over me like one of Abby's blankets. "Let's just go home. To your house. Wherever."

In the parking lot, I saw Blevins. Or didn't. A glimpse, and then he was gone. His presence, real or imagined, affected me no more than the cars in the parking lot.

"It's okay, Mom. I fixed the hole." Abby said.

"I like grapes."

"And bananas," she said.

"I think you both need a doctor," Evelyn said.

"We should go to the laundromat," Abby said. "We need to get Livvy's quilt."

I didn't care where we went. I was just along for the ride.

I FELL ASLEEP on the couch and woke up covered by Livvy's quilt, clean and smelling of lavender. Abby and Evelyn sat on the love-seat, watching television.

"Gramma says we will order pizza for dinner," Abby said.

"Sounds good." Still swaddled in my weird cocoon, I didn't have any appetite. I would have liked to stay where I was, wrapped in the quilt, but when Jim came home, he motioned me into the kitchen.

I draped the quilt over Abby. She stood and wrapped herself in it.

"I like Livvy's quilt," she said.

I did too.

Jim filled me in on the situation at the house. It was a loss—big surprise. The investigators hadn't yet found the cause and were still looking.

"Blevins was there watching," I said.

"No one else saw him."

"You don't believe me."

"I told George. They're looking into it."

At least that was something. I didn't tell him about seeing Blevins again.

"What did Dr. Yates say?" I knew he'd get around to asking sooner or later.

"She said I was holding up well."

"And?"

"I might have migraines. Like my mom."

"Did you tell her about the blackouts?"

"I assumed you did that." Not an accusation, simply a statement.

"You had some tests?" He didn't admit to anything.

"Blood work tomorrow. An MRI this afternoon. She just wants to check on things before she gives me migraine drugs."

"How'd the MRI go?"

"The doctor hasn't seen it. Or hasn't called me about it. The technician confirmed I have a brain, but couldn't confirm it's functional."

"Did you talk to Abby's teacher?" He ignored my attempt to lighten the mood. His mood. Mine was still anesthetized.

"Your mom talked to her this morning. I haven't had a chance yet."

"I heard there was some trouble this afternoon. I told you she should have stayed home."

"This is the first I've heard of it. What happened? And who told you?"

"Mom called. Ms. Colley wants Abby to see the psychologist."

"She didn't say anything to me." The twinge of annoyance I felt at my mother-in-law was more habit than my usual irritation. If anything, my emotional stupor was getting worse.

"Frankly, I think you both should—"

"Jim! Something's wrong with Abby!"

He jumped and ran at his mother's shout. I followed, sure Evelyn was over-reacting to some typical Abby quirk—until Abby screamed.

37.
[THE CEILING MAN]

"You know, it's not leaving the spare key in the garage that's stupid. Okay, it kind of is. But really, with all the places to hide it out there, why in the world did you make it so easy to find?"

The woman strapped to the chair didn't answer him. He supposed the duct tape over her mouth made it hard to speak. The broken arm probably distracted her too.

"It's your own fault. You could have let me in. I really didn't expect you to be so resistant to my charms. I have a way with grandmotherly types."

"Maybe you used to," Blevins said.

«*Shut up. Remember our deal. Chuckles awaits.*» It was more threat than deal, but it made Blevins agree to stay quiet while he worked.

He opened the red toolbox he'd found in the basement, removed screwdrivers and pliers, lined them up on the coffee table next to the power tools from the garage, stood up, and admired his work.

"I heard you had all the cool tools. You really do." He kicked the unconscious man on the floor. "I might have hit you a little harder than I intended."

The woman whimpered like an injured animal.

"Don't worry. He's still alive. I like my food fresh. It's a health thing, fresh and raw or nothing. However, I refuse to go vegan."

He needed to do something with the man before he woke up, if he woke up. The quilt frame in the corner looked interesting.

He pulled it to the center of the living room.

"Do you think this is strong enough to hold him?"

She didn't even squeak.

"You know, it's rude not to answer a direct question. You could at least nod or something. Blink. Once for yes. Twice for no."

She shut her eyes.

"You're very bad at following directions, aren't you? We'll work on that."

He shook the wood frame, then put both hands on the half-finished quilt stretched across it and pushed.

"Nice quilt, but it could use a little more red."

She didn't offer an opinion.

"I should apologize. I don't usually play with my food. It's unseemly. But you two, well, you get to be special. Since you're such good neighbors and all."

Her eyes opened, and she tracked his movements. He picked up the man and laid him on the stretched quilt. Not a perfect fit, but it would do.

"Seems sturdy enough. Is it an antique? The modern stuff is all made of matchsticks."

"Such cool tools." He picked up the nail gun.

"Have you ever read anything by Temple Grandin?"

Her eyelids fluttered. More than two blinks.

"I'll take that as a no. I sent my friend Chuckles to the library. I thought Miss Grandin might help me with a little problem I'm having. Now, where can I plug this in?"

He located an outlet.

"She might have, but Chuckles brought me the wrong book. Something about Mayan architecture. He had to steal it—no library card—so he didn't ask for help. And he's not very bright."

He plugged the gun into the wall socket and examined it.

"Looks easy enough." He pressed the tip against the cherry wood mantel above the fireplace. The gun made a satisfying *ker-chunk* as it drove in the nail.

The woman groaned.

"Don't worry. This isn't for you. At least, not yet."

He laid the nail gun on the man's chest.

"Back to Miss Grandin. Or is it Ms.? Wait, I think it's Doctor. Doesn't matter. I saw her on television. Aside from first hand knowledge of my little problem, she seemed to be some sort of expert in slaughtering animals for food. I know a bit about that myself, but I have no interest in keeping you calm."

Sweat soaked the woman's thin nightshirt.

"But, maybe I'll make you a tad more comfortable. Now, where's your thermostat?"

He didn't think she meant to answer. Her head was still, but her eyes flicked to the left.

He found the thermostat in the next room and set the temperature to twenty-six. The furnace clicked off.

"You'll cool off now. Eventually."

Where was the girl? She should have shown up already.

"Did you know that your hamburger probably had a bolt shot into its forehead? Well, not *into*, but close enough. Sometimes they shock the beasts, but I don't mess with electricity. It scares me. I couldn't find a captive bolt gun. Pete doesn't have *all* the cool tools. The nail gun will have to do."

He was enjoying himself, even more than he expected.

"It's been a long time since I had a real conversation. You really aren't holding up your end."

She didn't reply.

The girl. She didn't speak, but he sensed her. She watched. *Showtime.*

« *Took you long enough, Little Piggy. I was worried you'd miss all the fun.* »

"Hmmmm. Let's see." He turned the woman and her chair. "Maybe a little more to the center." He moved her over a foot. "And just a little bit closer."

Her fear invigorated him.

"You need a front row seat for this."

He spread the man's arms and lined up his hands on either side of the quilt rack. He picked up the nail gun and shot nails through his palms into the rails, first one hand then the other. The rack wobbled, but the man didn't flinch.

"I really *didn't* mean to hit you so hard." He felt the man's neck and found a weak pulse. "I may have to hurry things along. Shame. I was looking forward to a leisurely meal. Fine dining shouldn't be rushed."

Tears ran down the woman's face. She closed her eyes again.

«*Watch me.*»

Her eyelids shot up. She was weakening.

So was the girl.

"I wonder what kind of tools *you* have?" Her sewing box, bigger than the toolbox, stood on four feet next to him. At first, he'd thought it was a table. He opened it.

Inside the lid was a row of shiny scissors and craft knives. A box of long t-pins held possibilities.

"You seem like the type to keep your blades sharp. Hmm. I think I'll start with this one."

He made a long incision on the man's chest and flayed him.

"I knew these would come in handy. Hope they're sharp." He opened the box of pins. They slid smoothly through the man's skin as he pinned it to the quilt.

"I think we'll call this pattern *Devoted Husband*." He sniffed. "Oh, really. Did you have to? I'm about to eat here."

The woman's bowels had released.

"Did you ever eat lobster? I'll bet you're one of those dainty ones who crack the shell and carefully pick out the meat, leaving all the best parts behind."

He picked up the top piece of folded fabric from the basket next to the sewing box. All pale pinks, blues, and greens, the pieced quilt top was a miniature version of the blanket she gave the girl.

"Were you making this for a baby? How sweet." He tied the unfinished quilt around his neck like a bib.

"If I ate dead things, I'd be one of the messy ones. I would rip that lobster apart."

The quilt, soaked with blood, sagged in the center of the rack. He needed to get busy before the whole thing collapsed.

"*Bon appétit*. That was for me, not for you."

The woman's terror was good, but the girl's pain was better. It filled him, provided seasoning, spice, that extra dollop of flavor he craved.

He dove in.

"Delicious," he said. He moved around the quilt rack and knelt in front of the wife.

"Now, you, young lady, are a problem."

She stared at his face, not looking into his eyes but avoiding the quilt frame and what it held. Bits of her husband clung to her hair and blood dotted her face.

"Sorry. I didn't mean to be so sloppy, but sometimes I get carried away when I eat."

He prodded. Explored. There wasn't much left inside her. Her terror swallowed any other thoughts or emotions.

«*Blink. Twice.*»

She did.

"There are a lot of things I could do to you, and some I even want to do."

«*Nod your head.*»

She complied.

"But I really don't have time for fun and games right now."

«*Do the hokey pokey.*»

Her arms and legs heaved against the restraints. He stopped her before the chair toppled over.

"What's important is, how can you best serve my needs?"

«*Don't breathe.*»

"I'm talking long term here, not immediate. Well, long term as far as you're concerned."

She was completely his. At least for the time being.

He wanted her as a witness. He wanted her to tell exactly what he'd done to her husband, but he didn't want her to identify Blevins. Despite his threats to Blevins, he didn't have the time to break in a new host. Not until he took care of the girl. Unless—

"Hey!" Blevins said.

«*Shut up or you'll be gone and I'll be walking around with lady parts.*»

"I need to clean up. Maybe find some new clothes. Hubby is about the correct size. Was about the correct size. He's lost some weight. Stay right here and wait for me, okay?"

Her face was purple.

"Oh, if you really must, go ahead. Breathe. See you soon."

THE EYES ARE *the windows to the souls.*

He didn't believe in souls, but eyes were windows to something. Whatever it was, wifey had it back.

He nudged. She twitched, but her face didn't change. Not fear. Her expression was pure hatred. Some of these creatures were so resilient.

"Got your groove back, huh? Too bad. You're no use to me now."

Tears and mucous mixed with her husband's blood and ran down her cheeks and over her duct tape gag. On her nightgown, a pink stain blossomed.

"Oh, don't be a baby. I'm not going to eat you."

He picked up the nail gun and stood behind her.

"This is your own fault, you know." He pressed the gun to the base of the woman's skull and pulled the trigger.

"Cool tools, indeed."

"Can I talk now?" The girl's screams almost drowned out Blevins's words. Almost, but not quite.

«*I really wish you wouldn't.*»

38.
[CAROLE]

ABBY STOOD IN THE MIDDLE OF THE LIVING ROOM. LIVVY'S quilt puddled around her feet. Her eyes showed only white. Her mouth stretched open wider than I thought possible, and her screams filled the room and thickened the air.

The scene went red. *Not now.* Abby's shrieks battered me and pierced my shell. All of the pain and fear I'd lost in the last twenty-four hours hit me like bricks.

My house is gone. My daughter's next. I couldn't breathe. The red darkened to black, and Abby's screams faded.

No. I fought the pressure, but it was too much. I had to give in, let it crush me.

No more dirt and pennies. Abby's voice. I lashed out and pushed against the blackness. Something snapped. The dark lifted, and the room came back. Sami barked, and the television blared.

Abby still screamed. It couldn't have been her I heard.

Evelyn babbled in the background. "She just jumped up and started shaking and—"

Jim spoke. I couldn't understand what he said, but I hoped he was telling his mother to shut up. If he did, she didn't listen. None of them did. The noise pummeled my ears, and a dull ache spread through my body.

Abby still screamed. Her lips turned blue.

"Everybody shut up! Abby! Breathe!" I couldn't stop myself. I grabbed her and shook her.

She didn't flinch, but her screams became a wail. Not the sound of terror or grief, a howl of torment. I didn't hear it. I felt it. I let go of her and fell to my knees.

Paralyzed by her agony, I watched her face go from deep red to purple and knew I'd lost her.

Jim ran around us and grabbed her from behind, his arms around her waist. *The Heimlich manuever. He thinks she's choking.*

Sami jumped and snapped at him. I wanted to tell him it wouldn't work. She wasn't choking. She was drowning and I was going down with her, but I couldn't force the words out.

A quick movement from Jim, and Abby's body jerked.

Her wails stopped, and my head cleared.

It worked.

Jim let go, and Abby dropped to the floor.

She sat cross-legged in front of me. Her eyes returned to normal, but remained lifeless. She stared straight at me, but I didn't think she saw me. Sami quit barking and lay down beside us. She stuck her nose in Abby's lap, but got no acknowledgment from Abby.

"Breathe, Abby. Breathe." I used my meltdown voice although this was beyond any meltdown I'd seen. She didn't move. The deep color drained and left her face pale, almost transparent.

Someone finally shut off the television. Behind me, Jim questioned his mother.

"What were you watching?"

"*Little House on the Prairie.* It wasn't even one of the sad ones." Evelyn's voice shook.

Abby sat ramrod straight, but she still looked limp. I picked up one of her hands. It was icy, and when I let go, it flopped back to her lap.

Sami whimpered and nuzzled her. Abby opened her mouth, and I leaned forward to hear her. She didn't speak. Her mouth opened and closed, not quite in silent conversation.

"Jim, call an ambulance." I'd watched my grandmother move her mouth the same way hours before she died.

"Are you sure there was nothing that could have scared her?" He hadn't heard me.

"No, it was the episode—"

"Jim! Call 911!"

In an instant, he was on the floor next to me.

"This isn't a meltdown. I don't know what it is. She needs help. Get an ambulance."

"Abby?" He spoke softly, but Abby turned to him.

"Daddy? Help Livvy." Her voice was hoarse.

All that screaming.

"Abby, tell me what you're talking about," Jim said.

"No more Pete. No cool tools. Livvy needs the Woodsman." She gulped air between her toneless words.

She's going to hyperventilate. Or scream again.

"Too much red. Help Livvy. Help Livvy. Helplivvy. Helplivvy. Helplivvyhelplivvyhelplivvyhelplivvy..." Her eyes rolled back.

As she chanted, her breathing steadied. I no longer worried she'd hyperventilate, but I didn't know how to help her.

"Jim. Evelyn. Somebody call an ambulance."

Jim got up.

"Abby, come back." I took both her hands in mine. Still limp and even colder than before. Dead. *No.* I rubbed her hands in mine. Their chill crept into mine.

"Jim?"

"Helplivvyhelplivvyhelplivvyhelplivvy..."

"Just do a drive through the neighborhood. Check on the neighbors—the ones across the street." Jim gave whomever he was talking to Pete and Livvy's address. "I know. I'll explain later, but with everything that's going on, just do it. Please." He paused. "Thanks."

"Abby? I called the station. A policeman is going to check on Pete and Livvy. They are safe." Jim tried to wrap Livvy's quilt around Abby's shoulders.

She pushed it off.

"Too late. Too red. Pete's gone. The Woodsman can't help."

"Abby? Look at me." I got no response. Instead she retreated to—not Abby-land. When she went there, I could still see *her.* Wherever she'd gone, the Abby in front of me was a blank. She sat and she breathed. Other than that, she was a mannequin. A bad, expressionless mannequin.

"Abby?" Jim didn't get a response either.

"Did you call the ambulance?"

"We'll take her to the hospital ourselves. It's faster."

"I'm going with you," Evelyn said.

I'd forgotten she was there.

Abby stood when we pulled her up. Jim and I shepherded her to the car, him on one side of her and me on the other. She didn't resist when we tucked her into the backseat and buckled her seatbelt.

Evelyn tried to tuck the quilt around her. Abby flinched, and her strangled gasp communicated more than words could have. Pain and fear hit me like a jolt of electricity.

Evelyn snatched the quilt away and threw it on the ground.

In the front window, Sami watched us back out of the driveway.

EVELYN SAT UP front with Jim. "We really weren't watching anything scary," she said.

"It's not your fault." I doubted Jim's words had any effect on his mother. They didn't reassure me.

In the back seat with me, Abby sat motionless and silent.

"Can we hurry it up?" I said.

"I'm going as fast as I can."

No. As fast as you're willing. I wanted to scream and jump out of the car, to run and drag my daughter along with me. Instead, I took Abby's hand. She didn't flinch or pull away. Slumped in the seat, she was vacant.

We stopped at a red light. We were the only car at the intersection. *Just go through it.* I bit my tongue. Screaming at him wouldn't help.

"What good is it to be married to a cop if you can't have lights and sirens when you need them?" Not a joke, a whispered plea, too quiet for Jim to hear.

We finally made it to the hospital and pulled up at the emergency entrance.

"You take her inside while I park," he said.

Evelyn and I got Abby out of the car and steered her inside. Puppet-Abby went where we guided her. No resistance.

The woman at the check-in was engrossed in her computer and didn't look up when we entered.

"My daughter needs a doctor. She had a...seizure." *Seizure* was the best word I could come up with.

"Just a second." Her name tag said *AMBER. Patient Liaison.*

"Now." Port Massasauga Medical Center had a terrible reputation, especially the emergency room.

Amber looked us over. Evelyn wasn't her usual immaculate self, but she looked respectable enough. Abby was propped up between us, limp and glassy-eyed, but dressed in her new pajamas. I looked like an escapee from a meth lab. None of which should have made any difference. It did to Amber.

"There's no need to shout."

I didn't think I was.

"Why don't you take her to the chairs and sit down while I get some information. Now, do you have your insurance card?" The latter was addressed to Evelyn.

"I'm her mother. I don't have my card. Please, we need to see a doctor now."

"The triage nurse will be out soon. How about some form of identification?"

"I don't *have* my insurance card or identification. My husband is parking the car. He has that stuff. I want to see a doctor." I hoped Jim had his card. Mr. Always Prepared made it out of a burning house with his wallet and phone. There was no reason he shouldn't have his wallet and card.

"If you don't have insurance, I have a few forms for you to fill out."

"We need to see a doctor. Now."

"Without insurance, I need to see some form of identification."

Couldn't she hear me? Or was she just not listening?

"I didn't forget it. I have insurance. I don't have the card with me. My husband will give you the information. My daughter needs a doctor. Now." *How the hell long does it take to park a car?*

"I'll have someone here soon to evaluate her. Is there anybody who can bring your card to you?"

"Listen up, Amber. I don't *have* it. My house burnt down last night.

Insurance card? Ashes. Drivers license? Ashes. My husband-the-Boy-Scout still has all that stuff. He will be here in a minute. Get someone out to see my daughter now."

"Problem here?" A large orderly and a security guard appeared next to me.

Amber looked up from her computer screen. "A fire? Are you—"

"Amber. Joe. Perkins." Jim nodded greetings. "What's the hold up here?"

"I was just doing my job," Amber said.

"I hope you have your wallet," I said to Jim.

There were benefits to being married to a cop. Amber knew him. Joe knew him. Perkins knew him. The staff all knew him. We were in a room with Abby in no time.

Jim had his wallet. He gave it to his mother and sent her off to appease Amber.

UNLIKE AMBER, THE nurse who joined us was sympathetic or at least acted like it.

"Be careful," I said when she picked up the blood pressure cuff. "She's autistic. She doesn't like to be touched."

"She doesn't seem to be minding."

"That's part of the problem."

I told her everything I'd seen. Jim didn't have much to add.

"What happened before she started screaming? Any physical changes?"

"I don't know. I wasn't there. They were watching TV. *Little House on the Prairie.*" Irrelevant, but all I knew.

Jim suggested she talk to Evelyn.

"I'll do that, and a doctor will be in soon."

When she left the room, Jim started to follow her.

"No. Stay with us," I said.

Abby lay on the gurney, stiff and unmoving. If not for the slight rise and fall of her chest, it would have been hard to tell she was alive.

"She looks so small," Jim said.

"She's still screaming," I said. "We just can't hear her."

THE NURSE CAME back, alone.

"Where's the doctor?" I said.

Before she could answer, an alarm went off. The noise startled me, but the smooth electronic tones weren't frightening. Jim's reaction was.

He tensed beside me, and he and the nurse exchanged looks. *Some secret hospital code.*

"I'll be right back," he said.

"No—"

"I promise. I'll be right back."

"I'll stay with you," the nurse said.

She'd introduced herself, but I couldn't remember her name. "What's going on?" *I don't want you. I want my husband.*

"No!" Abby screamed. Her arms shot out from her sides and her back arched. She flailed her arms and bent her knees.

"Abby!" *Convulsions. She's having convulsions.*

Her lips turned blue.

The nurse—Jenna, that was her name—leapt into action. She must have hit another alarm. I didn't hear it, but two more nurses and a man in a lab coat—*finallyadoctor*—burst into the room.

"Get her out of here," Lab Coat ordered.

Where are they taking her?

He meant me, not Abby. A nurse—not Jenna—took my arm and dragged me away from my daughter.

"No—what's happening?"

Jenna turned Abby on her side.

"What's wrong with her?"

"Shhhh. We need you to stay calm and wait outside. It's the best way you can help her." The nurse pulled me into the hall and shut the door.

"Nonononononononono..." The door between us muffled Abby's cries, but I heard and felt each one.

"Can I wait here?"

"No." Not-Jenna grabbed my arm and dragged me away from the door.

One step down the hall, she shoved me against the wall.

Two EMT's, accompanied by lab coats and nurses raced toward us.

A gurney. They pushed a gurney. *Red. Why are they using red blankets?*

They closed in on us, and the thing on the gurney laughed. As they passed us, it screamed.

"Hey Little Piggy! How ya feeling now?"

My knees buckled.

Livvy. It was Livvy's voice.

39.
[THE CEILING MAN]

"Cool," Blevins said.

Cool wasn't an understatement. It was wholly inaccurate.

Legs apart, he leaned forward and braced himself against the dumpster behind the hospital. He panted and gasped, not minding the stench of garbage that filled his nose, his mouth, his throat. Flames rippled through his body, counteracting the bitterness of the falling snow. He imagined the chill metal of the dumpster glowing red beneath his hands.

Not *Cool*.

Intoxicating.

Invigorating.

Arousing.

The pleasures of human flesh held no interest for him—not in the usual sense. His hungers lay elsewhere.

As he'd ridden the girl's pain, his own strength blossomed and grew. It rose and expanded, unconfined, until he thought he'd burst.

He didn't. He flew, unfettered, from mind to mind throughout the hospital. Anywhere he wanted to go. He brought shivers to those normally out of his reach. He *felt* their discomfort and relished it. And, when he found the quilt woman—he'd left less of her alive than he intended, nothing for him to control, and it didn't matter. He didn't quite reanimate the dead, but close enough. His thrust inside her brought sensation so intense he couldn't help but laugh. He said his piece and slipped out. He left her useless, and he was stronger than ever.

The mother's fear—just the memory caused a stir between his legs.

"Whoa. That hasn't happened in a looooong time," Blevins said.

« You have no idea. »

The girl wasn't just a watcher—she was a catalyst. An energy source. Everything he'd ever done or been paled in comparison to the power and exhilaration he found when he mounted her fear. And he'd done it all from outside the building and across the parking lot.

He was invincible.

He wouldn't kill her quickly. Not until he'd wrung everything he could out of her and absorbed it. Made her his. Made her him.

She was damaged. Broken. She no longer had the strength to interfere with his plans. Her mother would bring her to him, and it would be her own idea. Once he had the girl, what she had would be his. If she could do this to him—for him—over distance and through walls, what would it be like when she was his? When she stood before him in agony?

The volcano inside roared, and its molten heat flowed. He trembled. Blevins groaned.

He'd drain her. Everything she had would be his. Then, he'd take her, consume her, and leave nothing behind.

"Can we have some fun with her first? *My* kind of fun?"

« Don't be crass. »

"Be a shame to waste that big honkin' thing in our pants." Blevins's usual mocking snarl was little more than a rasp.

« Oh, my pet. This is going to be so much better. »

The girl was still inside the building. He had time to go back for another taste. An appetizer. Something to tide him over until the main course.

He swelled in anticipation, and Blevins moaned.

40.
[CAROLE]

"ARE YOU OKAY?" THE NURSE PROPPED ME UP.

I couldn't answer. The walls rippled. The room—hallway—*where was I*—vibrated.

"Carole?" Jim reached for me, and I shrank into the wall.

Daddy is the Woodsman. Breathe. The floor quit moving.

"Why is the hallway red?"

"We need to get her to a chair," the nurse said.

Jim grunted, and together they led me down the hall to the waiting area.

"I don't want to sit."

"I'll take care of her," Jim said.

Daddy is the Woodsman.

"I'll send someone out to check on her as soon as I can." The nurse disappeared.

I collapsed against my husband, and he held me until I stopped sobbing.

"Abby. What's happening with Abby?" I said.

"I don't know. No one's told me anything."

"They wouldn't let me stay with her. They dragged me out. And Livvy. Jim, what happened to Livvy?"

"I don't know."

"Tell me." I always knew when he was lying.

He let go of me and backed away. He stared at my feet, not my face, and in a monotone, he relayed the news. Pete was dead, and Livvy—she was in the trauma room. Other than that, he didn't know anything. His contacts had a limit.

He wasn't lying, but he held something back. Whatever it was, I didn't want to know, at least not yet.

"It was Blevins," I said.

"I already told them to look for him."

"You believe me?"

"Shit. I don't believe any of this, but…I don't know."

"How did Abby know?"

Neither of us had an answer.

"How long have we been out here?" I searched for a clock. The walls of the spartan waiting room were bare. Not that it would have done me any good to find one. I didn't know what time they threw me out of Abby's room. Two people sat in the plastic chairs. One was Evelyn.

I'd forgotten about her. Her usual perfect posture was gone. Huddled and forlorn, she appeared to have aged ten years. I felt sorry for her.

"Jim. Your mother."

He flinched. Guilt. *He forgot about her too.* There was no triumph in the thought.

Together, we went to her.

"We were only watching TV." For the first time since I'd met her, she both looked and sounded like an old woman.

"It's not your fault." I sat down next to her and took her hand.

"I'll go see if I can find out anything," Jim said and left us alone.

"Why aren't you with Abby?" Evelyn said. Not an accusation, a simple question.

"She…they are taking care of her. They said I need to wait out here."

"It's bad, isn't it?"

"I don't know." The lie was for both of us.

"It was only *Little House on the Prairie.*"

"It's okay. She loves that show," I said.

We ran out of small talk. *What's taking Jim so long?*

The waiting area might have aimed for cheerful, but it missed. A sickly shade of pale yellow covered the concrete brick walls. The orange of the hard chairs was cautionary rather than bright. In the corner, an old man in filthy clothing slept off a drunk. He mumbled and fidgeted in his sleep. Even passed out, he looked uncomfortable. I knew how he felt.

Evelyn slapped at the back of her neck and shivered. "How can this place have mosquitos at this time of year? We should have gone to Mercy County."

"This was closer." Evelyn had a point. People threatened to have *In case of emergency, take me anywhere but PMMC* tattooed on their bellies. I'd made that threat.

Livvy had made that threat.

The drunk in the corner grew louder. I thought I heard him mutter something about *Little Piggy* and *burn your house down*. It had to be my imagination.

Livvy. I couldn't think about her. Or Pete. What ever happened to them, it didn't have anything to do with Abby. It couldn't.

The large orderly—I never found out whether he was Joe or Perkins—and a young woman entered the room. Instead of bringing me news, they headed for the pop machine. The woman wore burgundy scrubs. Red enough to make my heart pound.

I couldn't look at her, but I listened.

"I don't care. I won't be here tomorrow," she said.

"You can't just walk out with no notice," Joe-or-Perkins said.

"When I leave tonight, I'm outa here. People dead. People missing. That couple tonight? They lived across the street from that house that burned down. Where Jason died. This town is fucked up." Her nasal voice rose and carried, full of anger or hysteria or both.

"Keep your voice down," Joe-or-Perkins said.

She had a point. Focused on Abby, I never gave a thought to anything else, other than how it related to me and mine. The list of deaths and weird events was long, longer than Ms. Burgundy Scrubs knew, and I was afraid it *all* related to me and mine.

"What are they gonna do? Fire me? I'll stay 'til the end of my shift. But that's it. When I get in my car, I'm outa here. Straight to my mom's in Cleveland. Not even going home."

"Evelyn. We need to leave," I said.

"What about Abby?"

"No. I mean leave Port Massasauga. When we get out of here, we need to take Abby and go to my parents." They were in Cincinnati. Farther away from Port Massasauga than Cleveland. We should have gone there weeks ago. "You can come too."

"What does Jim say?"

"I haven't told him yet. No matter what he says, Abby and I are leaving." Running away wasn't his style, but he had to see it was the best thing. The only thing. We didn't even need to go back to Evelyn's. We could leave the hospital and drive.

"What about Abby?"

"She'll be okay." *Please. Please let her be okay.* "And there are doctors in Cincinnati too."

"You always say she doesn't like change." Evelyn's arguments were halfhearted. Habit, not conviction. I didn't like the sad old woman persona. I didn't want her to sound weak. I wanted her to be *Evelyn*. Disapproving, scornful, Evil-lyn. I wanted her to blame me, not herself. I missed my nemesis. I wanted things to be normal.

"She'll be okay. She loves her grandparents. All of them." I squeezed Evelyn's hand. "Come with us."

"We'll see."

"Little Pig, Little Pig! Let me come in!" The drunk was awake and yelling.

Joe-or-Perkins and Burgundy Scrubs ran to him. He vomited on the orderly.

I wanted to find Jim, but couldn't make my legs work to get out of the chair. My stomach churned, and not just from the smell of puke.

Little Pig. He heard Livvy's scream. Somehow, it penetrated his alcohol-soaked fog and made its way back out. That was all. Nothing else.

"I am so fucking out of here," Burgundy Scrubs said.

Me too, lady. Me too.

"Are you okay?" Jim stood in front of me.

"We need to get Abby and go."

"The doctor's coming out to talk to us."

"We need to leave Port Massasauga."

"What are you talking about?"

"It's not safe here."

"We'll talk about this later." I couldn't tell if he thought I was crazy or was considering leaving.

I recognized the doctor—the man who threw me out of Abby's room. He introduced himself. Dr. Horvath. I stood and leaned against Jim. Whatever he had to say, I wasn't going to listen to it sitting down.

"We sedated her. The seizures have stopped, but she's still agitated. She's asking for you. We want to do an EEG, but she won't let us. She keeps pulling the electrodes off her head. Even after we restrained her, she wouldn't stay still."

"*Restrained her?* Did anyone tell you she's autistic?" The image of Abby, restrained and wired to a machine infuriated me.

"That may explain some of her behavior. You're sure this is the first time she's had seizures? Are you her main caretaker?"

I hoped he was a good doctor, because otherwise he was a pompous prick in a lab coat.

"I'm her mother. And yes, this is a first. Can I see her now?"

"I'd like to get a CT scan, but don't know if she'll cooperate."

"Is she still restrained? I want to see her." I hated the smug bastard.

"Wait here and I'll get an aide to take you back."

"I'll just follow you." I was fed up with waiting. Waiting for whomever was supposed to check on me and never showed. Waiting for the doctor. Waiting for anybody to tell me *anything.* I wasn't going to wait to see my daughter.

Dr. Officious didn't want me tailing him. "Britanny!"

Burgundy Scrubs appeared. She hadn't left town yet.

I followed her to Abby. Jim followed me. Evelyn didn't. The walls of the hallway stayed where they belonged.

41.
[CAROLE]

"Hi, Mom. We need to go home now." Abby tried to get out of bed, but her wrist and ankles were tethered to the bed rails.

"Let her loose."

"We didn't want her to injure herself." Not Jenna, a different nurse.

"Where's Jenna?"

"She's with another patient. Dr. Horvath wants to—"

"Untie her or I'll do it myself."

"We need to go home now," Abby said.

The nurse didn't move. I freed Abby's feet. It wasn't hard. I was angry enough to rip the restraints apart if I needed to, but they were padded leather fastened with buckles. Easily undone.

She sat up before I had her last wrist free.

"We need to leave now," she said. She sounded fine. Looked fine. Alert, obsessive, and repetitive. Her usual self.

"Dr. Horvath said you sedated her. What did you give her?" The Abby we brought in acted more drugged than the one in front of me.

"The doctor needs to give you that information," the nurse said.

"The doctor's an ass."

"Carole, take it easy," Jim said, not very convincingly.

"We need to leave now," Abby said.

"We are." I undid the last cuff, and she started to climb out of the bed.

Jim put his hands on her shoulders and gently sat her back down.

"Too late. The Woodsman cannot help," she said.

"The doctor wants to do some tests, to make sure you are okay," he said.

"Livvy's gone. We cannot stay here." She tried to get up, but Jim held her down.

Livvy's gone. "We need to go. We can come back for the tests to-morrow." By tomorrow, we'd be in Cincinnati, with or without Jim.

"Where are her shoes and pajamas?" I was ready take her out in the hospital gown if I had to, but the nurse handed me a plastic bag with Abby's clothes.

"I am *not* a Little Piggy," Abby said.

"That's it." I pushed Jim aside, and Abby and I walked out of the exam room.

THERE WAS PAPERWORK. There was always paperwork. Jim took care of most of it while I took Abby into the bathroom to change into her own clothes.

"Button your pajama top," I said.

"No more cool tools."

"Shoes." I handed her a sneaker.

"I am not a Little Piggy."

"No, you are not."

"I am a banana."

"You are, and I love bananas."

"The Ceiling Man says bananas bruise easy."

I would have left without signing anything, but Jim had the car keys. I signed the paper he stuck in front of me without reading it.

"Let's go."

While we were inside, it had begun to snow. Not a lot, but big, lazy flakes floated down and stuck to the car and parking lot. Late snowstorms were the worst. One spring, at the end of April, two feet of snow fell overnight. It was seventy degrees the next day, and Abby and I wore T-shirts while we built snowmen. We built a dozen. We had plenty of time since we couldn't get out of the driveway. The snow—and the snowmen—were gone by sundown. Abby and I would be gone before sunrise.

Jim told us to wait. He'd get the car and pick us up at the door, but Abby wasn't having any of it.

"We need to go home now," she said and headed for the parking lot.

Jim grabbed her arm. She pulled away.

"No. We need to go home now."

"We will. The car is this way," he said.

Abby let her dad lead her to the car.

Evelyn and I followed. Abby slipped once in the snow, but her father caught her before she went down.

"We need to get out of here before this gets worse," I said.

"What did Jim say about leaving?"

"Not much." It didn't matter what he said, and I wasn't waiting until the next day to discuss it.

Abby and Evelyn settled into the backseat while I helped Jim brush the snow off the car.

"Did you hear a weather report?

"Lake-effect warning," Jim said.

Lake-effect warnings meant either a whole lot of snow or nothing. I never counted on the *nothing*.

"We need to take Abby and go to my parents."

"We'll talk about it tomorrow."

"No. Tonight. Before we get snowed in."

"I'm not in any shape to drive that far tonight. Neither are you. When was the last time you had any sleep?" Jim had been up for over twenty-four hours.

"I had a nap this afternoon. Your mom can help drive. You can sleep on the way."

"We can't just up and leave. There's too much to be taken care of."

"Fine. Abby and I will go. You can stay here and do whatever you need to do."

"You're not driving anywhere tonight. Besides, you don't have a car."

"Go by the house. I'll get my Jeep. Give me your key."

"Not tonight. We'll talk about this tomorrow."

I knew I was arguing with a rock, but I also knew where Evelyn kept her keys. One way or another, Abby and I were getting out of Port Massasauga. And soon. The snow was picking up, and Evelyn's

Lincoln didn't have four-wheel drive.

"No. We need to talk about it now." We didn't, but if I gave in too easily, Jim would know I was up to something. I badgered him the entire drive.

THE DRIVEWAY WAS an unbroken expanse of white. Maybe an inch of snow, but it had come quickly.

Jim stopped by the back door. "You all get out, and I'll put the car away." Evelyn never left the Lincoln out in the snow.

"I don't have keys."

"Neither do I," Evelyn said.

I knew where her spare keys were.

Livvy's quilt was where we left it, a small white mountain in the grass. Evelyn picked it up and shook it out, and I wondered if we should take it with us. Livvy was beyond comfort, but I had a feeling Abby and I would need a lot—if the quilt still held any comfort.

Jim unlocked the door. Sami waited inside. No barking. She just whimpered.

"You can leave the car in the driveway," Evelyn said.

"No. You like it in the garage. He can put it away." If it sat out, I'd have to clean the snow off before we left. The longer it took to get away, the better the chances of Jim stopping us.

"Gramma's car always goes in the garage. Mom likes the heated seats," Abby said. "Livvy doesn't need her blanket now. It won't help."

"I'll put the car in the garage," Jim said.

We need to leave.

"I'M SLEEPING IN Abby's room."

Jim didn't attempt to talk me out of it. Whether he'd forgiven me for trying to hurt her or was just too tired to fight, he helped me settle Abby in and left for the spare room. From the looks of him, he'd be asleep as soon as he crawled between the covers. I hoped so, and I hoped Evelyn wasn't a light sleeper.

My last cup of coffee was hours before, but I was too much-caffeine-woman, painfully alert and exhausted at the same time. My plan was simple. It wasn't as if we had anything to pack. I would give Jim and

Evelyn time to fall asleep, really asleep, take Abby, and leave. We would take Sami with us. I couldn't risk her waking Jim before we were well on the road—or even out the door.

"Daddy is the Woodsman." Abby sat up.

"Lay down. Go to sleep." I didn't intend for her to sleep long, but it would be easier to get her quietly to the car if she was groggy.

"We need to read," she said.

"You need to go to sleep."

"We need to read."

"Only if you lay down and close your eyes."

Little Women was gone, along with everything else. Most of the books on Jim's shelves weren't Abby-fare. Mysteries, horror—books from his high school and college years. *No wonder he became a cop.* I found an old Hardy Boys tucked into a corner. The mystery wouldn't be gruesome. If it didn't put Abby to sleep, maybe it would lull her into drowsiness.

"Lay down and we'll read," I said.

"I do not want to be a Little Piggy."

42.
[ABBY]

I think the Ceiling Man is here, but I cannot find him. He does not talk to me, but he is here.

My mom says, "Abby, go to sleep." I think she is wrong. I think I must stay awake. I think I should not leave my mom alone. I think I should not sleep when the Ceiling Man is here.

My mom is reading, but I do not like this book.

"Jo and Amy are better," I say. She is reading about Joe, but it is not my Jo. My Jo is very brave. I think I should be like Jo.

"I'll huff and I'll puff." The Ceiling Man talks to me, but I cannot find him.

I do not want to be a Little Piggy.

"Abby, you're making me seasick," my mom says.

That is what Ms. Colley says. I do not answer my mom. I do not stop rocking. I cannot find the Ceiling Man.

"Now's as good a time as any," my mom says.

The clock by my bed says 1:07. I do not know why 1:07 is a good time.

My ceiling clock that makes blue numbers is burnt up. The clock by my bed shows me red numbers. I hate red.

Gramma Evelyn says, "Do not say hate. It is a very strong word."

"I love bananas," the Ceiling Man says. He should not say that. Only my mom should say that.

"I do not want to be a banana," I say.

"I like grapes," my mom says. "Where are your shoes?"

"Bananas bruise easy," I say.

"Abby, get up. We're going for a ride," she says.

"I think we should sleep now." I close my eyes. I do not want to sleep, but I think we should not go for a ride. I think a ride is what the Ceiling Man wants.

The Ceiling Man laughs. I hear him, but I cannot find him.

"We're going to go see Gramma and Grampa," my mom says.

"The mother of your husband is in bed. I do not have a Grandpa Evelyn."

"No, honey, Gramma Bev and Grampa Lou." My mom laughs.

The Ceiling Man laughs too.

I do not know what is funny.

"We'll have an adventure," my mom says.

My windows rattle. The wind is crying. It is too loud and I put my hands over my ears.

"This night is too noisy. We should stay inside," I say.

"It's just the wind," my mom says.

"He will huff and he will puff and he will blow our house down," I say. My house is burnt down. I do not want Gramma Evelyn's house to blow down.

"It's just the wind," my mom says. "We need to go before the snow gets bad."

"The Ceiling Man is bad," I say. I think my mom will say *Abby, who is the Ceiling Man?* I will try not to say *Idunno*, but I think that I will say it anyway.

I do not want to go outside.

My mom does not say *Abby, who is the Ceiling Man?*

"Put this on," she says and gives me Gramma's coat.

Sami sticks her cold nose in my lap. She whines. I scratch behind her ears but she does not wag her butt.

"We should take Sami on the adventure," I say. If I cannot take Sami, I will not go on the adventure.

Sami yips. A yip is a small bark. I think maybe she is saying please because she wants to go with us.

If Sami barks loud she will wake up my dad.

Maybe he will say, "Abby, you do not have to go outside."

Maybe he will say, "Carole! What the hell are you doing?"

I will not wake up my dad. I do not want him to yell at my mom.

Sami yips again.

"Hush," my mom says. She is not talking to me. She is talking to Sami.

"I guess we'll have to," she says to me.

My mom sounds funny. I think she has a headache.

The Ceiling Man is laughing.

"Where is Daddy? He should come with us," I say.

"Daddy's asleep."

"Daddy is the Woodsman," I say.

"Come on, Abby. It's time to go." My mom's words sound like tears but her face is dry.

If I wake Daddy up, I think he will yell at my mom and hurt my ears. I think Daddy should wake himself up and come on our adventure but no yelling.

The red numbers say 1:14. It is time to sleep. I think 1:14 is a bad time for an adventure.

"I think we need the Woodsman," I say, but I get up and follow my mom downstairs. I do not want my mom's face to get wet like her words.

The kitchen is almost dark. Gramma Evelyn has a Man in the Moon nightlight. The nightlight smiles at me, but I do not smile back. My mom takes Gramma Evelyn's keys out of the green teapot cookie jar. It has a face, but no cookies. Gramma keeps her spare keys and exactly one hundred dollars in it.

My mom takes her husband's mother's money out of the teapot.

"Five twenties," I say. "Exactly one hundred dollars. Gramma says, 'for emergencies only.'"

"Shhhhh. Indoor voice," my mom says.

The green teapot cookie jar smiles at me, but it does not make me want to smile. Gramma's kitchen is full of smiles but my mom and I are not.

My mom puts the money in her pocket. Stealing is bad, but my mom is not bad.

The Ceiling Man is bad. He is not in the kitchen. I do not know where he is.

"Are we in an emergency?" I say.

"Come on." My mom is whispering.

I think we are in an emergency.

Mrs. Livvy's quilt is on the floor. I pick it up. It is wet, but I will take it on our adventure. It is an emergency and I think we need comfort.

I think we are having too many emergencies lately.

"Hurry. We need to get out of here before the snow gets worse," my mom says.

She is whispering. Maybe she does not want the Ceiling Man to hear her.

I cannot find the Ceiling Man.

WE DO NOT get out of here before the snow gets worse. The driveway is disappeared.

"March storms are the worst," I say.

My mom does not answer. I am wearing my pink sneakers but no socks.

"My ankles are cold. We need to go in," I say.

"Hush," my mom says. "It will be warm in the car."

Gramma's car has heated seats. I do not care. I stand still. My feet are in the snow and they are cold. The snow is sticking to Sami. Her black fur is turning white. I do not think she likes it.

I do not think we should go to the garage.

"Sami is cold. We should go in the house," I say.

My mom pushes the button on Gramma's keychain. The garage door opens.

"When Gramma opens the door the light comes on," I say. The garage is dark. The wind is loud and cold. My ears hurt outside and inside. I do not want to go into the garage.

Sami is growling. I think she does not like the dark garage.

"We should not go into the garage," I say.

"Since when are you afraid of the dark?" My mom uses her perky voice.

Daddy says, "Uh-oh. Perky. We're in trouble, kid."

I think my mom is afraid. I think we are in big trouble.

"We should take Daddy with us," I say.

"Come on. The sooner we get in the car, the sooner we can get warm and get out of the garage," she says.

I stand still. My feet are cold.

"Daddy is the Woodsman."

I do not know what time it is.

"Where are you going?" my mom says.

"I need my watch."

"There is a clock in the car. It has blue numbers." My mom grabs my arm. I almost drop Mrs. Livvy's quilt but I do not.

My mom pulls me and I try not to move my feet but I do not want to fall in the snow.

I smell dirt and pennies and I cannot get away.

43.
[CAROLE]

TIME SLOWED TO A CRAWL, YET THINGS HAPPENED TOO FAST to absorb. Sound was muted by the swirling snow, yet reverberated in the cold air. The sky was moonless, yet the falling white reflected light.

I felt as if I was inside a snow-globe. *Just so nobody picks it up and shakes*.

Heavy, wet snow covered the driveway. More than when we got home, but I couldn't tell how much. Shin-deep drifts bordered spots of bare pavement. I couldn't tell if the snow still fell, or if the wind picked up and rearranged what was already there.

"March storms are the worst," Abby said.

Yeah. And driving is going to be a bitch. I considered going back to the house. Waiting for morning. Talking Jim into going with us.

If we stay in Port Massasauga, we won't make it through the night. I didn't know where the knowledge came from, but I believed it more than I'd ever believed anything. I didn't want to leave Jim behind, but with him or without him, Abby and I were gone.

A gust of wind cut through my thin jacket, and I shivered. Somebody shook the snow globe. I grabbed Abby's arm, afraid she would disappear into the white. Or that I would.

When I was young, my father scared me with stories of people vanishing in snowstorms.

"They'd head for the outhouse and lose their way," he said. "They weren't seen again 'til spring, when the snow melted and revealed their frozen corpses. True story. Happened to my grandfather's cousin."

Sometimes it was his uncle's neighbor. As a child, I couldn't decide if he was telling the truth or trying to make me appreciate indoor plumbing, but at that moment, I believed his story.

Like many of the older homes in the area, Evelyn's garage was built well after the house. Attached garages were a modern invention. A barn once stood in the garage's place, but it wasn't all that far behind the house, maybe sixty feet. We had to be halfway there, but I couldn't see it through the swirling white. If I got turned around, we'd end up in the backyard instead of the garage. My sense of direction wasn't great in the daylight.

The sudden whiteout died down. Sami's black coat was covered in snow. The poor dog leaned against Abby's legs and whimpered. Abby didn't move.

"We need to go," I said and pulled her forward. We both slipped and nearly went down.

The corpses weren't found until the snow melted.

I fumbled with the Lincoln's key fob. I didn't want to hit the panic button. The alarm would wake up Jim. I must have hit the lock button first. Tail-lights flashed. At least we still faced the dark garage. I found the unlock button, and the inside of the car lit up. *Bless you, Evelyn.* The white leather interior made the Lincoln a beacon. I aimed for it.

"Come on," I said.

Abby didn't move.

"The sooner you get in the car, the sooner we can get out of the garage." I used my syrup-voice.

Cajoling didn't do any good. Fed up, I dragged her to the garage. She didn't fight, but her passive resistance was as good as a fight. We slid and slipped our way forward and somehow managed not to end up on our rear-ends in the snow.

The Lincoln's passenger door wasn't quite shut. *Jim must have left it unlatched.* It was unlike him not to make sure everything was securely locked up, but after the hospital, understandable. *If someone tried to open it, the alarm would have gone off.*

Abby stood next to the car and swayed. Sami growled—I assumed because I grabbed Abby. She was protective of all of us, but Abby was always her first priority. I resisted shoving Abby into the car—the last thing I needed was a dog bite—but my patience was used up.

"Get in the freaking car." Sami's growl had nothing on mine.

44.
[ABBY]

"Get in the freaking car," my mom says. It is not her perky voice. It is her fed-up voice.

I get into the freaking car. It smells like dirt and pennies.

"Little Pig, Little Pig, let me in."

My mom screams.

A man is in the backseat. He is smiling, but I do not think he is happy. I think he is mean.

I do not like his smile. He is missing a tooth.

"You should go to the dentist," I say. My mom needs to call the dentist. It is time for my appointment. I do not want to be missing a tooth.

Sami is growling.

"Little Pig, Little Pig, let me in," the man says. He says it with his mouth but I hear it with my head.

Sami is barking. My mom is shouting. My ears hurt. I cover them with my hands.

"Little Pig, Little Pig, let me in."

The Ceiling Man is in Gramma Evelyn's car. I think he wants to be in my head.

I do not want to be a little piggy.

My mom is shouting. She calls the man *Blevins*.

He is not called Blevins. Devon did not write *Blevins* on his list.

Sami is barking. She is on my lap. I think she wants to be in the backseat. I think she wants to bite the man. I think she should.

Gramma's car is honking. My ears hurt.

"Shut up," the man says.

Sami stops barking. She is heavy on my lap. I think she is crying.

I am crying. Mrs. Livvy's quilt is not working. I think the comfort is all used up. Mrs. Livvy is all used up and maybe her quilt does not work anymore.

"Little Bunny Foo Foo, hopping through the forest." The Ceiling Man is singing.

"Stop," I say. I know I am not the bunny. I am the piggy.

"Scooping up the field mice—"

"No." I know I am not the mouse. I am the piggy.

"And bopping them on the head."

My mom drops Gramma's keys. She falls down fast on the garage floor and puts her hands on her head. I think her head hurts. I think my mom is a field mouse.

My head hurts too. I know where the Ceiling Man is.

"He is not called Blevins," I say. "He is called the Ceiling Man. Devon wrote it on his list."

I do not think my mom hears me.

I do not want the Ceiling Man in my head.

I do not want to be the piggy.

45.
[CAROLE]

"Little Pig, Little Pig, let me in."

The first time he spoke, it didn't fully register. Abby'd talked about pigs and woodsmen and wolves for so long, I wondered what happened to her voice.

Blevins popped up in the backseat.

"Little Pig, Little Pig, let me in," he said.

"Abby! Out of the car! Run for the house!"

Her hands covered her ears, and her eyes were shut tight. Overload signals. She was blocking out the world. A meltdown was on the way. On Abby's lap, Sami barked. If she even noticed the dog, she didn't show it.

Stay calm. He's not violent. Just an asshole.

"Blevins—"

"Little Bunny Foo Foo—" He sang, but his mouth didn't move.

Sami's barking had to be torture for Abby. *Why didn't Sami just jump to the backseat?*

«*Hopping through the forest.*»

Blevins's mouth moved, but not in sync with the song.

How is he doing that?

His mouth stretched into a wide, toothy grin. Other than one missing front tooth, he looked like Batman's Joker.

I hated the Joker.

"Blevins—"

«Scooping up the field mice—»

It's not him. There's someone else here. I fumbled with the key fob. The light inside the car went out. *The panic button.* I blindly jammed all of the buttons on the fob. One of them would make the car light up and the horn blare. Jim would hear it. He'd wake up.

Daddy is the Woodsman.

«And bopping them—»

Pain slammed the side of my head, and the darkness closed in. The sickly sweet smell of something dead and rotting overtook the garage smells. My stomach heaved, but nothing came up. Bone-chilling cold spread from the soles of my feet up my legs. The floor swayed and I fell. *Somebody shook the snow-globe.*

Abby was in the car with Blevins.

The pain in my head pulsed with the blare of the Lincoln's horn. Evelyn's keys lay in front of me. I must have found the panic button. I needed to get up, but my body wouldn't listen. The cold concrete floor held me like a magnet.

« You'll move when I tell you to move.»

The words thundered in my head.

Thunderclap pain. Cerebral aneurysm. No. I can't die now—Abby. I need to get Abby.

«You're not going to die yet.» Not Blevins's voice. Someone else was there.

"The Ceiling Man." Abby's voice was soft and toneless, but like the other, it echoed inside my skull.

My mouth filled with dirt and pennies. The wind howled and snow gusted into the garage, hitting my face like icy needles. Sami barked and the car's horn bellowed. Pain hammered my head. I gave up. *Sink into the floor. Silence. Peace. No Ceiling Man. No Blevins.*

"Mom. You should breathe."

My arms and legs wouldn't budge, but I managed to lift my head. Looking into the lit up Lincoln was like looking into the sun. My eyes burned. I strained to see around the bright spots floating in front of me.

Blevins was still in the backseat. His mouth moved, but I couldn't hear him.

Abby rocked in the front seat, right where I'd put her, Sami half in her lap. Her eyes rolled back in her head. Livvy's quilt covered her up to her neck. The quilt rippled. I knew she fluttered her fingers in front of her.

«Mom. You should breathe.»

I heard her speak, but her mouth never moved.

"Abby. Get out of the car and run." She rocked faster.

Sami scrambled into the driver's seat and barked and snarled at the man in the backseat. I wanted her to rip out Blevins's throat. She lunged between the front seats. She didn't make it. With a yelp, she bounced back and hit the dash. In a second, she was on her feet again, barking and snarling.

«Pick up the keys and get into the car.» Not Blevins, the other voice.

"And get rid of the fucking dog." Blevins. His voice, I recognized.

"I have cash. In my pocket. Take it and go."

"Too late for that," Blevins said.

«Pick up the keys and get into the car.»

"You should have been nice to me, bitch," Blevins said. "All I wanted was coffee."

I can't move. I need to get Abby out of the car. Get away. Back to the house. Get Jim.

«Pick up the keys and get into the car.» The voice filled my head. The same voice that told me to drug Abby. To bring her to him. To hurt her.

46.
[ABBY]

I think it is CODE RED HOSTILE INTRUDER ALERT.

Devon's list says, "PROCEED TO THE NEAREST SECURE SPACE."

I do not think Gramma's garage is a secure space. I pull Mrs. Livvy's quilt to my chin. It is soft and not scratchy and it is dirty but it does not stink. I want to pull it over my head, but I think that is a bad idea. I do not know why, but I am sure it is a bad idea.

The man in the backseat laughs. I hear him with my ears, but I hear the Ceiling Man with my head. The man in the backseat is not the Ceiling Man, but the Ceiling Man is the man in the backseat.

My mom says, "Abby, you can't be in two places at the same time. It's just not possible."

The man in the back seat hurts Pete and Livvy. They are dead and gone and will never come back.

The Ceiling Man hurts Pete and Livvy. He laughs and makes them dead and gone and they will never come back.

I cannot think about Pete and Livvy or I will cry and scream. I do not think this is a good time to cry and scream so I shush my Pete and Livvy thought.

"Dead and gone and never coming back," the Ceiling Man says.

The Ceiling Man and the man in the backseat are two people in one place at the same time. I think my mom would say, "Abby, it's just not possible."

I think it is not possible but it is true. Not possible means *no it absolutely cannot happen*. True means *real and not a lie*. I think the Ceiling Man is both.

My mom is crying. I hear her with my head and with my ears.

The Ceiling Man is hurting my mom. I do not want my mom to be dead and gone and never coming back.

"Mom. You should breathe," I say. I think I say it with my mouth, but I am not sure.

Maybe the HOSTILE INTRUDER is the man in the backseat.

Maybe the HOSTILE INTRUDER is the Ceiling Man.

Maybe the HOSTILE INTRUDER is both.

It is not possible but it is true.

Devon's list does not say what to do when the HOSTILE IN-TRUDER is in the backseat.

Devon says, "Mrs. Lamb's brain blew up."

"You did it," the Ceiling Man says.

"No. You did it," I say.

The Ceiling Man tells my mom to get into the car.

"You should not listen to him, Mom. He is a bad man. I think he is two bad men." I do not think my mom hears me. Maybe I do not talk with my mouth.

My yellow bricks are cracked and my wall is broken. I think the Ceiling Man hurts my mom and I do not think I can protect her.

"I huffed and I puffed and I blew your wall down," the Ceiling Man says.

I do not think I can protect me.

"Leave my mom alone."

The Ceiling Man's laugh scrapes my ears like Sami's growl.

I should make new yellow bricks and stack them up and up and they will reach the sky and my mom will be safe behind my yellow wall. My brain is talking in the Fast Voice, but I do not think I am Headed for a Meltdown.

I think I am headed for something else.

"Time for an adventure." It is not my mom saying *adventure*. I think the man in the backseat says *adventure*. I think the Ceiling Man is laughing, but maybe he says *adventure* too.

"Little Bunny Foo Foo—"

I know it is the Ceiling Man singing because he is louder than the man in the back seat. I put my hands on my ears but it does not help. The Ceiling Man is in my head not in my ears.

"Leave my mom alone." My wall does not grow. I try to concentrate but I cannot. "Focus, Abby, focus," I say, but it does not work. My yellow bricks are crumbly and they fall apart.

"Scooping up the field mice—"

"I am not a field mouse. My mom is not a field mouse. I am Abby and my mom is my mom and you should leave us alone."

"And bopping them on the head." The Ceiling Man sings low and growly and I do not like it.

I think my mom's head is full of thunder. She makes a squeaky noise and puts her hands on her head. Thunder-snow fills my mom's head and thunder-snow fills the garage.

I am not the field mouse. My mom is the field mouse.

I do not want my mom's brain to blow up like Mrs. Lamb's.

I do not want my brain to blow up like Mrs. Lamb's.

I do not want Devon to write *Good-bye Abby* on his list.

I hope *Good-bye Abby* is not the something else I am headed for.

"Leave my mom alone."

"We'll go for a little ride," the Ceiling Man says. "Maybe we will stop to see Twyla."

"Twyla does not like to leave town. She does not travel well," I say.

I think I have a spring inside my chest.

"But she does like red," the Ceiling Man says.

I see red ceilings at Twyla's house. I do not think the Ceiling Man wants to take Twyla with us.

When the Ceiling Man talks, the spring in my chest gets tight. It does not feel good. It does not feel right.

"You and I need to spend a little time together." The Ceiling Man is breathing hard.

I think that is not just a bad idea but a very bad idea which is even worse than a bad idea and means if I do it I will be in bad trouble.

"ABBY. GET OUT of the car and go into the house." The Woodsman is here.

I do not ignore him, but I do not get out of the car. The spring is getting very tight. I am like a Jack-in-the-Box in a red box.

I do not like boxes and I hate red and I cannot get out of the car.

"Daddy is the Woodsman," I say.

When I am little and Gramma Evelyn gives me a Jack in the Box and I do not like him, Daddy takes the Jack in the Box apart.

Daddy says, "See, Abby. He's just a spring. Nothing to hurt you."

I think it is a bad thing to have a spring inside his chest and I do not like the Jack.

"Carole? Can you get up?" My mom does not answer my dad.

"Blevins, get out. Slow. With your hands in the air." Daddy uses his Mad Dad voice. The man in the backseat laughs.

"He is not the wolf," I say.

The Ceiling Man laughs. I think he will sing the Bunny Foo Foo song and hurt my dad. My spring is very tight. My mom should tell me *Breathe, Abby. Breathe.*

"All around the Mulberry Bush." I sing but I am whispery. I am a Jack in a Box, but I do not like the Jack. I know he will pop and jump but I do not know when. Waiting for him makes a squeal in my head and a thump in my chest and I cannot breathe.

I do not think it is good to be a Jack. I do not think even the Jack likes being the Jack.

"The monkey—"

"Little Piggies don't sing."

I am not a little piggy. I am a Jack in a red box and I am angry and my brain is stuck in the Fast Voice and the Jack song will not go away. I cannot breathe.

My mom should say *breathe Abby breathe* but she does not say anything.

"I said get out of the car," the Woodsman says.

"Fuck you," the man in the backseat says.

"—chased the weasel." I am Jack in my box and my spring is very tight and the spring in my chest makes the Fast Voice in my brain sing the Jack in the Box song. I think maybe my mouth sings too.

Daddy pulls the man out of the car and hits him. I think the Woodsman is angry. I do not like angry and I do not like fights and I cannot breathe but I must keep singing.

I am the Jack.

I think I must be the Jack even if I do not like it.

"The monkey stopped to scratch his nose." I do not think anyone hears me singing. Sami is barking. The garage is full of red screams. I think Daddy cannot breathe. I think maybe the Ceiling Man can hear me but he is ignoring me because he is busy trying to eat the Woodsman.

The wolf does not eat the Woodsman.

I think the spring in my chest will go POP and I will hit my head on the ceiling of Gramma's car.

I hope the ceiling will not be red.

"This is going to be fun," the Ceiling Man says. His hands are on the Woodsman's neck and his mouth is open and I do not know where he got so many teeth. It is not possible but I know it is true.

I am not a little piggy and I am not a bunny or a mouse or a Jack. I am Abby in a red box. I hate red and I am angry and my spring is too tight and my brain talks too fast but it says *breathe Abby breathe*.

The wolf does not eat the Woodsman.

"POP goes the weasel." I sing loud with my mouth and with my head and there is thunder and there is lightning and my ears hurt but I do not hit my head and the ceiling is not red.

The garage is quiet now, but I think it is too late.

47.
[CAROLE]

ABBY. TRAPPED WITH BLEVINS. I NEEDED TO GET UP, TO GET TO her, to grab her and run, but my frozen limbs refused to listen to me. Dense fog blanketed me. My breath caught in my throat. My chest heaved. My lungs screamed for air. I was dying.

No. I was inside in a nice warm bed, asleep and dreaming. Abby was safe and Jim was—

Jim. Jim is here. Blevins. Jim pulls Blevins from the car.

Thunder. A flash and—a dream. A nightmare. Not real.

It is not possible but it is true. Abby's voice. *Breathe, Mom. Breathe.*

My tongue thickened. The fog turned to sludge and engulfed me. Crushed me. Suffocated me.

Breathe, Mom. Breathe. I clung to Abby's words and fought for air. *Breathe, Mom.* Bit by bit, I dragged myself out of the mire and back to consciousness. The concrete floor swam into clarity, every sharp detail of its sandpaper texture magnified. I was awake and in the garage. Not a dream.

My throat and chest cleared, and I breathed in the foul and metallic air.

Dirt and pennies.

"Abby?" The memory of pain ricocheted in my head and drowned out her answer, if she gave one. I struggled to get up, but my heavy body didn't cooperate. The concrete stung my hands, and familiar pins and needles shot up my arms. *Not numb. Not paralyzed.* I'd lost all sense of time, but however long I'd been on the cold floor, it was long enough for my arms and legs to go to sleep. *Not a stroke.*

"Abby? Jim?"

Jim. Blevins's hands on Jim's neck. Teeth, thunder, and—

It is not possible but it is true. Someone was dead.

If Jim was there, why didn't he say something? If he wasn't, if he was dead, it was my fault.

Abby did it.

No. I brought Abby to the garage. My fault.

Breathe.

The roar in my ears faded, replaced by the howl of the wind. A high-pitched wail soared above the sound of the wind. Abby.

My arms and legs burnt, but they were mine again. I took it slow and fought through the pain and pushed myself upright.

The garage light was on. *When did that happen?* Snow billowed in the driveway and drifted in through the open door. Abby, covered up to her chin in Livvy's quilt, sat in the front seat of the Lincoln, right where I'd left her. Sami sat next to her, ears cocked, on high alert.

And something else. Something I wasn't ready to take in.

One of them is dead. Abby did it.

Not possible.

It is not possible but it is true.

I tried to stand, but my legs weren't yet ready to hold me and I sank back to the floor. Abby was safe. Sami would watch over her. I had to get my bearings, ground myself, before I faced what I feared—what I knew—lay in front of me.

Breathe, Mom. Breathe.

On the garage walls, garden tools hung in a neat row. Only one hook stood empty. Evelyn's garage was as neat and organized as her house.

In the car, Abby rocked. Sami's glare wasn't aimed at me. She bared her teeth. I steeled myself and followed her gaze.

In front of me, Jim. *Alive.* The wave of relief nearly sent me back to the floor. *Breathe. Breathe.* The thought came in Abby's voice, not my own. Jim knelt, not looking at me, but at the ground between us.

I made myself face the thing that didn't belong, the thing I didn't want to see. Between us, crumpled on the floor like a discarded rag doll, lay Blevins.

He wouldn't break any more windows.

The Ceiling Man. I glanced up. *No red.*

The red was in front of me, not above me. The dark pool edged toward me, a blemish on the once spotless floor. *Evelyn's not going to be happy.* I swallowed the acid in my throat. *I will not be sick.*

"Jim?" He didn't look up from Blevins.

Dead Blevins.

Abby pushed him. Impossible.

Jim is here. Shouting. He opens the back door of the car—I see his mouth move, but the white noise in my head drowns out his words.

The wind howling. Yelling. Sami barking. Jim grabbing Blevins, pulling him out of the car. Blevins laughing.

Different laughter. Another man.

I hadn't seen another man. If he was still there, he was hiding.

"Jim. There's another one."

"No, there's not." His eyes held mine a little too long.

I didn't know how Blevins ended up on the floor, broken. I didn't know why he was in the garage in the first place. I didn't know where the pool of red came from. Most of all, I didn't know if what I'd seen was real.

"What happened?" I didn't want to know, but I needed to know. "You saw it."

Abby pushed Blevins. She killed him.

"No." I addressed both Jim and the nagging voice in my head. The crazy voice.

The ice and steel in Jim's eyes weren't directed at me. *It's his cop face. That's all.*

"Yes, you did."

Think.

Jim hits Blevins. Blevins laughs, and Jim hits him again. Why doesn't Blevins go down? Blevins puts his hands on Jim's neck.

Abby screaming—no, singing.

"*POP goes the weasel!*"

A flash of light, an explosion.

Blevins in the air.

Blevins bounces off the wall and lands on the floor.

It isn't possible but it's true.

"You saw it," Jim said. "He attacked me. I knocked him down. He hit his head."

Pop goes the weasel. Blevins in the air.

No. Jim's explanation was possible, so it must be true.

"Is he going to be all right?" I asked, but I wanted Blevins dead. I wanted confirmation. Most of all, I wanted Jim to reassure me, to drive out the impossible scene playing over and over and over in my head.

Jim stood. Dark stains covered his pant legs. *Red. Blood. Blevins's blood.*

Abby killed him. Abby killed him. The sing-song thought taunted me. The harder I tried to block it out, the louder it trilled.

"He's gone," Jim said.

Abby stopped her wailing. "The Woodsman is gone," she said.

Blevins was dead. He couldn't hurt us.

"Carole?" Jim held out his hand, stained to match his pants.

I shook my head and got up on my own.

"Take Abby in the house. You don't need to look at that," he said.

The compulsion to look was intense, and Jim's attempt to shield me made it worse. I had to take it in, to make sense of what I'd seen. What I thought I saw.

It is not possible but it is true.

Blevins sprawled on his back, arms and legs akimbo. *Heads don't attach to bodies at that angle.* The dark trickle at the corner of his mouth didn't account for the widening puddle of red.

A wide rake—not a broom-like leaf rake, but a steel-tined garden rake—lay in the middle of the dark halo. *The empty hook.* The tines pointed upwards. In the center, Blevins's head. Impaled.

Jim took my arm. I imagined his bloody handprint eating through my sleeve, burning my skin, entering me. I swayed, but Jim caught me before I fell.

"How...what..." I couldn't find the words.

"Karma," Jim said, grim. Predatory.

Involuntarily, I jerked from his grasp.

"You're safe. Abby's safe," he said.

The Woodsman is gone.

"I'm just—cold." My teeth chattered. The imprint of Jim's touch burned like acid on my arm. *Blevins's blood. We are all stained.*

"Shock," he said. "You need to take Abby inside. I'll be in in a minute."

In the car, Abby no longer rocked. Her stony face gave no clue whether her hard eyes were the result of fear or fury.

Abby did it.

It is not possible but it is true.

For a second, I was afraid of my daughter.

"Time to go in," Jim said.

Abby's expression didn't change. Sami snarled.

"It's safe now. You can get out of the car," I said.

"It is not safe," she said. "The Woodsman is gone."

"I'm here," Jim said. "Come on, honey. Time to get out of the car." He reached for Abby, and Sami leapt.

Abby screamed, and Sami bounced off Jim and hit the floor.

Blevins bounces off the wall and lands on the floor.

It isn't possible but it's true.

"Fucking dog!" Jim collapsed against the side of the car. His arm torn, his blood mixed with Blevins's.

Dirt and pennies.

Abby put her hands to her ears. "Help is coming," she said.

Sirens screamed in the distance and grew louder. Nearer. *Evelyn must have called 911.*

"I hate red." Abby wasn't talking about the blood. The lights at the end of the driveway flashed red. *Township, not city.* It didn't matter. I didn't have to wonder if Jim was in the car. My automatic—normal—reaction comforted me.

"The lights should stop now. They hurt my eyes," Abby said.

All I saw through the blowing snow was the strobe of cherry lights as a second, a third, a fourth vehicle pulled up and stopped. *They really called out the troops.* I wondered if one was an ambulance. Blevins was beyond help.

"They should help Sami," Abby said.

The dog lifted her head and whimpered at her name, but didn't get to her feet.

"I think your dad needs some help."

"I'm good," Jim said.

"He is not good." Abby was out of the car. "It is still Code Red Hostile Intruder Alert and we are not safe." She sat down next to her dog.

"Daddy took care of the bad man, and the police are here. We are safe." The sirens stopped, but the red lights were all I'd seen of the police. What was taking them so long?

"No. It is still Code Red." Abby took Sami's head into her lap.

I knelt and put my arm around her shoulders. She jerked away. Sami bared her teeth and growled.

"On the ground! Face down! Arms straight out to your sides!" The garage filled with blinding light, but I understood. Police, with flashlights. And guns.

"Abby, it's the police. Do exactly what they say," I whispered.

"Shit," Jim said.

"The Woodsman cannot help us anymore," Abby said.

48.
[CAROLE]

THE GARAGE SWARMED WITH POLICE.

We stood outside in the still raging blizzard and answered questions. Abby cocooned herself in Livvy's quilt, its bright fabric muted beneath a layer of wet snow, and refused to—or couldn't—speak. Between the wind and the wet, I was frozen to the core, and between the shivering and the shaking, I could barely squeeze out answers. Jim asked the cops to take Abby and me into the house.

"I think we can finish this inside," one of them said.

A mute nod was all I could muster, but I was grateful to Jim for suggesting it and to the officer for agreeing. Township or city, they were all cops and knew each other.

Three uniformed cops escorted us inside. I didn't know any of them. Jim stayed outside, taking the police through what happened. He was one of them. They would believe what he told them.

He would protect his daughter.

"He attacked me. I knocked him down. He hit his head." I tried to convince myself Jim's words were true.

"A few more questions and we'll have you write out your statements and leave you alone," the cop in charge said. His name was Gillespie.

"The Woodsman is gone." Abby clung to me.

"Daddy is fine," I said. "He'll be in soon."

"No. He is gone." She buried her face in my shoulder.

"He's fine. Remember, he's the Woodsman."

"Not anymore," she said, bereft.

"Can we do this later?" I asked Gillespie.

"The sooner we get started, the sooner we'll be done."

I could have made a fuss and refused to let them talk to Abby alone and probably gotten away with it, but I wasn't sure what Gillespie would ask me. I wasn't sure I wanted Abby to hear my answers. I compromised and let them separate us, but insisted we be able to see each other. Abby and a woman officer named Weber went to the dining room. Gillespie stuck with me.

In the living room, I sat on the couch wrapped in an afghan. Gillespie remained standing.

"This won't take long." He was kind, but I knew he was lying.

Jim would say *it'll take as long as it takes*. As far as I was concerned, it was already taking too long.

"How did the rake end up on the floor?"

"I don't know. It may have been there when we went in. I didn't notice."

I couldn't get warm. The scene outside seeped into the living room. The whine of vehicles coming and going merged with the sound of the wind. No sirens, but their red lights flashed through the sheer curtains and lit up the room. Like Abby, I'd come to hate red.

Evelyn and her interrogator were in the kitchen, and the smell of coffee drifted through the house. I wondered if they'd taken Blevins's body away. I hoped so. Even dead, I didn't want him anywhere near us.

Abby shredded a piece of paper and stared at me while she answered questions. Abby's stare could mean so many things, and I wasn't sure what this one meant, but I assumed she was answering. Weber kept her voice soft and low, and Abby matched her tone. Their murmurs reached me, but not their words.

I knew Abby's story would be exactly what she'd seen, if she'd seen anything, and I was sure Weber would dismiss it. She'd assume Abby was incompetent or crazy. If I told Gillespie what I saw, he'd assume I was incompetent or crazy or high.

I hoped Abby would just answer *Idunno* and refuse to talk and wished I could do the same.

I kept my story simple. Believable.

"Blevins attacked Jim. Jim knocked him down." I wanted to believe

Jim, so I repeated his story and hoped Gillespie believed me.

"What?" I'd drifted off and missed something Gillespie said.

"We're just going to go over this once more. What did you see when you entered the garage?"

Abby shifted her gaze from me to Weber, her eyes narrow and her mouth shut tight. I recognized the expression. She was pissed.

"I really should be with her."

"As soon as we're done here. She'll be fine," Gillespie said.

He asked me the same questions over and over.

I gave the same answers over and over.

"Why would Blevins be in your garage?"

"How would I know? And it's not my garage. It's my mother-in-law's."

"Did he have a weapon?"

"I didn't see one."

"Has he bothered you before?" Gillespie threw in a new question.

"He used to come into the downtown Senior Center. I work there. Worked there."

"Other than that?"

I hesitated. "I think he was there when our house burned down. I'm not sure it was him. There were a lot of people around."

"When was that?"

I had to stop and think. "The night before last." An eternity ago.

"Why were you outside?"

"I was taking Abby and going to my parents."

"Why?"

"With all the crap going on around here, don't you want to leave?"

Gillespie didn't answer my question. He kept on with his. *Where were you standing? Where was your daughter? What brought your husband to the garage?*

I longed to pull an Abby and end the conversation with an *Idunno.* Or start yelling and screaming.

I did neither. I stuck to short simple answers. *Just the facts, Ma'am.* I wasn't standing. I was on the floor. I didn't know how I ended up there. Maybe I had a panic attack. Maybe I'd blacked out for a few seconds or minutes. Time was fuzzy.

I left out the other voice, the one I'd heard in my head.

I didn't tell Gillespie about the flash of thunder and lightning that filled the garage. The thunder and lightning I'd felt, not heard or seen. Had Jim felt the same thing, or was it only in my head?

"Pop goes the weasel," Abby sang in the other room, loud and off key as ever.

Blevins in the air. He hits the wall. The garage shakes. Blevins on the floor in a pool of blood. Silence, until Abby wails.

"Daddy was the Woodsman." Abby's Fast Voice. Not a good sign.

"I need to be with her."

"We're almost done here. Do you think you could write out your statement? Just put down everything you've told me." Gillespie's question wasn't a request. It was an order. He handed me a clipboard and a pen.

"Hey. Can she write a statement?" Weber directed the question to me, but Abby answered.

"I am not stupid. I am autistic." Abby was defiant, more fed up than pissed.

"There you go," I said. *We'll get through this.*

"I have very neat handwriting," Abby said.

"That'll be a change from the usual." The corners of Gillespie's mouth twitched.

"Don't laugh," I said. "Her handwriting's better than mine."

"I have a nephew a lot like Abby. Weber's going to get schooled if she isn't careful."

I liked Gillespie. Weber, not so much, but I wanted them both gone.

I wrote everything, from the time Abby and I found Blevins in the garage to the time the cops arrived. Almost everything.

"He attacked me. I knocked him down. He hit his head." If I wrote down Jim's story, maybe it would become the truth.

I read my statement, decided spelling didn't count, signed the form, and handed it to Gillespie.

"Am I done?"

"For the time being," he said.

He followed me to the dining room. Abby handed her statement to Weber.

"Officer Weber said I should write everything that is true," Abby said, "so I made a list. It is not as good as Devon's lists, but it is true. I do not think Officer Weber believes me."

I told her I was sure whatever she wrote was fine.

"This is my list," she said. "One. Daddy was the Woodsman."

"It doesn't make a lot of sense," Weber said. She handed Abby's statement form to Gillespie.

"Two. The Woodsman tried to save me."

"She's been stuck on a couple of fairy tales lately," I said.

"Three. The Ceiling Man is dead."

"Who is the Ceiling Man?" Gillespie said.

"Four. The Ceiling Man is not gone."

"I don't know," I answered.

"Five. The Woodsman is gone."

49.
[ABBY]

MY LIST IS NOT A LIE BUT I DO NOT THINK IT IS THE TRUTH.

My mom says, "Abby, sometimes leaving things out makes the truth act like a lie."

I do not think the truth should act like a lie. My list is the truth but I think if I do not leave things out Officer Weber will think it is a lie. I think maybe she thinks I am stupid and I think I bother her.

Daddy says, "Ignore those silly people. They see what they want to see and nothing else. It's their problem, not yours."

Officer Weber is a policeman even if she is not a man. Policemen are not supposed to be silly people. I do not think Officer Weber likes me.

Daddy is a policeman. Daddy is the Woodsman. The Woodsman is gone.

I think if I tell Officer Weber the Ceiling Man hurts my dad and I am Abby in a Box and my spring is too tight and I do not have a meltdown instead I go POP and the man in the backseat is dead on the floor and the Woodsman goes away but the Ceiling Man does not, she will not believe me.

I do not think Officer Weber can keep us safe even if I do not leave things out.

"It's a very good list," my mom says.

"I do not like the spring and I do not like to go POP." I hear my Fast Voice.

"Abby, breathe. It's a good list, and we're safe now," my mom says.

I think it is an okay list but I think my mom is wrong. We are not safe now. Maybe we are not safe ever.

I do not want my mom to be wrong.

Officer Weber shakes her head. I do not know if her head-shake means, "No, it is not a good list" or "No, we are not safe now" or something that I do not understand. Head-shakes are slippery. I want to tell Officer Weber to use her words but I do not because it might be disrespectful and rude.

Adults do not like it when I tell them to use their words. Except my mom and Daddy. They laugh when I tell them to use their words. I want my mom to laugh and I want her to be not wrong but I do not tell her to use her words.

"She didn't see anything," my mom says. "She was in the car, and I didn't want her to see the—the thing on the floor."

My mom is wrong. I see the thing on the floor. The thing on the floor is broken and red. The thing on the floor is the man in the backseat. The thing on the floor is the man my mom calls Blevins. I think he is dead and I think it is my fault. People who make people dead are bad people and are in trouble. I do not want to be in trouble.

My head-shake is slippery and I do not think my mom knows what it means.

Officer Weber hands me my list. "Do you know how to sign your name?" she says.

Of course I know how to sign my name. I think Officer Weber is disrespectful and rude. It is her problem and not mine.

I do not know what I did in the garage or how I did it. Maybe Officer Weber knows Blevins is dead and it is my fault. Maybe she will put me in jail. I take her pen and sign my name on my list.

I do not want to be in jail.

I think my problem is worse than Officer Weber's.

"Well, I think we're about finished here." When my mom's policeman smiles at me I like his smile. I do not like Officer Weber's slippery smile or her slippery head-shakes.

I think she knows I did a bad thing. I want her to leave.

"I hope Jim's about finished," my mom says. "It's freezing out there."

"Daddy is finished," I say.

"He should be in soon," my mom's policeman says. Officer Weber does not say anything.

Jim is Daddy. Daddy is the Woodsman. The Woodsman is gone.

I need to rock but if I do my mom will say, "Abby, now is not the time."

"You should leave now," I tell Officer Weber. "You can stay," I say to my mom's policeman.

They laugh. I did not mean to be funny. I cannot help it and I am rocking.

"Come on, Abby. Let's go see your grandmother," my mom says.

I think she means I should not rock, and I follow her into the kitchen. Gramma Evelyn is drinking coffee with her policeman.

"That smells heavenly," my mom says.

Gramma Evelyn offers coffee to everyone but me. She is very polite, but my mom's policeman says, "No thanks, we need to get back outside."

I am not polite and do not say good-bye to Officer Weber. The policemen go out and the Ceiling Man comes in.

"Damn, it's cold out there," he says.

I wait for Gramma Evelyn to tell him *Do not say damn* but she does not. She is too busy giving him hugs.

Daddy says bad words when he is Mad Dad or when he is fixing the sink but he does not say bad words in front of Gramma Evelyn. She does not like Foul Language and she is his mother so he must respect her.

I do not know why Gramma hugs the Ceiling Man when he says *damn*. Maybe even if the Ceiling Man looks like Daddy he does not have to respect her. Gramma Evelyn is not the Ceiling Man's mother.

"It's over," he says. His smile is slippery.

My mom's face is wet. I do not think she is sad because *It is over*. I do not think *It is over*. I think the Ceiling Man lies.

My mom hugs the Ceiling Man.

My mom should not hug the Ceiling Man.

The Woodsman is gone and I am shaky inside.

"Ouch. Watch the arm," the Ceiling Man says. His arm wears a bandage.

Sami is Velcro-pup and she growls at the Ceiling Man. Maybe she wants to bite him again. Maybe the Ceiling Man makes Sami shaky inside too.

"Abby, come join the celebration," Gramma says.

I cannot look at the Ceiling Man and I do not think we should celebrate.

I pull Livvy's quilt tight around me. It smells like wet and garage and only a little bit like purple flowers, but it does not smell like dirt and pennies.

"Abby, why don't you give that to me until we can wash it again," Gramma says.

I do not answer and I do not give her Livvy's quilt. I think as long as it smells a little bit like purple flowers, maybe it has some comfort left.

"Leave her with it," my mom says.

Gramma does not argue.

"Things are not what they seem," I say, but no one listens to me.

"I'm listening." The Ceiling Man does not talk with his mouth and I do not think my mom or Gramma hear him.

My mom says, "Abby, you really need to try to pay attention to details. Details are important."

My mom says, "Your grandmother's hair always looks exactly the same. I don't know how she does it. It's like she gets it trimmed every day."

Gramma gets her hair trimmed every three weeks, not every day. Three weeks is twenty-one days. Sometimes she must wait twenty-eight days and her hair gets very long and I see it. That is a detail. It is a small thing, but I do not think it is an important thing.

The man my mom and Gramma hug is not my dad. He is the Ceiling Man and that is not a small thing and I think they do not see it. They are not paying attention.

"Big things are important too," I say.

"How bad is the arm?" my mom says.

"Not bad."

"Does it hurt?"

"Not much."

"Anybody hungry?" Gramma Evelyn says.

"Famished," the Ceiling Man says.

"How about waffles?" Gramma Evelyn does not use the toaster to make waffles. She uses her waffle iron which is different from her clothes iron. Gramma Evelyn's waffles are one of my daddy's favorite things.

Daddy is the Woodsman and the Woodsman is gone. The Ceiling Man is here and he is hungry.

I do not think he is hungry for waffles.

50.
[CAROLE]

FEAR DRAINS. AFTER A BRIEF SUPER-CHARGE OF ADRENALINE, all that's left is the need to sleep. Or cry. Relief operates the same way.

The police left as the sun came up, and I came down. Blevins was dead. We were all safe. Whether it was fear or relief, I hit the sleep or cry or both stage. The reason didn't matter. I couldn't give in to exhaustion or tears. Not yet. Not until I'd spent time with my family and made sure they were okay inside as well as out, as much for me as them.

Despite my attempts at denial, I needed to make sense of what I'd seen.

I wanted to talk to Jim, but not with Abby or Evelyn hovering. The EMTs had bandaged his arm and urged him to go to the hospital and have it examined, maybe get stitches and an antibiotic.

"It's just a surface wound," he said. "Barely a scratch. I told them I needed to stay with you and Abby and promised to get checked out later."

Abby and I were both scheduled to return to the hospital that morning, me for blood work and Abby for tests. We could make it a family outing, but I doubted any of us would bother. *Maybe tomorrow.*

"You should have gone with them," Abby said.

"And leave you?" He reached for her, but she evaded his touch, just as she did when he came in.

"It's one of those mornings," I said. I was just grateful Abby wasn't in meltdown. Hell, I was happy I wasn't in meltdown.

We all sat at the kitchen table while Evelyn bustled around making breakfast. Waffles and bacon, and not the microwave kind. I offered to help, but she shushed me and told me to sit.

The smell of breakfast and the warmth of the kitchen wrapped around me like fog. Not the suffocating mist of the garage, but a wonderful anesthetic. I was numb but safe. Both were good.

After an idiot reporter from the local paper called for the third time, Evelyn unplugged the phone. None of us wanted to talk to the press about what happened. We weren't even talking about it with each other.

Other than the hiss of the waffle iron and the sizzle of bacon in the skillet, the room was quiet. The storm died out just before dawn, and left the world outside the windows tranquil. The morning sun made the snow sparkle. As much as I hated snow when it was falling, and as ugly as it was when tracked up and dirty, I had to admit the brief pristine period in-between was beautiful. I hoped school was canceled. Abby hadn't brought up the subject yet—and I wasn't about to—but there was no way she was going. If she had a snow day, I wouldn't end up the bad guy.

Evelyn refilled my coffee cup. When she called 911, she told them I was stealing her car. She apologized. I forgave her. Not that there was anything to forgive. I *was* stealing her car.

"I don't care why you called them. I'm just glad you did." I hugged her. She hugged back.

I was even more thankful she woke Jim and sent him out to stop me. I didn't want to imagine what might have happened if Abby's Woodsman hadn't arrived.

Denial was my friend. Blevins was gone. We were safe.

Relief and exhaustion made me benevolent. I promised myself to sneak Evelyn's cash back into the cookie jar before she noticed it was gone.

Jim wore clean clothes. I had a vague notion the police took his bloodstained clothes, but wasn't sure whether it really happened or I imagined it. I felt that way about a lot of the night. Eventually, I would ask Jim what was real and what wasn't and hope it made sense. He was ragged. If the EMT's hadn't checked him out, I would have worried. A thin coat of sweat gave his forehead a slight sheen. His color was off, not quite gray, but not his usual robust glow. His eyelids drooped, as if his lashes were too heavy for his lids. His cheeks sagged. He'd aged overnight. *Not overnight.* How long since he slept? Two days? And, he'd just killed someone.

Abby killed him. I pushed the crazy thought away, visualized putting it in a box and locking it up. Nothing would burst my happy-comfort bubble. *Safe. We are safe.*

Abby would have nothing to do with her father. She didn't look at him and sat as far away from him as possible, with Sami by her side. The dog's fall only knocked the air out of her. She'd recovered, but wouldn't let Jim near her. Abby, she still protected. She gave a small growl when Evelyn set Abby's plate of waffles in front of her.

"Oh, hush," Evelyn said.

I swore I saw her slip Sami a piece of bacon. I wasn't sure who had taken over my mother-in-law, but I liked it—and wondered how long it would last.

Evelyn set Jim's overloaded plate in front of him, and he pushed it away.

"Not hungry."

"You have to eat something," his mother said.

"I *said* I wasn't hungry."

Evelyn took a step back, and Sami growled.

Abby finally looked at her father. "No red ceilings," she said.

Jim smiled.

"What are you talking about?" Evelyn said.

"Idunno." Abby took a bite of waffle and stared at her father while she chewed.

I told myself she meant no *more* red ceilings, or ceiling men, or anything else horrible.

Blevins was dead. We were safe.

"Abby, don't stare at your father."

Blevins is dead. It's over.

Jim's smile turned to a smirk.

Don't be ridiculous. He's just exhausted.

Evelyn put a plate in front of me. I drenched everything in maple syrup and dug in.

We were safe.

51.
[THE CEILING MAN]

"I *SAID* I WASN'T HUNGRY."

Oops. From their reactions, he didn't sound much like darling daddy. He flashed the old bitch a big toothy smile. She smiled back. *Oh, Gramma, what big teeth you have.* Too bad for her—his were bigger.

"No more red ceilings."

He couldn't tell if the brat spoke aloud or only to him. Not good. He couldn't let anger and frustration get the better of him. Cloud his perception. His judgement.

His anger was directed as much at himself as the brat. Maybe more so. She'd taken him by surprise. He let her.

If it hadn't been for Daddy's split second of shock when Blevins went down, he'd be dead along with his asshole former host. The jump was pure self-defense. Unthinking reaction. He was unprepared, and the move sapped his energy.

"Jim?" One word from the mother, packed with so much concern and love it sickened him.

Not the emotions he craved.

"I'm good." He picked up his coffee cup, pretended to drink. He'd play along with the happy family act until he had a plan.

A plan. What was it, his fifth, sixth since discovering the brat?

This one would be the last.

First step, assess the situation.

The kitchen pained him. Everywhere he looked, he saw *cheerful.* Yellow flowers on the walls. Blue ruffles on the windows. On the counter, next to a wooden block full of knives, a freaking teapot with a face grinned at him. He choked back the urge to smash it.

He sat at the head of the table. Royalty. The conquering hero. They had no idea.

Across from him, the girl swayed slightly—almost imperceptibly—in her chair, but there was no waver in her glare. He couldn't see the dog, but heard its growl. Next to the girl, maybe at her feet.

He needed to watch the dog. It knew. It would go first.

"Abby, don't stare at your father. He's boring," the mother said. Chipper, but he knew her well enough to know it was contrived. She'd aged since he first found her, something he was happy to take credit for. When he made the jump, he'd left her alone, but it shouldn't be hard to regain control. Mom was the least of his problems.

The brat was another matter. Alert and on edge, she didn't break her stare.

Both mother and daughter seemed to be waiting for something, but where mom appeared expectant, the brat appeared wary.

Abby. He had to remember to call the brat *Abby.* Not *the girl* or *the brat.* Even with Blevins gone, it would be too easy to slip up and call her *the little retard.* Abby's loving daddy would never say that. Probably never even thought it.

Fucking saints. Blevins was gone, but he'd left his mark.

Gramma said something about syrup. He didn't catch it, but figured a quick smile and a *that's fine* would do, and it did. She turned back to the stove. The old bitch was an unknown quantity. She'd resisted him once, with the brat's help.

The brat put her fork down. He gave her a nudge. Nothing. Either she resisted or he was too weak to get through that thick skull of hers. The effort brought hammering inside his head, and her steady stare made him itch.

"Abby. Eat your breakfast," he said.

"You're not the boss of me."

"Abby!" Mom and Gramma spoke in unison. Shock and disapproval. As far as they were concerned, he was The Dad.

"It's okay. Rough morning," he said. "But remember, little girl. I am your father, and I *am* the boss of you."

«No you're not.» Her mouth didn't move. She spoke to him alone. The pounding in his head increased.

He needed to feed.

He needed more than food.

The brat was *more*. She was his plan. How great would her pain be when forced to watch darling Daddy rip apart and devour her beloved mother and grandmother? His earlier joyride would be funereal in comparison. A tremor took him. Coffee sloshed from his cup.

"Jim—" The mother's concern amplified, echoed.

"Tired," he croaked. He ached to ride the girl's pain, bask in it, grow with it.

The girl was his goal and his obstacle. If she understood what she did in the garage, repeated it, he'd never get near the women. She needed to be contained. Restrained. His longing surged. *Get a grip*. Daddy's body never reacted like that at the thought of his darling daughter.

He reached out and nudged. Nothing. He pushed harder, got nowhere. She'd closed her mind to him.

«*Little Pig, Little Pig, let me come in.*»

She cut a bite-sized piece of bacon, placed it on a neat little square of waffle, and primly forked it into her mouth. She chewed intently, eyes on him all the while.

Didn't the brat blink? What was she, part lizard?

She was taunting him.

He thrust again—and he was in. She couldn't keep him out.

«*We're going to have some fun, Little Piggy.*»

She didn't answer or change her expression.

«*The Woodsman's gone. Gramma's next.*»

Something snapped. White noise surrounded him.

He had her.

Caution tempered jubilation. No more surprises. He concentrated. Not noise. She was humming.

Not the song from the garage. *His* song. The one she hated.

The humming stopped, and she sang out loud. The noise filled the kitchen. She really couldn't carry a tune, but it was all good.

Too good. Anticipation and desire shook him, weakened him. *Not yet*. He gathered his strength and focussed.

"Abby, don't sing at the table," the old woman said. "It's rude."

The girl sang louder, and he knew he had her. The kitchen reverberated with her racket, but in her head, she sang with *his* voice. He joined in, a duet with himself.

"Scooping up the field mice and—"

Fuck.

52.
[ABBY]

THE CEILING MAN IS NOT THE ONLY ONE WHO CAN SING *BUNNY Foo Foo*.

He is quiet. His face is in his waffles and syrup and his voice is not in my head.

I cannot see his smile.

I think I should be sad I hurt my dad, but I did not hurt my dad. Only bad people hurt people. I do not think the Ceiling Man is people. I am shaky inside, but I am not sad.

Daddy is the Woodsman. The Woodsman is gone.

When I am five years old and small, Daddy says, "I'll eat you up!"

When I am five years old and small, I think getting chewed up and swallowed will hurt. I scream and I scream and I cannot stop until there is red and black in my head.

Daddy says, "Abby, I am very sorry. I didn't mean to scare you. I will never say...the scary thing again." He stretches his lips. I think his teeth will chew me up and I cannot look at him.

Every day, Daddy says, "Abby. This is my smile. It means I love you very much and I will never, ever hurt you."

I cannot look at him.

Daddy says "Abby, this is my smile" forty-two times on forty-two days. On the forty-third day, I look at him and I think maybe his teeth will not chew me up. He says it every day anyway.

Every tenth day, he says he loves me very, very much.

When I am twelve years old and big, Daddy says, "Abby, what does my smile mean?"

"You love me very, very much and you will never hurt me."

Today, Daddy does not say, "Abby, what does my smile mean?"

Today, Daddy's smile says, "I'll eat you up."

Today, Daddy's smile is not Daddy's smile.

The Ceiling Man is quiet but he is not gone. He is breathing. I must find him but I do not want to wake him up and I do not like it inside his head.

I want the Ceiling Man to be gone.

"Abby. Abby. Listen to me," a Daddy-voice says.

I think it is a trick. The Woodsman is gone.

"Abby. It's me." The Daddy-voice is in my head and not in my ears. I think it is the Ceiling Man's friend pretending to be my dad.

"You be quiet. You are not the Woodsman." I try to shut the door but it will not budge. I think shutting the door is something the Ceiling Man must do, but he is asleep in his breakfast and he is quiet. I cannot hear him, but I can feel him and he feels mad.

Mad Dad.

The Ceiling Man is not my dad.

"Abby, you have to listen to me," the Daddy-voice says.

The Ceiling Man's friend is called Blevins. The dead man in the garage is called Blevins.

"Abby. The dill pickles count as vegetables," the Daddy-voice says.

I do not think Dead Blevins knows about the dill pickles.

"Daddy?" My face is wet.

Outside my head, the Ceiling Man sits up. He has syrup on his nose. His nose is Daddy's nose but his eyes are not Daddy's eyes.

Inside my head, the Ceiling Man says, "You little brat."

"The wolf always dies at the end," the Daddy-voice says.

«Shut up,» the Ceiling Man says.

Something says thunk and Maybe-Daddy is gone.

"The wolf does not eat the Woodsman," I say.

Gramma is screaming. She does not use her mouth.

"It is okay, Gramma. It is not Daddy," I say with my mouth. "Daddy is the Woodsman. The Woodsman is gone. Dead Blevins cannot trick me."

"Evelyn, call 911," my mom says.

The Ceiling Man sits up. "No need," he says with Daddy's mouth and it sounds like *noneeee*.

« Good try, Little Piggy, but I've been at this much longer than you have,» he says with his head.

The right side of Daddy's face is droopy. The Ceiling Man only makes one half of a smile with Daddy's mouth. His left-side-only smile says, "I'll eat you up."

Gramma holds the phone but it is unplugged because we are tired of talking to stupid reporters. When people say I am stupid, my eyes burn but I do not cry.

I am not stupid. Maybe the Ceiling Man and Dead Blevins and Officer Weber think I am stupid, but they are wrong.

"Evelyn, don't call 911," the Ceiling Man says. His words are mushy and he says *doan* instead of *don't*. I think maybe he needs to see Mr. Lanham the speech therapist.

Gramma stands very still. The phone is in her hand but it is not plugged in and she does not move it to her ear and mouth. Her eyes are very big. I do not know what her eyes mean. Maybe they are burning. Maybe she is surprised. Maybe she is scared. I wait for her to talk. I wait for her words to tell me what her eyes mean.

Gramma does not talk.

My mom says, "Your grandmother has something to say about everything and anything."

But my grandmother does not say something about anything or everything and I think there is a lot of anything and everything in her kitchen right now. I think it is the Ceiling Man's fault and I should help her.

« Go ahead, Little Piggy. Help her like you helped Mrs. Lamb.»

Mrs. Lamb is dead. I did not do it.

I do not want Gramma Evelyn to be dead.

"Oh, you did it, Little Piggy," the Ceiling Man says. "Do it again."

I cannot tell if he is talking with his mouth or with his head. My mom is talking with her mouth, but I only hear the Ceiling Man.

I did not hurt Mrs. Lamb, but I did hurt the man in the garage. The man is named Blevins and he is dead.

I think maybe I made the Woodsman go away.

"You did it," the Ceiling Man says.

I hurt the Ceiling Man and he did not go away.

Gramma Evelyn does not move but she is standing up so she is not dead. Maybe the Ceiling Man is right and I made Mrs. Lamb dead. The right side of the Ceiling Man's face is droopy and does not move when he talks with Daddy's mouth.

Right also means correct. Right is a slippery word and I do not like slippery words.

I do not care that the Ceiling Man is droopy on his right side and I do not care that maybe I hurt him but I do not want him to be correct. I do not want to make Gramma Evelyn dead like Mrs. Lamb.

I do not know what to do.

"Evelyn," my mom says.

Gramma does not move. Her eyes are big and I do not know what is wrong with her, but I think it is not my fault. It is the Ceiling Man's fault.

Gramma screams in her head.

Mrs. Lamb screams in her head and I make her stop.

I do not make Gramma stop.

"Do it," the Ceiling Man says.

I do not know what my mom wants Gramma to do and I do not know what I should do.

The Ceiling Man-Daddy smiles. Only the left side of his mouth smiles. I do not see his teeth, but I know that they are there.

I will be like Pete. I think Gramma and my mom will be like Pete and I do not think Gramma will like her ceiling red.

"Abby." The Daddy-voice is a whisper but I think it is a trick.

Daddy is the Woodsman and the Woodsman is gone.

"Abby, don't listen to him." The Daddy-whisper does not say *doan* instead of *don't*.

I should tell my mom.

My mom says, "Abby, use your words."

Ms. Colley says, "Abby, use your words."

My words are stuck in my chest. My words are all mixed up.

Daddy says, "I love you very much and I will never, ever hurt you."

The Ceiling Man says, "I will eat you up."

"Abby, can you hear me?" the Daddy-whisper says.

"Idunno," I say.

Maybe the Woodsman is the Ceiling Man's new friend. Maybe the Woodsman is still here and he is not the Ceiling Man's friend. Maybe it is not possible but it is true.

My mom says, "Abby, just because you want something to be true does not make it true."

Daddy is the Woodsman.

The clock on Gramma's stove has blue numbers.

I do not know what I should do.

Daddy is the Ceiling Man. The Ceiling Man is Daddy.

I do not want my mom to be dead.

I do not want my gramma to be dead.

I do not want to be dead.

"It is 7:57," I say. "I do not think I should go to school today."

53.
[CAROLE]

ABBY, ASHEN AND STILL, STARED AT HER FATHER. TEARS RAN down her face. He stared back, their gazes locked in silent battle. *Don't be ridiculous.*

"Abby. Go to the living room." Whatever was happening to Jim, I needed to shield her. Protect her. She'd already seen enough—too much.

"No." The steel in her voice belied her fragile appearance.

I couldn't cope with Abby in stubborn mode, so I didn't.

My mother-in-law stood rooted to her spot, dead phone in hand, eyes dull and unfocussed.

"Evelyn, you need to plug the phone in." Nothing. Inside, I screamed *why the hell are you just standing there—do something* but outside, I stayed calm. "Evelyn—"

Jim shifted his attention from Abby to me, and my words died in my throat. His mouth hung open. Only one side of his face moved. The other drooped, lifeless. I saw him melting away, a wax figure left in the sun. Spit gleamed at one corner of his mouth, and from the other, the dead side, drool trickled to his chin. The living side of his mouth stretched into a rictus of...what? Not a smile. The leer of a predator about to crush his prey.

It's not Jim. He's gone.

My eyes burned and my chest constricted. Desolation spun with panic, and my veneer cracked.

He's gone. I'm alone.

"Leave my mom alone." Abby brought me back to reality, but I didn't have time to figure out what she was talking about. I took a deep breath and pictured the poster on the wall of the Senior Center. *Warning Signs of Stroke. Act FAST!* It was too late for speed, but *FAST* was an acronym.

F-Face. Jim's non-smile and sagging face fit the bill.

A-Arms. "Jim, can you lift both arms?" I shouted at him, as if volume would force him to answer me. It didn't. Two out of four, and Evelyn still hadn't moved or called 911.

Jim's eyes gleamed. His lopsided smirk terrified me. Sami snarled. I struggled to breathe.

"Leave my mom alone."

Bright lights zig-zagged in front of me, and the familiar jagged crescent appeared in the corner of my vision. The once comforting odor of bacon and waffles turned sour and nauseated me.

"Relah. Jus go with eh." Jim's mouth barely moved, and his words oozed like mud.

S-Speech. Slurred speech. Not making sense.

My vision narrowed. Far away, at the end of a tunnel of red, I saw myself, my hands around Abby's neck. I clenched my hands, and my fingernails cut into my palms. The pain brought me back. The tunnel disappeared.

«*Don't fight. Go with it.*»

"Mom. Breathe." The bossy voice. Abby was the only one holding herself together.

The lights flickered, and the room wavered.

I needed to be the adult. The mom. Do something. Get help.

A flash of light and the kitchen brightened. The glint of sunlight on the stainless steel sink pierced my eyes like barbed wire. The glaring yellow of the cupboards assaulted me, and the simpering cookie jar echoed Jim's leer. I didn't see my surroundings. I felt them, in overwhelming detail.

«*Don't fight. Relax.*»

Jim was right. I wouldn't fight. I'd slip away to somewhere dark. Soft. Quiet.

"Leave my mom alone."

Concentrate. Fight. Stay with Abby. Help Jim.

T-Time. How long since Jim collapsed? I strained to see the clock, but all I saw was Evelyn. She hadn't moved, and her face was wet with tears.

"It is 8:02. It is time for our long night to be over." Abby's words hammered my ears and drove spikes into my head.

I felt sound as well as light. *Fight it.*

I got up to take the phone from Evelyn. A block of knives stood on the counter behind her. Instead of the phone, I reached for the largest knife. I would end Evelyn and end our long night.

A bolt of pain sent me back to my chair. I couldn't move. Couldn't see. I was back on the garage floor, cold and paralyzed.

"Leave my mom—"

"Jus go wi—"

Abby and Jim spoke at the same time. Their words rolled over me. Crushed me. *I'm dying. Jim's dying.*

"Dead and gone. He's dead and you might as well join him," Evelyn said.

Abby will be alone.

"I'll finally be rid of you."

"Do not listen to him, Mom."

Him? What was Abby talking about? Evelyn's voice dripped with years of hatred, and for the first time, I wanted to listen to her.

"Mom. Breathe. Breathe. Breathe."

The pain drifted way. I watched it evaporate, wisps of red steam. In its place came overwhelming drowsiness. *Dorothy in the Field of Deadly Poppies.*

When was the last time we read *The Wizard?* Dorothy's shoes were silver in the book.

Abby doesn't like red.

My eyelids are weights and my arms tingle with electricity. I will melt into my chair and disappear. The cookie jar smirks. The air thickens with a sweet, heavy stench. *Poppies.* I know poppies have no scent, but I know it is poppies I smell.

It is not possible but it is true.

267

I will give in to their drug. More than anything, I want to give in to their drug.

"It is okay, Mom. Breathe," Abby says. Her whisper is the sound of the ocean.

A soft rumble. Thunder. No. Jim—or maybe Evelyn—speaks, their words a tremor I don't understand.

"We need to go to Oz," I say. "The man behind the curtain—"

"I know," Abby says.

My daughter is wise.

"Mom, breathe."

I obey. The saccharin perfume fills my nose, my lungs, my head. The kitchen tilts and fades, and I am surrounded by waves of crimson.

Poppies are red.

"No red," Abby says, and the soft scent of lavender replaces the reek of the poppies.

54.
[THE CEILING MAN]

THE BRAT HAD HER MOTHER. THE WOMAN WAS OUT OF HIS reach.

For a while.

He'd lost the battle, but not the war.

He never lost the war.

Syrup dried and stiffened on his face. Its sticky sweetness soaked his pores and sickened him. A napkin lay in front of him, but his useless body refused to reach for it.

It really wasn't fair. All the years of taking only throwaways, he finally landed in a healthy, well-fed human—this guy had all his teeth for fuck's sake—and it didn't even last him a day.

It was his own fault.

He should've killed the brat the first day he discovered her watching him. Or ignored her and moved on. But no, he had to hang around. Cats weren't the only creatures felled to curiosity.

The slight rise and fall of the mother's chest said she still lived. The brat had her stashed somewhere out of his reach, and if he couldn't get in, she was as good as dead for his purposes.

"Leave my mom alone." The brat was stuck on repeat.

« *You killed your mother.* »

"You should go away now."

She didn't know her own strength. He needed that strength.

He craved it.

He had Gramma locked down, but didn't know for how long. He couldn't underestimate the girl again, nor could he let himself be distracted by the thought of pleasure.

He should have finished her off back at the hospital, when she was weak. *Should've, would've, could've.* Except—he was no longer sure she was weak, even then. His stunt with the neighbors hurt her, that he was sure of, but it also made her stronger.

She wasn't a catalyst. He hadn't fed on her energy. It was all her. He'd piggybacked on her pain and rage, not fed on it. The sensations were a drug. They made him greedy.

The pleasure...*now. While she's distracted with her mother.* He nudged Gramma. She reached for the knife the mother had failed to get ahold of. It was in her hand.

«Stop.»

At the girl's silent command, the knife clattered to the floor.

Not so distracted after all.

He'd never been a hedonist. Lust was so human. He was disgusted with himself. Disgust didn't kill the yearning, but survival was his first priority.

Daddy would soon join Blevins, and he needed to move on.

He didn't have many options, and he had to choose carefully. He only had one chance to get it right. *Little Bunny Foo Foo.* The girl was a fast learner.

Who was the easiest target? Wrong question. He needed the best target.

She loved her mother and grandmother, but wearing either of them wouldn't protect him. Wearing Daddy hadn't. Taking either of the women was likely to piss her off even more, and he couldn't afford another hit.

He certainly wasn't moving to the damned dog.

A seventeen-year-old girl hardly fit his lifestyle, and with what he planned to leave behind, the whole country would be looking for her. He could wear her long enough to go get Chuckles. Leave her at the hotel and wear the moron long enough to get out of town. Maybe feeding would give him the energy for one more jump.

Maybe *she* would give him the energy for one more jump.

Or kill him.

His worst option was also his best option. Like Artie the penny-ante gambler, he needed to think positive. *I won forty dollahs!* This was no penny-slot. He was in the high rollers room.

Time to hit maximum bet. All or nothing.

"You should go away now."

"We'll both go. I promised you an adventure and an adventure you're going to get. It'll be the time of your life."

"I do not think I need an adventure."

She sounded pretty sure of herself. *Sounded.* They were speaking. He wasn't inside her head. She'd shut him out, and he hadn't noticed.

"Little Piggy, you're just like me. We are going to have so much fun together."

"I am not a little piggy and I am not like you."

Confident. He only had one shot at her. It better be a good one.

"Abby, what does my smile mean?" The words echoed in the back of his head. *Shit.* Daddy was awake.

"You love me very, very much and you will never hurt me." The brat still spoke aloud, but her voice quavered.

Good. Maybe Daddy would come in handy.

"Don't you want to go on an adventure with Daddy? There's only one way you'll see him again, my Little Piggy."

"Don't listen to him," Daddy said.

"The wolf does not eat the Woodsman." The brat narrowed her eyes.

He couldn't tell what she was thinking, and he didn't like it. It made him feel powerless.

He wasn't powerless. Not yet.

"But he does eat Gramma." He let go of the old woman, just long enough for her to hit the floor with a satisfying thunk.

The girl jumped.

"Abby—" The mother started to speak, but stopped when the brat looked at her.

"Gramma, what big eyes you have," he said.

"Leave my Gramma alone." The brat's eyes flickered toward her grandmother. Her mother sat up straighter.

That was it. She couldn't shield both women—and with any luck, herself—at once. Not yet, anyway. Distract her and his odds would improve. Too bad Artie wasn't around. He'd be proud. *Thinkin' positive. Gonna be a winner.*

"I think we'll take Gramma with us."

"*Abby. Ignore him.*"

The brat pushed her unfinished breakfast aside and leaned forward, elbows on the table.

«Daddy?» She didn't speak aloud. Her eyes brightened. *Hope?*

"*Don't listen. He doesn't mean what he says.*"

Blevins was irritating, but Daddy was dangerous.

«*I don't have time for this.*»

He kicked the door shut on Daddy, but instead of a slam, it snicked shut with a whisper. Maybe the girl's work, but he suspected he was weakening fast.

Daddy would be back. Blevins always managed to get out, and Daddy wasn't the waste of skin his predecessor was.

"Don't worry. As long as you have me, you'll have Daddy. As long as you behave yourself."

The spark disappeared from her eyes, and the laser stare returned.

"So, who's coming with us? Your mother or your grandmother?"

"You should go away by yourself."

"Who do you love best?"

"Idunno."

"Aw, come on. Pick one."

"Idunno."

"Here's the deal, Little Piggy. It's you, me, Daddy—and either Mommy or Gramma. You get one. Who do you want to tuck you in at night?"

Her eyelids fluttered. Her eyes rolled back in her head.

"I think you should go alone. Now."

"Not going to happen, Little Piggy."

Her mouth clamped shut, and she rocked in her chair. He nudged her. Whether her twitch was a reaction to him or just a coincidence, it didn't matter.

He was getting to her.

55.
[ABBY]

I AM NOT LISTENING TO THE CEILING MAN.

"Pick one, Little Piggy," he says, but I ignore him.

I think I must build a new wall. My yellow bricks are broken and crumbly, and I do not think I have enough to build a wall.

"Abby." The Daddy-whisper is back.

I do not answer.

"Abby. What did you do in the garage?"

I am Abby in a Box and the Woodsman is gone, but I do not tell the Daddy-whisper. I do not want to be in trouble.

"Can you do it again?" the Daddy-whisper says.

I do not think I should do it again. I think it was a Bad Thing, and the Woodsman would not want me to do a Bad Thing. I think the Daddy-whisper is not the Woodsman.

"Idunno," I say. It is the truth. I do not know if I can do it again, but I know I do not want to do it again.

The Daddy-whisper is in a box, but I can hear him. When the Ceiling Man's friend is in the box I cannot hear him. Blevins is the Ceiling Man's friend. Blevins is dead and I think I killed him.

I think Daddy is the Ceiling Man's new friend.

"I know who the Ceiling Man is," the Daddy-whisper says.

"I do not know who the Ceiling Man is. I only know he is, and I think you should not be his friend," I say.

"I am not his friend."

I want to believe the Daddy-whisper, but I do not think I should.

"Abby, what goes best with peanut-butter?"

"Dill pickles. They are vegetables." I whisper, but I do not want to be an Abby-whisper.

"What does my smile mean?"

"You love me very much and will never hurt me." The Daddy-whisper says the words with me, but I say *you* and *me* and he says *I* and *you.*

I think maybe the whisper is my dad. I think I want the whisper to be my dad. I think I need the whisper to be my dad. I think sometimes what I want and what I need are the same thing.

"One goes with us. One stays behind," the Ceiling Man says.

"Abby," my mom says, but I shush her. She should not talk now.

"Abby," my gramma says, but I cannot listen.

«*Pick one, Little Piggy.*» The Ceiling Man laughs.

"Abby, breathe," the Daddy-whisper says.

My mom should say *Abby breathe*, but I breathe and the Ceiling Man stops laughing.

"I spy something tall and strong," the Daddy-whisper says.

"My brick wall," I say, but my wall is broken.

"No, Abby, you," the Daddy-whisper says.

"I need more yellow bricks," I say, "but no crumbly bricks."

"Abby, why yellow bricks?" the Daddy-whisper says.

"Because they are not red," I say.

"Your turn, Abby," the Daddy-whisper says.

We are playing I Spy with My Little Eye.

"I spy with my little eye something warm and safe," I say.

Daddy and I are not good at I Spy. He never sees what I see and it takes me a long time to see what Daddy sees. Sometimes we play for one hour and sixteen minutes and nobody guesses right.

I do not think we have one hour and sixteen minutes left.

The Daddy-whisper does not guess what is warm and safe. He does not even try to guess.

"Take care of your mother and grandmother," he says.

"I am," I say.

"Remember, silly people see only what they want to see," the Daddy-whisper says.

The Ceiling Man is not silly but maybe he sees what he wants to see. I know what the Daddy-whisper wants me to do. I do not hear his words, but I feel them. They are in my chest, and I should not let them out.

I do not know if I can do what the Daddy-whisper wants me to do.

"I do not want my mom and Gramma to go away. I do not want red ceilings, and I do not want to be Abby-in-the-Box," I say.

The Daddy-whisper says something, but I cannot understand him. My head is full of fog, and my mouth is full of dirt and pennies.

«*Daddy can't help you, Little Piggy,*» the Ceiling Man says. «*He's gone.*»

"Abby." I hear the Daddy-whisper, but he is far away.

"Peek-a-boo," he says and I cannot find him.

"Wait for the Woodsman," he shouts.

«*Enough,*» the Ceiling Man says, and the Daddy-whisper is shushed.

The Daddy-whisper is the Woodsman and the Woodsman is gone. I am alone.

"I am not lost in the woods," I say.

56.
[CAROLE]

ABBY IS ROCKING. NOT HER SELF-COMFORTING ROCK AND NOT her furious rock.

Her rhythm is methodical, focused. She's concentrating. Her mouth moves and her face suggests a heated argument, but she doesn't make a sound—at least not one I hear.

Rather than dancing her fingers, she grips Livvy's quilt, pulling the blanket so tight that I picture the taut fabric shredding. The strained seams burst and the colored patches rip loose, flutter away, and disappear. Except the red ones. The red ones float to the ceiling. They cling and spread until the white ceiling turns blood-red.

"Do not do that." Abby pauses her rocking and speaks.

I don't know what I did.

Across the table, Jim sits motionless. No, he's not still. His mouth opens and closes in slow motion. He's trying to tell me something, but all I hear is the empty howl of the wind.

I need to help him. Call an ambulance. Do something, anything, but I can't move. My husband is dying, and I can't help him.

"He is not the Woodsman," Abby says. "We should not go on an adventure."

I promised Abby an adventure. *So had someone else. Blevins? Blevins was dead.*

"We have a hostile intruder and we must go to a safe and secure place. It is on Devon's list."

Abby's mouth stops moving, but I hear her speak. Her tone soothes. Her words don't. I sway, matching her steady cadence.

The kitchen fades. The yellow tulips on the walls, the blue curtains on the windows, and Evelyn's silly smiling teapot cookie jar are all still here, but I see through them, to somewhere else. Somewhere I don't recognize.

I'm reminded of the slide shows of my youth, faded transparencies of my parents' past vacations projected on a white screen, bright and transparent. My father steps in front of the screen and blends into the images of beaches or mountains or amusement parks. He is in two places at the same time.

Abby and I stand in front of the screen. The kitchen is a wavering image, projected from a point I cannot see. It warms my skin and repeats and reflects around me, an infinite number of grinning cookie jars.

I am here, but I am no longer here.

"Abby, we cannot be in two places at the same time," I say. Familiar words. I've said them a thousand times.

"It is not possible but it is true," she says.

"Is this Abby-land?" I wonder at my sense of peace and know it's unnatural. I don't care.

"Maybe. I do not know."

In the kitchen, Jim's face is twisted and cold. He reaches out to me but does not break through the screen. He's in pain. I have to help him, but I'm absorbed into the flickering Kodachrome of maybe Abby-land and I can't reach him.

"Mom, you have to help," Abby says. "We must build a wall. You and Gramma must be safe."

At my feet, a pile of yellow bricks. I didn't notice them until now. I don't know if they were there all along or if they just appeared.

I don't know anything.

"We must build a wall," Abby says.

Yellow bricks. "Are you Dorothy?" I ask.

"I am Abby."

"Listen to her," Jim whispers, but I can't find him.

The fog closes in on me. Not fog. Something dense, viscous, odorless. It invades my ears, my nose, my mouth. I can't—

"Breathe, Mom. Breathe."

The magic words. The fog returns to mist, and I breathe. The mist is heavy with the scent of cookies. *Oatmeal chocolate chip. Abby's favorite.*

The slideshow speeds up. The kitchen is gone. Snapshots of Abby's past flash by. Some too fast to see. Some pause, flicker, and melt into the mist. Some I recognize. Some I don't. So much information in no order. *Third grade. Abby sits behind a boy with red hair. David Besom.*

Colors swirl around me, but I don't see them. I feel them, taste them, breathe them. The yellow bricks radiate warmth. The blue air is sweet and cool. The purple is a scent. Purple flowers. Lavender. The scent of comfort. No red. *Abby hates red.* I am in Abby-land, but I don't know how or why. I should be frightened. Terrified. Instead, I'm serene. Accepting.

Insane.

"Abby?"

"This is the secure place," she says. "Devon's list says *proceed, if possible, out of line of sight of windows and doorways and to the nearest classroom or secure space.*"

Abby is no longer my Abby. Alice stands before me, brave and strong in the madness that is Wonderland.

"I am Abby," she says, and she is.

Dreaming. I'm dreaming and I need to wake up.

"You need to build the wall," Abby says.

I've fallen down the rabbit hole or through the looking glass, and I've lost count of the impossible things I've believed before breakfast.

"You should be brave like Alice and I will be brave like Jo," Abby says.

Abby's always liked Little Women *better than* Alice. The thought is inane, but so is the situation.

"Listen to her," Jim says.

"I must get Gramma. You must build the wall."

She is gone.

I kneel and pick up a yellow brick. Its warmth comforts me. I will build Abby's wall.

The warmth flares and pain sears my hand. The brick crumbles. The fiery dust turns orange then red as it filters through my fingers and disappears into the mist.

Laughter fills my head.

"The Ceiling Man," Jim whispers. "Ignore him. Listen to Abby. She'll protect you."

I have no words to answer him. I reach for another brick. I don't know what else to do.

57
[ABBY]

Gramma's face is blue and purple.

«*You wouldn't choose, so I chose for you,*» the Ceiling Man says.

"No," I say, but it does not help. Gramma's eyes are bulgy and round like hard-boiled eggs and I do not like them. The Daddy-whisper says I am tall and strong but I think I am small and weak.

«*Oh my, Grandmother dear, what big eyes you have,*» the Ceiling Man says.

"Breathe, Gramma, breathe," I say but it does not work.

"You are strong and brave," the Woodsman whispers.

"I am Abby-in-the-Box," I say.

The Ceiling Man laughs, and he disappears.

My gramma breathes.

58.
[CAROLE]

ABBY IS BACK, AND THE QUEEN OF HEARTS IS WITH HER. I WAIT for her to shout, "Off with her head."

"No red," Abby says.

The Queen is gone and Evelyn is here. An image of the kitchen flickers across her face. It's pale, as if there is too much light in the room or the projector's bulb is going dim. The blue glow of the oven clock stands out amidst the washed out tulips of the wallpaper. I strain to read the numbers, and the kitchen fades and disappears.

"I brought you help," Abby says.

I need help. Only three bricks lay end to end. The rest burned and crumbled, leaving my hands blistered and raw.

"The wall will keep us safe," Abby says.

Three bricks are not a wall. How can it protect us? I want to ask but can't find the words I need.

"Trust Abby." Jim's whisper comes from above me and below me.

"Look," I say and hold out my hands. I'm not sure who I am showing them to, Abby or her grandmother, but it doesn't matter. The blisters are gone. My palms are pink and healthy.

"You'll be fine," Evelyn says. She kneels beside me and reaches for a yellow brick. It crumbles in her hand just as they do in mine. If they burn her, she gives no sign.

Abby stands behind her grandmother.

"You should build the wall," she says. "We must keep the wolf away."

The brick she holds is firm and whole, but she makes no move to place it on the wall.

"Abby, where are we?" I ask.

"Idunno."

There is a *snap* behind us, and the mist is gone. The air shimmers, waves of heat rising from the scorched asphalt of a summer parking lot, but I'm bathed in pleasant warmth. I feel no pain when the bricks flare and crumble in my hand.

Evelyn and I turn from our thankless task. Livvy's quilt hangs behind us. It is Livvy's quilt, but it's either grown or we have shrunk. It moves back and forth, swaying in a breeze, but the air is still. *It's rocking, like Abby.* I am looking at the pale blue backing, but through it I see the intricate patchwork of the quilt top. The colors glow. The red is gone. The bottom edge is stained with mud and grease.

"I'll never be able to get those stains out," Evelyn says.

"Seriously?" I turn to my mother-in-law, unsure whether I am relieved or irritated at her injection of reality into my—what? Dream? Hallucination? Insanity?

I expect to see Abby standing behind her. She's not there.

"Abby!"

"She left," Evelyn says.

I know that Abby is on the other side of the quilt and in danger. I must go to her, but Evelyn wraps her arms around me. Not a hug. A trap.

The harder I fight, the tighter she clings.

"Let me go. Abby's not safe." I cry and scream. She doesn't listen.

"We need to stay here." She's calm. It takes no effort for her to hold me, no matter how hard I fight.

"I need to get Abby!"

"Jim said we should stay here."

"Jim's dead," I say. It's not true. I hope it's not true, but I want to hurt her, to shock her. I want her to push me away and let me go.

"I know," she says, her serenity unbroken.

My sobs overtake me, and I collapse against her. Her embrace is warm. I stop fighting. The steel bands melt away and I smell lavender.

"Please let me wake up," I say.

59.
[ABBY]

Daddy says, "Peek-a-boo! Where is Abby? Is she lost? I can't find her!" I am small and under the blanket and do not want to be lost.

"Here I am!" I say.

My mom and Gramma should not say, "Here I am!" They are not small and they are not lost. I must keep them safe.

I think I should stay with my mom and Gramma. Behind Livvy's quilt, it is warm and safe and smells like cookies and comfort. In front of Livvy's quilt, it is cold and scary and smells like dirt and pennies.

The Ceiling Man is not behind Livvy's quilt.

My mom says, "Is this Abby-land?" I do not know what Abby-land is. Abby-land is what my mom says when she thinks I am not paying attention to what is happening around me.

I think the Ceiling Man wants to go to Abby-land but I do not think he should go there.

Ms. Colley points at the map of the United States on the classroom wall and says, "This is Maryland. Its capitol is Annapolis." Maryland is yellow. Maybe Mary is a girl and she is like me and Maryland is where she goes when she rocks.

I am rocking but I cannot stay behind Livvy's quilt. I must be brave. I must leave Abby-land.

"Here I am," I say, and Livvy's quilt is behind me.

I think the Ceiling Man is here but I cannot find him.

I must wait.

The Ceiling Man says, "I'll take you on an adventure. It'll be fun. You'll see, Little Piggy."

I am not a Little Piggy and I do not think we will go to Maryland.

Abby-land is not on the map and I do not know what color it is but it is not red. Maybe it is blue. Maybe it is yellow like Maryland. I do not think I should let it be red.

I want to go find the Ceiling Man but I know I must wait.

Daddy says, "Patience, Abby. Patience."

I am being patient, but it is hard.

When I am small and angry and not patient and cannot stop screaming, Gramma Evelyn says, "Look at the state she's in!" but she is not pointing at a map. State is a slippery word. Maybe Abby-land is a state.

I think the Ceiling Man will come and the Woodsman will go away. I will be the Ceiling Man's new friend and live in a box.

I do not want the Ceiling Man to go to Abby-land. Maybe if it is not on the map he will not find it.

There is no clock, and I do not know how long I must wait.

I am not the Ceiling Man's friend and I do not want to be the Ceiling Man's friend. I do not want Abby-land to be red and I do not want to be Abby-in-the-Box and I do not want to be lost.

The Daddy-whisper says, "Abby, you must be brave and strong. I know you can do it," but I know I am remembering Daddy talking. He is quiet now.

I hope Daddy is not gone. The wolf should not eat the Woodsman.

«Which one, Little Piggy?» The Ceiling Man is in my head but not in Abby-land.

I do not want him in my head but I must be patient. I ignore him. If Abby-land is a state maybe I am the capitol and I can make the rules.

Rule One: Abby-land is warm and safe.

I am not warm and safe.

Rule Two: No bad guys can come in.

I want Daddy to say, "I love you very much and I will never, ever hurt you," but he does not say anything.

Rule Three: Everyone is safe and no red is allowed.

I think maybe I am alone. Maybe the Ceiling Man is giving up and going away. I do not think so, but maybe he is.

Rule Four: Everybody lives happy ever after.

"So, Little Piggy, have you made up your mind?"

I hear the Ceiling Man with my ears and with my head. I am not alone.

Devon should write my rules on his list. When Devon writes it on his list it is true. Devon is not here.

I must be brave like Jo.

"I do not have to make up my mind," I say.

My mom reads, "Jo never left her for an hour since Beth had said I feel stronger when you are here. She slept on a couch in the room, waking often to renew the fire, to feed, lift, or wait upon the patient creature who seldom asked for anything, and 'tried not to be a trouble.'"

I think I would feel strong if Jo was here but Jo is not here. Jo is in my book and my book burned up in my house. Jo is brave and strong and takes care of Beth. I must be brave and strong and take care of my mom and Gramma Evelyn.

«*Beth dies anyway,*» The Ceiling Man says.

I hear a noise and it hurts my ears but I do not put my hands over my ears.

«*You can't hide them from me, Little Piggy.*»

A piece of Livvy's quilt falls in front of me and lands by my feet. It is a small piece but it is red.

Ms. Colley says, "Abby, concentrate. Focus on what is in front of you."

I think I should focus on what is behind me. I cannot let the Ceiling Man hurt Livvy's quilt.

"No red," I say.

«*Pick one, Little Piggy. Who do you want to tuck you in at night?*»

Jo makes stories. In Jo's stories the bad guy dies and everyone is safe. Stories are not true but they are not lies. I cannot make stories.

"I do not need to be tucked in at night," I say, but I do not tell the Ceiling Man that I like to be tucked in at night.

My mom says, "What you need and what you want are two entirely different things."

I do not think that is always true.

Livvy's quilt shines like the sun on my back and makes me warm. I smell purple flowers. I think my mom and Gramma are safe and I hope they are comforted.

I hope they do not have to miss me.

I do not want to be an adventure.

I do not want to go away.

Devon should write, *Abby is brave and strong*. I think it is too late for Devon to write *Abby is brave and strong* on his list.

Beth comforts Jo but Beth dies and Jo is sad.

"I do not want anyone to be sad," I say.

Sami is Velcro-pup at my side. She growls. I put my hand on her head and I am comforted.

«*If you won't choose, I'll have to choose for you,*» The Ceiling Man says.

"You cannot choose. They are warm and safe," I say.

I taste dirt and pennies. I do not see red but the red covers me and my skin burns.

"Now!" the Woodsman says. He is not a whisper and his voice hurts my head and Sami barks and I want to scream but I do not.

I breathe and I step behind Livvy's quilt.

The quilt snaps and screams but it does not rip.

"I am not a Little Piggy. I am not Beth. I am Abby and I am strong," I say. My mom and Gramma are crying and hugging me and it is okay.

Livvy's quilt is strong and we are safe.

"It is 8:13," I say. "I am tired and I think I should sleep now."

Devon does not need to write *The Ceiling Man is gone* on his list. It is true.

60.
[THE CEILING MAN]

HE HIT THE PATCHWORK WALL AND BOUNCED INTO...NOTHING.

The body he left behind was dead, and there was no going back. The girl, and her mother, and grandmother were out of his reach. He couldn't even get to the damned dog.

He'd gambled and lost.

Blevins's voice came back to him. "Ha ha, asshole. Taken down by a little girl."

Shit.

Like a virus that cannot survive outside a host, he was gone.

61.
[CAROLE]

Jim died before the EMTs arrived. He was gone before we called them. The autopsy said he died of a cerebral hemorrhage.

Natural causes.

Neither Evelyn nor I disputed the coroner's findings. They went well with our account of what had happened. *Jim collapsed into his breakfast. He regained consciousness, but was confused. Not himself. Before we were able to call 911, he collapsed again.* Both of us told the same story.

"There was nothing you could have done," the doctor said. "It was quick."

"It is not a lie," Abby said.

It wasn't the whole truth, but it was a truth.

The hours we spent with Abby's Ceiling Man, like a bad dream, were only minutes in real time, and like a dream, the more I thought about that time, the less sense it made.

"Abby, where were we?"

All I got out of her was *Idunno.*

The official story was a truth I could handle and one I wanted to believe. Evelyn threw herself whole-heartedly behind the official account. When we were alone, I tried to find out what she'd experienced during the time we were in—wherever we were.

"I'm sure I don't know what you're talking about," she said.

Maybe I had imagined it all, except—

As soon as she had the chance, she took Livvy's quilt to the laundromat and washed it herself. She brought it back smelling of lavender, but one edge still bore mud and grease stains.

"I told you I'd never be able to get those stains out," she said.

What happened next is popularly referred to as *sharing a moment*, but we never again discussed our shared dream.

Instead of Abby and I going to my parents, they came to us. They wanted Abby and me to stay with them in a motel, but I convinced them we should stay with Evelyn.

"She's lost her only son." A believable excuse. I couldn't explain my need to keep Evelyn, Abby, and I together.

My father oversaw the cleaning of the garage. My mother pampered us all, and Evelyn let her.

I planned a funeral.

The police, the fire department, and the town council turned out for the services. More than half of the residents of Port Massasauga—I think anybody Jim ever met and some he hadn't—showed up. Many were there out of curiosity. The police hadn't found evidence to tie Blevins to all of the Port Massasauga killings, but they had tied him to Pete and Livvy, and Blevins died in our garage. Rumors flew, each one wilder than the last. None approached the truth.

At the funeral home, before the service, Evelyn and I stood in the receiving line and accepted condolences and platitudes from the endless parade of friends and strangers.

"He was a fine man."

"We'll all miss him."

"At least you have Abby."

"How are you holding up?"

Abby sat in the corner, flanked by Twyla and Devon. The three of them held hands. Twyla wore blue from head to toe.

"It's her new favorite color," Abby said.

Sweet Mrs. Gardner, from the Senior Center, stopped to talk to Abby and bent over to give her a hug. Abby stiffened. Twyla and Devon held onto her hands. She couldn't hug back, and the result was awkward. Mrs. Gardner backed off.

"It will be all right," she said.

"Yes. Devon wrote it on his list," Abby said.

He had. When he arrived, he showed me his new notebook. The first list had three entries.

1. The Ceiling Man is gone.

2. Everything is all right and everybody is safe.

3. Everybody lives happy ever after.

"When Devon writes it on his list it is true," Abby said. I hoped she was right.

A lot of people thought she hadn't absorbed her father's death and didn't understand he was never coming back. I thought she understood more than the rest of us could or ever would.

My parents left, and we settled into a routine. I didn't know how long the peace between Evelyn and me would last, and I didn't want to think about it. We would stick together for a while. We needed each other, and we both needed Abby.

I bought a new copy of *Little Women*, and Abby and I finished it. "We should read the *Alice's* next," she said. "Because you like them."

"Maybe we should find a new book."

Jim got his wish. I went back to my own bed—my new bed—and left Abby alone.

I dreamt I was back in Abby's secure place, but even in the dream, I knew it was a dream. Scenes from Abby's life swirled around me, but only happy ones. School. Peanut butter and dill pickle sandwiches. She and her father made brownie sundaes. A scoop of ice cream hit the floor, and Sami lapped it up. Abby and Jim giggled.

Jim stands beside me. "It will be all right," he says.

"I know. Devon wrote it on his list."

I woke and went to check on Abby. I couldn't help myself.

She was awake and rocking. Her eyes were closed, but I suspected if I could see them, they were rolled back. Her smile was beatific. Wherever she was, it was a happy place. Abby-land from before the Ceiling Man invaded our lives, but watching her brought back all my fears of the last few months.

When she rocks, he can find her. Tension twisted my gut and bile rose in my throat.

Breathe.

The Ceiling Man, whomever or whatever he was, was gone. He couldn't get to her or any of us anymore. *They all live happy ever after.*

I knew I had to let her have this small comfort.

Knowledge and emotions are entirely different things.

I wondered how long it would be until I could watch Abby being Abby without fear. As if she heard my thoughts, she stilled and opened her eyes. Her big loopy grin lit up her face, and she spoke.

"It's all right, Mom. Daddy says we'll be okay now."

ACKNOWLEDGMENTS

ALTHOUGH WRITING IS A SOLITARY PURSUIT, IT DOESN'T happen in a vacuum, and I have many people to thank.

The Ceiling Man served as my thesis for Seton Hill University's MFA in Writing Popular Fiction program. (And that is *Hill*, not *Hall*.) Had I not been accepted into the program, I doubt if this book would exist, and even if it did, I know it would be a lesser book. I owe thanks to too many faculty members, fellow students, and alumni to list here, but I am grateful to all of you.

There are, however, a few people who need to be singled out.

SHU-WPF legend has it that we get one fuzzy-Muppet-cheerleader mentor and one mentor who tortures us in ways we never imagined. I got cheated. I never got my fuzzy-muppet. Instead I got Scott Johnson and Tim Waggoner. Both, in different ways, pushed me to look deeper at my project and to become a better writer. Thanks, guys.

I had a wonderful list of critique partners: Jessica Barlow, Kenya Wright, Cody Langille, Daniel Goddard, Tanya Twombly, Amber Bliss, Stephanie Brown, and Michelle Lane. I would have never made it through the program or finished the book without the friendship and support of The Tribe: Alex, Anna, Crystal, Gina, Jeff, Jessica, Kenya, Lainey, Lana, Matt, Michelle, Penny, Tyler, and Valerie. Thank you all.

Huge thanks to everyone in my very first SHU workshop, led by Will Horner, who suggested I turn my short story, "Abby," into the beginning of a novel.

Medals of Valor go to my beta readers and proofreaders, both in and out of SHU: Douglas Anderson, Lana Hechtman Ayers, Valerie Burns, Vera Kitchen, and Jennifer Ryan, and to the members of AWFUL who read early bits and pieces.

Last, but the opposite of least, thanks to Liz and John Coblentz and my cousin Jennifer, for love and encouragement and margaritas as needed. John, I miss you.

ABOUT THE AUTHOR

PATRICIA LILLIE GREW up in a haunted house in a small town in Northeast Ohio. Since then, she has published six picture books (not scary), a few short stories (scary), and dozens of fonts. A graduate of Parsons the New School for Design and Seton Hill University's MFA in Writing Popular Fiction program, she is a freelance writer and designer addicted to coffee, chocolate, and cake. She also knits and sometimes purls.

The Ceiling Man is her debut novel.

You can visit her on the web at www.patricialillie.com or follow her on Twitter @patricialillie.

The text of this book is set in Garamond Premier Pro, designed by Robert Slimbach for Adobe. Garamond Premier Pro is Slimbach's reinterpretation of the roman types of Claude Garamond and the italic types of Robert Granjon, which he first explored in Adobe Garamond (1989).

Titling is set in Veneer, designed by Ryan Martinson for Yellow Design Studio. A popular digital display font, Veneer gives the impression of distressed, vintage letterpress type.